Twilight: Midnight Sunburn

A light parody of Midnight Sun

by Anna Jones Buttimore

Preface

The *Twilight* series by Stephenie Meyer was a huge international phenomenon, giving rise to fervent fandom. For many years it looked as though the final book, *Midnight Sun,* would never be completed. With fans clamouring for it I decided to whet their appetites a little and write a stopgap book. Copyright law allows parodies – humorous spoofs based on the original book – but I love *Twilight* so the humour in this book is quite gentle, respectful, and inoffensive. My hope was that this book would be just true enough to *Midnight Sun* to satisfy the screaming hordes of *Twilight* fans, and just enough of a parody to satisfy the copyright lawyers.

Happily, Stephenie Meyer announced in May 2020 that she would finally be publishing the long-awaited *Midnight Sun.* That means that this parody, *Midnight Sunburn,* no longer has a purpose, and I considered withdrawing it from sale. However, as with all my books my author royalties are donated to Heart Mothers (www.heartmothers.net) which cares for young girls rescued from sex trafficking in Cambodia, and it has so far raised hundreds of dollars for these survivors. So for now, at least, I will continue to make it available.

If you enjoy this book, please do check out my others – all royalties from them also go to the charity. If you enjoy historical fiction try *Her Ladyship's Secret* (a regency romance) or *Fields of Glory* (a World War II thriller) and if you're in the mood for a light comedy you might enjoy *The Husband Hunt.*

Of course, if you're a Twilight fan, you really should buy *Midnight Sun* by Stephenie Meyer.

Chapter One

If you're going to get stuck for eternity at a certain age, seventeen is not the age you should go for. Thirty-two would be about right, or maybe even thirty-five at a push. Old enough to be respected.

Old enough to not have to spend eternity in High School.

I often wondered whether this was purgatory, and I was paying for my sins by having to sit through all these tedious classes, but people supposedly got out of purgatory once their atonement was finished, and there was no sign of my personal atonement ever ending. Maybe it was just plain old hell, Gehenna, the underworld, Gre'Thor, or Detroit.

Why the heck couldn't Carlisle and Esme just say I was home schooled?

To make matters worse I was afflicted with the noise of several hundred voices in my head, all day, every day.

"Phew! It was a silent one – but can anyone smell it?"

"I'm not gay, but for Edward Cullen I'd make an exception."

"I'll be there for yoooouuuu, when the rain starts to fall. I'll be there for yoooouuu…"

I tried to shut out the various earworms, insecurities and fantasies by making patterns out of the cracks in the paint on the wall, but most of the boys were mentally undressing the new girl who had arrived just that day, and their combined thoughts gave a volume which refused to be ignored to the image of the pale little brunette girl randomly shedding her clothing, for no reason whatsoever.

Alice called my name and I thankfully tuned into her thoughts. She was worried about Jasper, and since I could see into his mind she relied on me to let her know how he was getting on. Quite why Esme and Carlisle thought it appropriate to send *him* into a building with several hundred happy meals on legs I would never understand, despite my mind-reading abilities. I placated Alice, kicked Jasper's chair to remind him that I was watching his thoughts, and then fell back into my emo misery.

Hearing my name in Jessica Stanley's mind I was brought back to reality. She had taken the new girl under her wing, it seemed, and the new girl had noticed us. Hardly surprising, really, when we were incredibly good-looking, deathly pale, and most of us were already paired up. Given that our cover story is that we were all the adopted children of the town's doctor and his wife—a story Jessica Stanley was already regaling the new girl with—it was only to be expected that people would be curious. What would they ask?

Why do they all look so alike when they're adopted from different families?

How the heck did Carlisle and Esme Cullen ever get approved to adopt teenagers when they're not even in their thirties?

Seriously, would it have killed Carlisle to give a bit more time and effort to his cover story? I mean, he's a doctor, right? Couldn't he have said that we all had some rare illness he was an expert in and we were living with him so that he could study us?

I told Emmett that Jessica was telling the new girl about us. "I hope she's making it good," he laughed in his head, and when I discreetly

4

explained that she wasn't, he asked what the new girl thought of what she was hearing.

I tried to tune into the new girl. I strained to pick up her curiosity, her interest, her nervousness, anything. Nothing. I checked that she was still in the room, sitting next to Jessica Stanley, and my eyes locked with hers. *Awkward.*

I endeavoured to hear her thoughts, but she was as completely empty-headed as I'd expect her blonde friend to be. It was somewhat disconcerting, especially with everyone else in the room screaming their attraction for her, jealousy of her, or annoyance that I had noticed her when I ignored them.

She looked away first. *Yay, I won!* Blushing, she asked Jessica Stanley about me, and then sneaked another look at me from the corner of her eye. Jessica gave some dismissive reply typical of her, telling the girl not to waste her time thinking about me. Which, apparently, she wasn't. Or at least, not strongly enough for me to be able to hear it. She wasn't thinking about *anything.* She was a void, an abyss, a vacuum in the brain department. She could have run for congress.

She was clearly an android sent to destroy the puny humans.

I liked her already.

Rosalie suggested we leave for class, so we stood up, en masse as usual, and strode handsomely in slow motion across the cafeteria, a light indoor breeze blowing our hair into attractive ripples as we basked in the adoring and admiring looks of the vulnerable children.

My next class was biology. I already knew everything there was to know on this subject, as well as all the others taught in this backwater school. This fact made school even more boring than it already was for everyone else, as well as making me unbearably smug. I settled into my

5

habitual seat and prepared to entertain myself by listening to all the ways in which the other students misunderstood what Mr Banner said.

Bella—the new girl—was in this class. Her name in her fellow students' minds preceded her entry to the classroom, but the real fanfare which announced her presence came when the heating duct sent a jet of warm air across her and toward me.

Her scent hit me like a wrecking ball. It was apple pie cooling on a window sill. It was diesel fumes on a dusty road on a warm day. It was Beyoncé's latest overpriced perfume creation with some poncey name like "White Heat".

It was the reason I existed. It was all I wanted at that point, and all I could imagine ever wanting.

So, she wasn't an android after all, then.

In that instant I had to have her. My throat ached with agonising thirst, as though no other source of nourishment had ever existed for me. It ceased to matter that I was in a classroom full of innocent human children: whatever carnage might result would be worth it to get a taste of that rich, oily blood.

Except that Alice had only just bought me this Ralph Lauren shirt and she'd kill me if I got blood all over it.

A random motion wafted un-Bella-scented air over me and I snapped back to my normal, restrained self. Never mind Alice, Carlisle would be very disappointed in me and I'd set back all those years of carefully practiced self-control. I wanted to be better than that; I wanted to be true to the self I had built for so many decades.

Bella stumbled awkwardly, then settled down noisily on the only empty seat in the room—beside me. I leaned away from her, trying to escape the all-pervading smell, and wishing someone in the room would fart so that there would be something to mask it. I spent the rest of the lesson holding my breath to avoid drinking in that hypnotic scent, and thinking about ways to kill her. It was pleasantly diverting, and made a nice change.

As soon as the lesson was over I fled to the sanctuary of my Volvo and played a CD of music which usually calmed me. The Police had been one of my favourite bands in the 80s, and as I listened to 'I like to eat my friends' I found that the moment of madness was passing. I switched my 6-CD multichanger to the Fine Young Cannibals and allowed the cool, damp air to clear away all trace of Isabella Swan's scent.

I didn't have to kill her. If I could avoid her—and her mesmerizingly delicious scent—then things could be as they had always been. I could continue in my mind-numbingly boring half-life as though nothing had changed. I only had to endure another brief year or so of high school, and then Isabella Swan would go off to college, and I would probably do the same, heading as far as possible in the opposite direction. I hoped she didn't plan on going to Alaska, or I would end up in Florida, and that really wasn't a vampire-friendly state, even if I really did love those river rapid rides at Disneyworld.

I left my shiny Volvo and headed for the school office, where Mrs Cope, the school secretary, fluttered her eyelashes at me and trembled slightly at my approach. She would be putty in my hands. All women were.

Unfortunately it seemed that I could neither switch to physics nor drop biology. Mrs Cope would have loved to give me everything I wanted—and several things I didn't—but she had to consider the teachers. *Maybe Home Economics,* she thought. *I bet he'd look just darling in an apron. Or maybe I could sign him up as the life model in the art class.*

She had something there. I'd certainly be very good at keeping still while the students created their masterpieces.

"Please Mrs Cope, isn't there some other section I could switch to?" I pleaded, putting aside our shared mental image of me artistically naked in front of a class of teenaged artists. "I'm sure there's an open spot somewhere. Sixth hour biology can't be the only option."

The door had opened while I was engaged in negotiations with Mrs Cope, but I hadn't heard anyone enter, so had ignored it. When it opened a second time, however, a gust of wind blew into the room, picked up a scent and hurled it angrily in my direction.

She was in the room. I felt the venom spring to my mouth, and my muscles twitched as the predator in me readied itself for the most satisfying kill of my eternal life. I whirled round and saw her there, clutching a piece of paper, her eyes wide as she looked at me. No wonder I hadn't heard the thoughts of the person who had entered—but she had heard every word I said, and I could see from her wide eyes that she understood—or thought she understood—the reasons behind them.

She was right. I was trying to get away from her, to avoid her. I was right to try. Every particle in my eternal body was designed to destroy and feast upon this girl, and it ached to do so. If she were to live, I had to be as far from her as possible.

Holding my breath had worked before. Using the last of the air in my lungs I gasped thanks to Mrs Cope, and fled to my car.

It was lucky the stunning shiny Volvo was also spacious, because Emmett, Rosalie and Jasper were in the back seat (Jasper between Emmett and Rosalie, just to annoy them) and Alice waited anxiously in the passenger seat, an expression of bewilderment on her face. "What the heck, Edward!"

"Ha! See? It's not just me!" Jasper jabbed at Alice.

"Did you nearly eat the nice lady?" Rosalie teased.

I slammed the superb, stunning, shiny, spacious Volvo into gear and tried to drown out my family's thoughts with the squeal of tyres as I sped out of the car park. If Bella had seen my hasty retreat she could have been left in no doubt that I was running away from her.

"So," Alice pondered, "Are you going to kill her or are you going to get out of Dodge? Because right now I can see both options."

So could I, in Alice's thoughts. I could see myself at Chief Swan's house, stalking his only relative, and I could see myself driving the superb, stunning, shiny, spacious, silver Volvo at break-human-neck speed to Alaska. I liked the latter better, and even as I decided it, the image became stronger, clearer. The only other vegetarian vampires we knew lived in Denali, and Kate, Tanya and Irina would welcome my company. It would be a suitably safe distance from the girl who could be my downfall. And I could have fun building a snowman, maybe an igloo, and seeing whether I could break my own snowball throwing record.

Chapter Two

I stayed only a week in Alaska. Despite the daft name, Forks felt more like home than anywhere I had lived before, and I wanted to return almost as soon as I left. I missed my family too, and in my race to get away I had forgotten to pack my charger. As I watched the battery power slowly, agonisingly, drain away, I knew I had to go back.

She was just a puny human girl, and I surely wasn't the first teenaged boy to find himself bewitched by a mysterious woman. It was almost cliché, the idea of the strikingly good-looking boy overcome with desire for the very ordinary girl who was somehow different from everyone else, unavailable and closed to him. It could give hope to clumsy, introverted, acne-ridden, ordinary teenage girls for years, until they realised that someday some equally ordinary man would love and cherish them, and that would be better than any fantasy.

It was time to man up and face this strange girl with the overpowering scent and the obscured thoughts. I had spent decades learning to overcome my base vampire nature, and now I had to face this new challenge head on.

Alice clucked around me like a mother hen as we sat in the school cafeteria, her thoughts no longer entirely on Jasper. He wasn't the weakest of us any longer, and on some level she was pleased by that, even if her concern was annoying.

I scanned the thoughts of all the children, looking for anything Bella might have said to them, but there was nothing more than the residual interest in the new girl, and I was disappointed.

I stiffened as Bella entered the cafeteria, accompanied by Jessica Stanley and Mike Newton. All my senses, acute as they were, tuned to her, and I felt renewed frustration that her mind was silent to me. I heard her say that she wanted only a soda because she felt a little sick, and found myself strangely alarmed. Why should it bother me if the girl had a churning gassy stomach? Was I worried that her burps or farts would smell as appealing to me as her body odour?

As she sat down beside her new friend I found myself looking at her. My eyes met hers, and she quickly looked away, but as though transfixed I couldn't stop staring at her. People were noticing. My brothers and sisters were rolling their eyes. Jessica was getting annoyed and pointed out my incessant gaze to Bella.

"He doesn't look angry, does he?" Bella whispered. She had assumed that I had something against her, then. She was bright – she had understood the scene in Mrs Cope's office, or thought she had.

"No," Jessica replied. "Should he be?"

"I don't think he likes me very much."

"The Cullens don't like anybody. Well, they don't notice anybody enough to like them. But he's still staring at you."

"Stop looking at him," Bella asked, and Jessica, seething with jealousy, obeyed. I couldn't stop looking at Bella as easily. I watched her that entire lunch hour, trying to glean the tiniest clues about her from her body language, her tone, the contributions she made to her friends' conversations. Once or twice I thought her eyes seemed tempted to flicker in my direction, yet she resolutely focussed on her small group of friends, even as I steadfastly ignored my apprehensive family.

Sitting on that hard plastic chair in a featureless room full of humans in a dull high school in a small obscure town, I found that I felt something I hadn't felt in a long time. *Happy.*

I stayed in the cafeteria long after the other students had left, processing what was happening. Something in my eternally interminable life was changing, and that little girl from Arizona was the reason why. She had awoken something in me. The terrifying predator, yes, but also something else. I wanted to find out what it was. I needed to spend more time with her, and my next class was biology.

Alice, who had waited with me, assured me that it was safe for me to go, that I was almost certainly not going to massacre all the students. I decided to hold my breath wherever possible, just to be sure, and hurried to class faster than was wise, worried I had tarried too long in the lunch room.

She was sitting at the desk doodling. I decided to start again, and smiled as I sat beside her. "Hello. My name is Edward Cullen." I knew she knew, but she didn't know that I knew that she knew, and she couldn't be allowed to know how I knew that she knew.

She looked up to acknowledge me, but didn't say anything. As our eyes met I said, "I didn't have a chance to introduce myself last week. You must be Bella Swan."

"How do you know my name?" she demanded.

I resisted the urge to say, "It's written on your folder" or "How often do you think a new student come to this school?" and instead settled for, "Oh, I think everyone knows your name. The whole town's been waiting for you to arrive."

She blushed, as though embarrassed to be the centre of attention. "No, I meant, why did you call me Bella?"

"Do you prefer Isabella?"

"No, I like Bella, but I think Charlie—I mean my dad—must call me Isabella behind my back. That's what everyone here seems to know me as."

Oops. Clue One. How would I know that when I had barely seen her?

We worked together on the lab, examining five slides of onion root in turns. Despite my checking each answer she gave, she was always correct. I had been right in my initial assumption: she was smart. At one point our hands touched as we both reached to remove a slide, and I wondered whether she'd noticed that my fingers were ice-cold. *Clue two.*

We finished the work before the other pairs. Bella had evidently done this topic before, as had I, numerous times. As we waited I found her looking at me. "Did you get contacts?" she asked suddenly.

"No," I responded automatically, confused at the left-of-field question.

"Oh. I thought there was something different about your eyes," she said.

Clue three. I had been hunting over the weekend, trying to satiate my thirst in preparation for the ordeal of Bella-induced craving. My eyes were now dark. Given that she'd seen so little of me last week, I was surprised that she'd noticed the change. I shrugged, and was pleased to see Mr Banner approaching us, ending Bella's opportunity to question me further.

"So, Edward, didn't you think Isabella should get a chance with the microscope?"

"Bella," I corrected him, and while I was on a roll, "Actually, she identified three of the five."

"Have you done this lab before?" Mr Banner asked Bella.

14

"Not with onion root," she replied, shyly.

"Whitefish blastula?" When Bella nodded he asked, "Were you in an advanced placement program in Phoenix? Well, then, I guess it's good that you two are lab partners."

She was smart. I had been right. Smart enough to put together the clues and figure out what was different about me? I decided to distract her with mindless, normal human conversation, just to emphasise how exactly like every other high school student I was.

"It's too bad about the snow, isn't it?" I said.

"Not really," she replied, surprising me. Not being able to read her thoughts meant that her reactions came as a genuine revelation.

"You don't like the cold," I said. Duh. Stupid thing to say when she'd just admitted that she liked snow. Snow is generally cold, and she liked it. If I was going to try to sound like a half-witted teenage boy I was doing a good job.

"Or the wet," she agreed, which was nice of her.

"Forks must be a difficult place to live," I observed.

"You have no idea," she said darkly, and I was intrigued.

"Why did you come here, then?" I was really rocking the rude and ignorant teenage boy thing.

"It's complicated."

"I think I can keep up." I really, really wanted to know what had brought this enigmatic and compelling girl across my path.

"My mother got remarried," she said.

I understood. Teenage girls and stepfathers were often a volatile combination. "That doesn't sound complex. When did this happen?"

"Last September."

"And you don't like him," I concluded triumphantly.

15

"No, Phil is fine," she smiled, throwing me for a loop again. "Too young, maybe, but nice enough."

Now I was genuinely confused, and that wasn't something I was used to. "Why didn't you stay with them?"

"Phil travels a lot. He plays ball for a living."

A bit more gentle questioning, and I was able to establish that he wasn't a major league baseball player that I might have heard of.

"And your mother sent you here so that she could travel with him?" I was assuming again, and assuming wrong, as it turned out.

Bella was emphatic in her reply. "No, she did not send me here. I sent myself. She stayed with me at first, but she missed him. It made her unhappy, so I decided to spend some quality time with Charlie."

"But now you're unhappy," I observed.

"And?" She really didn't care. Her mother's happiness was more important to her. She was smart and she cared more for others than she did for her own comfort. I could really admire this girl.

"That doesn't seem fair."

She laughed. "Hasn't anyone ever told you? Life isn't fair."

"I believe I *have* heard that somewhere before."

"So that's all," she told me. She seemed to be trying to draw our awkward conversation to a close, but I wasn't ready for that. I had this typical teenage boy thing *down*. I was going to keep pestering her until she went nuts and killed *me*.

"You put on a good show, but I'd be willing to bet that you're suffering more than you let anyone see. Am I wrong?" When she grimaced I added, "I didn't think so."

"What does it matter to you?" she demanded.

I only wished I knew. Why did I care about this girl's life story? "That's a very good question. Am I annoying you?"

"Not exactly. I'm more annoyed at myself. My face is so easy to read, my mother always calls me her open book."

That was ironic—her face might be easy to read, but in every other respect she was the most obscured person I had ever come across. I told her something like that, and she commented that I must be good at reading people.

Mr Banner called for attention. The other pairs had now finished their work, and it was time to turn our attention back to him. As Bella turned her head to look at the teacher, her hair wafted her alluring scent back towards me, and I found all my composure gone, my mouth running with venom, my heart once again that of the monster, my mind crying for her quick death. I struggled to put down the beast within me, holding my breath, reminding myself that I *had* resisted her, I *had* had a normal friendly conversation with her, and I *could* continue to see her, day after day, without succumbing to that overpoweringly seductive and tantalising fragrance. When that failed I imagined the poor cleaning woman trying to mop up the mess there'd be once I'd finished. I liked Roseanna, she worked hard and her thoughts were always happy. That did it.

I didn't hear much of the rest of the lesson. I sat abnormally still, wrestling inwardly with my monstrous urges and desires. It wasn't usually wise for us to remain so still, to not breathe, in case those around us noticed, but on this occasion it seemed safer than the alternative. If I had to divert even the smallest fraction of my capacious attention to mimicking the little traits which would make me look human it might release enough of my hold on my self-control to result in disaster.

"Cullen looks like he's desperate for a pee," I heard Mike Newton observe mentally. *"Or desperate for something else,"* and his thoughts conjured up an image of Bella and I that neither of us liked very much, he because I was part of it, and me because it was improper and obscene.

When the lesson ended Bella headed off to her next class—gym with Mike Newton himself—and I retreated again to the safety of my superb, stunning, shiny, spacious, speedy silver Volvo to listen to *Bring your Daughter to the Slaughter* by Iron Maiden. I sat there, practising my self-control in a way I hadn't had to since the nineteen-thirties, waiting for Bella to come out of school.

When she trudged carefully across the snow, clapping her hands together for warmth, she didn't even notice me watching her. The ancient Chevy truck a few cars down from mine turned out to be her vehicle. It really didn't suit her, but by this time I was used to being surprised by everything about her.

Chapter Three

I hunted with Carlisle again that night, knowing that I would see Bella the next day and wanting to do everything vampirely possible to protect her from the monster in me. I had considered running away again, but didn't want to either abandon or uproot my family. Besides which my pride wouldn't let me take this easy way out, and neither would my common-sense. What was to say that I wouldn't come across another human in the future with a scent which inflamed my senses? Was I going to run away every time someone smelled more delicious than usual?

So the following morning saw almost a reversed replay of the previous afternoon. I was getting out of in my car as I watched the ancient rusty Chevy truck drive into the school parking lot. Bella got out, earbud leads snaking from under her hair to her coat pocket, (has she ever even read the highway code?) and I watched as she bent down to look at her tyres.

At the same moment that she did so I heard the roar of Tyler Crowley's engine, almost drowned out by his thoughts. The snow had thawed overnight, and refrozen into ice, and Tyler had entered the parking lot at typically injudicious speed, his wheels had locked into a skid, and his mind screamed and reverberated the horror as his van headed uncontrollably in Bella's direction.

My internal screams echoed his: it would kill me if Bella died before I had decided whether to eat her or not. This could not be allowed to play out the way I was already seeing it in Alice's head.

I didn't stop to think more than that. I flew toward Bella so fast that I must have been barely a blur to any onlookers. I wrapped my right arm around her waist and pulled her to the side of her truck, out of the path of the careening van. The sudden jolt made her head fall back, knocking painfully against the pavement as she fell. Her earbuds flew out of her ears and I heard the tinny chords of *Maneater* by Hall and Oates.

With a sharp and painful thud and crunch, the front of Tyler's van met the unyielding strength of Bella's ancient rusty red Chevy truck. It ricocheted off, spinning again on the ice, and heading toward where the vulnerable girl lay startled in the embrace of the invulnerable vampire. Cursing physics, I stuck out my left hand and slammed it into the underside of the van, hoping I'd picked an out-of-sight spot to leave the imprint of my hand, simultaneously stopping the van's progress and lifting it so that it didn't crush Bella's legs.

Clue four.

Bella was staring up at me in shock. I found that I was so overwhelmingly relieved and happy to see those deep brown eyes alert and aware that it almost didn't matter that I had possibly exposed our family's secret, put us all in terrible danger, and mussed up my hair.

I asked if she was alright, and she dazedly replied that she was fine. Despite her assurances I warned her, "Be careful. You hit your head pretty hard." It had only been a little bump as I pulled her to safety, but it might not be a bad idea if she attributed any delusions of me streaking like The Flash across Forks High's parking lot and then single-handedly (literally) stopping a speeding van to her head injury.

"Ow," she confirmed, pressing a hand to her head. Then, "How in the… How did you get over here so fast?"

She had noticed. I decided to bluff it out. I blinked twice, the way humans do when they are being perfectly honest. "I was standing right next to you, Bella."

She looked up at me, searching my placid face for any trace of guile, then tried to stand up. "Just stay put for now," I advised.

"But it's *cold,*" she protested, and I laughed.

"You were over there," she said accusingly. "You were by your car."

"No I wasn't." How long had she been staring thoughtfully at her tyres before Tyler had skidded into the parking lot? Was it conceivable that I might have been walking at normal human pace toward her during those few seconds?

"I saw you," she insisted. She evidently didn't think so.

"Bella, I was standing with you and I pulled you out of the way."

"No."

I needed her to believe me. I had hoped that I could confidently bluff, make her doubt what she had seen, but she without being able to read which way her thoughts were going I found myself suddenly unsure, was she too smart, too perceptive or so dumb she'd swallow any line I fed her? So my next alternative was to turn on the charm and wheedle. I fluttered my eyelashes. "*Please,* Bella."

She demanded to know why she should accept my version of events, and I found myself promising (with my fingers crossed behind my back) to explain everything to her later. She grudgingly acquiesced, and I was able to give my version of events to the crowd of onlookers, and the EMTs when they arrived.

Charlie Swan sped into the parking lot at the same dangerous speed and angle Tyler had, but by dint of not being a foolhardy teenage boy, managed not to kill anyone. Seeing the cruiser unexpectedly alarmed me; I had trotted out my lies to the students, teachers and EMTs, but it felt wrong to be dishonest to the man who was not only the Chief of Police but also Bella's anxious father.

Charlie's mind was a turmoil of worry and questions, but as I listened in order to gauge my response to him it was difficult to make out specific thoughts. It was as though I was listening to a badly tuned radio: I could make out occasional words, but mostly it was a jumble of feelings and impressions. Curious that Bella's mind was entirely closed to me, and her father's was partially obscured.

Bella, wearing a neck brace and being loaded onto an ambulance, called reassurance to Charlie that she was fine, and his concern subsided enough for him to agree to follow her to the hospital in his cruiser rather than ride along in the ambulance. He didn't seem to want to speak to me, for which I was grateful, and I drove at some distance behind him as he tailed the ambulance to the hospital.

Following a cop car was a new one for me – generally it was the other way around. I did have a habit of driving extremely fast. For a human my speeds would be reckless and dangerous, but I had lightning-fast reflexes, and an internal early-warning system of any driver coming towards me on blind bends. So, like every seventeen-year-old boy ever I drove stupidly fast and made excuses about how I was a fantastic driver with special skills so the rules didn't apply to me

Once I saw, from a safe distance, that Bella was being cared for, I sought out Carlisle in his office. Of course, he wasn't there, because doctors are busy people and don't generally have time to sit around in their offices all day sharpening pencils. Listening to the hum of thoughts I identified Carlisle near the nurses' station looking through charts, and sought him out.

"What have you done now, Edward?" he groaned, seeing me in the hospital when I should have been at school. "You didn't—"

"Quite the opposite," I said proudly and yet with the slightest sheepishness as I remembered that I had endangered our family. "I saved her. But I think I did bad." I outlined what had happened and Carlisle rolled his eyes and tutted.

"I'll go pack," he said. "Esme'll be mad. She likes it here. She's joined this great ladies' craft circle and next month she was going to teach them all to make lavender sachets."

"Let me try to contain the breach first," I begged. "It's only Bella who suspects. No one else saw anything, and she took a bump to the head. I might still be able to persuade her."

Carlisle nodded. "Very well, I'm going to give you a chance to clear up your mess, but only because I was looking forward to seeing all those cute little lavender sachets. Now, I expect you'll want me to take a look at her?"

I was torn. Seeing Carlisle and me together would surely drop another big clue. Bella knew we weren't related by blood, yet we were both pale and perfect. To be honest, it was a miracle the entire town hadn't been asking for years how come we all seemed to have the same pallor. Esme and Carlisle were friendly with the locals – how was it that none of them had ever commented on our unusual appearance? Maybe they had wondered, but no human had yet had the benefit of all the clues I had inadvertently dropped for Bella.

Despite my misgivings, I trusted Carlisle's medical judgement, wanted Bella to have the best, and for some strange reason I really wanted Carlisle to meet her. It was important to me that the man I most respected should be introduced to the girl I… well, who seemed to be the flame to which I was irresistibly drawn. "Knock yourself out," I said finally.

"Like you almost did to her?" he shot back.

Oh ha ha.

Hospitals are not a comfortable place for vampires, and it had always amazed me that Carlisle would choose to work in one. Today it was easier for me than usual, however. My mind was entirely focussed on Bella, so much so that when I saw her lying asleep I almost failed to notice Tyler Crowley in the next bay being tended to by a nurse. His mind was filled with remorse, but I still felt angry with him. If he had just driven more responsibly Bella might not have almost been killed, and our family might not be facing the need to move on again.

It startled me that I should come across Bella so suddenly without realising that she was there. I had grown too used to having people's thoughts announce their presence. And yet Tyler's thoughts were loud and irritating but I hadn't noticed them in my single-minded searching for Bella.

Tyler looked up at me and started to say something, but I wasn't interested in his apologies. "Is she sleeping?" I asked.

Apparently she wasn't, because at the sound of my voice Bella's eyes flew open and she fixed me with an accusing look. She still wasn't buying my story, and she wordlessly demanded the explanation I'd promised.

"Hey Edward, I'm really sorry—" Tyler began, but I waved away his apology.

"No blood, no foul," I grinned. He wasn't the one I wanted to speak to, plus he was covered in blood; it was safer for me to remain very focussed on Bella. "So, what's the verdict?" I asked her, keeping my voice light.

"There's nothing wrong with me at all, but they won't let me go. Hey, how come you aren't strapped to a gurney like the rest of us?"

"It's about who you know," I said as Carlisle entered the room. "But don't worry, I came to spring you."

"So, Miss Swan, how are you feeling?" Carlisle asked. He hadn't introduced himself to her the way doctors are supposed to, but there was probably no need. Bella's mouth was hanging open in surprise as she looked from Carlisle to me and back again. There was no mistaking the resemblance, and yet she knew I was 'adopted'. *Clue Five.* I toyed with explanations in case Bella asked about it. "We've just got back from a vacation in Lapland, it's midnight sunburn - it makes you go paler", or "The whole family was in the car when we had an accident – we collided with a tanker of bleach", or "Esme's cooking is terrible, it makes us all really sick."

"I'm fine," she insisted, and then repeated her statement when Carlisle asked about her head injury. She allowed him to examine her scalp, insisting that it didn't hurt even when it clearly did. She was brave too, I noted.

"Well, your father is in the waiting room," Carlisle told her. "You can go home with him now, but come back if you feel dizzy or have trouble with your eyesight at all."

"Can't I go back to school?" she pleaded.

"Maybe you should take it easy today," Carlisle suggested

"Does *he* get to go back to school?" She glared at me.

You can handle this one, Carlisle thought to me.

"Someone has to spread the good news that we survived," I laughed.

"Actually, most of the school seems to be in the waiting room," Carlisle said, and Bella groaned, but insisted that she wanted to go, even

25

though she stumbled a little when she got up from the bed. I was just starting to feel the first hint of relief that Bella would soon be heading home with Charlie and I could collect my thoughts and work out how to bluff it out, when she made clear that she wanted to speak to me *right now.*

"Your father is waiting for you," I suggested hopefully. *Go home, Bella. Don't ask me about it. I haven't made up my excuses yet. A man needs time for these things…*

She was having none of it, and even as I walked to a quiet part of the hospital corridor, I felt that I was being dragged there by the ear, like a man discovered in a downtown bar when he'd claimed to his old lady that he'd be working late.

"What do you want from me, Bella?" I demanded, trying to hold on to the tattered shreds of my manhood and dignity.

She was calm even in the face of my bravado. "I want to know the truth. I want to know why I'm lying for you."

I was playing the role of henpecked man very well. Rule one: admit nothing until you ascertain what she suspects. "What do you think happened?"

"All I know is that you weren't anywhere near me—Tyler didn't see you either, so don't tell me I hit my head too hard. That van was going to crush us both—and it didn't, and your hands left dents in the side of it—and you left a dent in the other car, and you're not hurt at all—and the van should have smashed my legs but you were holding it up."

Oh. Right.

"You think I lifted a van off you?"

She nodded.

Henpecked man rule number two: appeal to the perception of peers. "Nobody will believe that, you know."

"I'm not going to tell anybody," she declared.

She looked as though she meant it. I was relieved. "Then why does it matter?"

"It matters to me. I don't like to lie—so there'd better be a good reason why I'm doing it."

Like you lying to your mother about wanting to spend time with your father? "Can't you just thank me and get over it?"

"Thank you."

"You're not going to let this go, are you?"

"No."

"In that case, get used to disappointment."

We glared at each other, but I was less convincing in my scowl because I found I rather admired her. She was fearless in confronting me, and unapologetic in declaring what she had witnessed, however impossible it sounded. She was also going to protect my secret, even though she was angry at me for keeping it. She was honest and honourable.

"Why did you even bother?" she spat.

I told her the truth. "I don't know." Why does anyone ever save anyone's life? It's a mystery.

With one final scathing look in my direction, she stalked off to find Charlie.

Chapter Four

"Inverness is very nice," Jasper suggested. "Lots of cloud and rain, great scenery, a big local problem with too many wild deer, and a fantastic second-hand bookshop."

"We could discover the Loch Ness Monster," Alice said. "I bet it tastes really good."

"What about Norilsk?" Rosalie asked. "I could do with brushing up on my Russian, and polar bears are so delicious."

"Do we *have* to go?" I pleaded.

Emmett was keeping up a monologue in his mind of all the insulting names he could think to direct towards me. *Moron! Jackass! Idiot! Fool! Lunatic! Chump! Sucker! Dope! Imbecile! Mug! Buffoon!* It was rather distracting, especially when he ran out of English words and started on other languages.

"I think it would look more suspicious if we leave at this point," Carlisle said. *You owe me for this, Edward. And the slightest hint of trouble and we're off.* "Alice, the girl told Edward she wouldn't say anything. Do you see her breaking that promise?"

Alice crossed her eyes for a second, then grinned. "No, she's not going to say anything, and she and I are going to be best buds! How fun—I can't wait to meet her."

"Best buds?" Rosalie said, aggrieved.

"We're going to be like that!" Alice held up crossed fingers.

29

"Well, thanks," Rosalie hissed sarcastically. "I thought *I* was your best friend."

"You can't be my best friend, you're my sister."

"I'm not really your sister."

"Well, no, but—"

"Are you saying that sisters can't be friends too? Are you ditching me for this pathetic little accident-prone human?"

"Rosalie, you're taking this the wrong way!"

I cut in. "Please, Rosalie, this isn't about you." Rosalie shot me a look which completely matched her thought: *Traitor! This is your doing!*

Alice tried hard to placate her jealous sibling. "Rose, you'll always be my very best friend, you know that."

"Really? That's not what you said a minute ago."

"Well at least I'm not as bad as Edward. Edward's going to be *in love* with her."

I stared at Alice, stunned into silence. Around me, Alice's words echoed in my family's heads. Except Emmett's. Emmett was still reciting *idiota! Идиот! Ηλίθιος!*

"In love with her?" I said, stunned.

"Aren't you already?"

If I thought about it, I had to admit that the signs were all there.

"Either that or you'll kill her."

Chapter Five

She was true to her word not to tell anyone about my apparent superpowers, and I had to add *trustworthy* to the list of qualities I admired about her. Qualities which, apparently, I would come to love, if I didn't already.

Perhaps it went partway to explaining why I had rescued her that day. My family generally obeyed the prime directive and didn't interfere with the natural state of human affairs, but in that moment I had known that Bella had to live, and it was nothing to do with the risk of how I might behave if her blood were to be spilled across the asphalt.

I let the days pass quietly, trying to let everything go back to how it had once been: the interminable days of going to lessons to relearn facts I already knew; listening to the imbecilic inanity of teenage thoughts; mentally counting off the days but all the while not knowing what I was counting towards, or why.

Bella and I mostly ignored each other. She greeted me indifferently that first day, after which we barely spoke. Her scent still tantalised me, so I held my breath in biology and tried to avoid her at other times—not easy when I couldn't detect her thoughts and use them as an early-warning system.

I could handle this. Another brief year of this, and our paths would diverge, probably never to cross again. Bella would go away to college, meet some handsome jock, move into his trailer and have his babies...

My complacency was destroyed by the spring dance. Mike Newton asked Bella to the dance during biology class, and I found myself suddenly tuned completely into their exchange, inwardly seething with more than just a desire for Bella's blood. The monster within, the one I had been trying to control for these last weeks, was now a green monster.

She turned him down, to my considerable relief, claiming she had plans in Seattle that day. I spent the rest of the lesson wondering what those plans might be, whether she was meeting someone else, whether she was just claiming them as an excuse not to go to the dance with Mike, or whether she just fancied a day in her pyjamas singing into her hairbrush and painting her nails. I had to speak to her.

"Bella."

"What, are you speaking to me again?"

"No, not really," I admitted.

"Then what do you want, Edward?"

Excellent question. What did I want to ask her? Why was I even talking to her? What was I going to say?

"I'm sorry," I said in the end, which was pretty lame. "I'm being very rude, I know, but it's better this way, really."

"I don't know what you mean," she said.

"It's better if we're not friends. Trust me." If was going to ignore her for the next year, it was probably good that I set the parameters for doing so.

She stared angrily at me for a moment, then said, "It's too bad you didn't figure that out earlier. You could have saved yourself all this regret."

I was confused. "Regret? Regret for what?"

"For not letting that stupid van squish me!"

I was astonished. Who could ever regret saving another person's life? What kind of a monster did she think I was? Because, even monsters have limits you know, I wasn't *that* bad, surely. "You think I regret saving you?"

"I know you do."

I took back all the times I had thought she was smart. "You don't know anything!"

Huffily, she grabbed all her books and stalked out of the room without even looking at me. She'd barely passed the doorway when I heard the crash of her textbooks hitting the ground. That was my Bella, endearingly clumsy as ever. I was at her side in an instant, picking up the books and handing them back to her. She growled her thanks in a tone as irritated as it had been at the end of our conversation, and I responded in the customary way with similar surliness.

It had not been the most satisfactory exchange, and yet I found myself curiously buoyed by it. It took me the whole of the next lesson to figure out why: I'd got to her. She felt something for me—mostly anger, but it was something.

I became aware from the thoughts of those around me that two more boys wanted to ask Bella to the dance and were psyching themselves up to do so as soon as school ended. I'd felt extremely jealous when Mike Newton asked her, but now that I knew I'd got under her skin I was curious to know what she'd say to these two boys. So curious, in fact, that I deliberately blocked the exit so that Tyler Crowley would be able to ask her after Eric had been turned down.

She was furious to be cornered, I heard in her tone. That amused me, almost as much as hearing her give the same excuse to Tyler as she had to Eric and Mike. She didn't want to go to the dance with anyone. Maybe she really was going to Seattle.

33

I wondered whether she'd accept if *I* asked her. Not only was that a really bad idea, but it was girls' choice, and so to do so would be crass. All the same, if three guys had asked her to a girls' choice dance, how many might be in line to do so when it wasn't?

I barely acknowledged my family when I arrived home. I'd seen my siblings at school, of course, but Esme liked to ask whether I'd had a good day, and since every day for the last five decades had been pretty much identical, it was getting to be a tough question to answer with any real meaning.

I debating staying in my room and doing my embroidery, but decided instead to go and watch Bella sleep. After all, with 200 television channels available to me, and a complete library of the best films of the last fifty years, not to mention the almost endless music collection I'd amassed, there was nothing more interesting to do than stare at Bella as she did nothing at all.

Maybe being in her presence would help me get used to her mesmerising scent, harden myself against its effects. Maybe her subconscious mind would be more open to me than her conscious one, and I might be able to share in her dreams. Or maybe I was just unhealthily obsessed with her and wanted to be in her bedroom for no acceptable reason at all.

Still, when I'd spent the last few weeks ignoring her, only speaking to her to tell her I was going to ignore her some more, this plumbing of new depths was entirely in character.

I entered her bedroom with ease. Finding out which of the windows was hers was as simple as tasting the air and jumping up to it; opening it wider so that I could climb in was hardly more difficult.

There she lay, hair scattered across the pillow, legs and arms carelessly splayed in all directions, drooling slightly from the corner of her mouth.

Her room was untidy. Underwear had missed the hamper, and candy wrappers had missed the trash can. CDs were spread across a desk, piled on top of papers which were probably homework. The closet drawer was slightly ajar, and an empty cereal bowl was under the bed, the dregs of the milk long since past the sour and lumpy stage and now crusted onto the surface.

So, a perfectly normal teenage girl, then. I settled down on the chair in the corner, sitting on top of the clothes Bella had been wearing today, watching as she snored and savouring her scent as though it were a fine wine.

I was training myself. Breathe the scent – feel the venom pool – stop breathing – let the craving abate – rinse and repeat. I would keep doing this, I reasoned, until my vampire nature was quelled; until my instincts had been conquered and the inner monster had learned to associate Bella's scent with restraint. And if I failed, at least I'd have a diploma in stalking under my belt. Or maybe with disappointment and frustration, the way so many teenage boys had to learn the real meaning of girls' perfumes.

I still couldn't hear her thoughts, which made it difficult to know for sure whether she was really asleep. Instead I listened to her heartbeat; slow, rhythmic, peaceful. It was quicker during the day when she was awake; at least, it was when she was with me.

She snored noisily but musically, occasionally snorted, drooled with abandon, farted when she rolled over, and mumbled words which even my super-human hearing couldn't make out. It was quite entertaining, in a daytime TV kind of way.

35

"Edward," she said, suddenly, clearly. Before I could stop myself I was crouched at her bedside, inches from her slumbering face. She hadn't taken off her make-up before she went to sleep. Her mascara had stained little dark bags under her eyes, and her cheekbones were imprinted on her pillow.

"Edward," she declared again. "I'm just testing fish."

I stifled a laugh, and decided that watching her at night was probably less entertaining than listening to her. Then I realised that she'd uttered my name, and a thrill ran through me. I was in her dreams. Her subconscious was trying to process my place in her life. I *mattered* to her, in the same way that testing fish did.

I hoped touchscreen phones never took off, and Blackberry never went out of business. iPhone screens don't respond to cold, dead fingers, and fiddling with my phone made the hours I spent in Bella's bedroom, sucking in her scent and conditioning my response, a little less dull.

Chapter Six

I was still following her around the next day at school, so closely that I was able to pick up her dropped car keys and hand them back to her almost before they hit the ground. That annoyed her, so I went on to accuse her of being exceptionally unobservant and utterly absurd, make it clear that I'd deliberately given Tyler the opportunity to ask her to the dance. Finally, I insulted her truck as a reason for offering to drive her to Seattle the following Saturday.

It's lucky I had my looks. I must have confused the heck out of her with all my crazy flip-flopping about not being friends but wanting to be friends. I could only attribute her acceptance of my offer of a ride to my vampire splendour, unless she was some particular kind of masochist who liked her men obscure and obdurate.

I remained within earshot of Bella the entire morning – I was never more than five hundred yards away from her. When lunchtime came around I arrived early at the cafeteria and eschewed the table I usually shared with my siblings, to Rosalie's annoyance, hoping that Bella might sit with me.

My plan backfired – Bella didn't see me at first, and it was only when Jessica commented that I was staring at her that her eyes sought me out, and found mine. I beckoned her over. I even winked at her. She looked astonished, but picked up her drink and left her annoying friend to stumble towards me at my lonely table.

"Why don't you join me today?" I suggested when she hesitated.

She pulled out a chair and sat opposite me. "This is different."

"Well," I replied, "I decided as long as I was going to hell, I might as well do it thoroughly."

She likes men who are incomprehensible I reminded myself when she commented that she had no clue what I was talking about. After some pointless small-talk about her friends wanting her to sit with them, I elaborated: "I got tired of trying to stay away from you. So I'm giving up."

"Giving up?"

"Yes—giving up trying to be good. I'm just going to do what I want now, and let the chips fall where they may."

"You lost me again," she said apologetically. Nice of her really, to pretend she'd ever actually understood any of our conversation.

"I always say too much when I'm talking to you—that's one of the problems." Probably a good thing, then, that I *hadn't* been talking to her for over a month.

"Don't worry, I don't understand any of it," she said. Hardly surprising really, when I was so given to speaking in incomplete and disjointed sentences about things she had no idea about.

"I'm counting on that."

We carried on in this vein for a while: me giving vague, ambiguous statements about things she couldn't possibly have any clue about, and her prompting me for answers which only grew more unintelligible. We'd had these circular and meaningless conversations before, and unless she made decent progress in figuring out what I actually was, we'd probably keep having them for some time. I prompted her, gently probed to find out what she'd pieced together from the clues, but although she could recite an impressive litany of my peculiarities, she really hadn't got any further than a superhero theory.

Whatever else I was, I wasn't *that*. I didn't have the skin-tight costume.

I was suddenly stricken with the realisation that she thought I was *good*. Nothing could be further from the truth. "What if I'm not a superhero? What if I'm the bad guy?"

"Oh. I see."

"Do you?" She was only acknowledging what I'd told her before.

"You're dangerous," she shook her head firmly; she didn't believe this, "but not bad. No, I don't believe you're bad."

I tried to set her straight, but she wasn't buying it. I wanted to argue with her, declare *I'm bad, I'm bad, I'm really, really bad,* but my enhanced vampire singing abilities would probably give the lie to my words.

"We're going to be late," she said, standing up. I thrilled to hear that word *we* until I remembered that this wasn't a date, this was biology class, and I wasn't going. Mr. Banner was blood typing today, and it wasn't a good idea for me to be around bleeding humans.

When I told Bella I wouldn't be in class with her, she demanded "Why not?"

I had no ready prepared excuse. There *was* no possible excuse except the truth, so I went with "It's healthy to ditch class now and then." I knew it sounded lame, but it was at least true, it would be healthy for the other students if I ditched this particular class. I worried slightly it would severely diminish straight-A-student Bella's opinion of me, but, on the plus side, now I sounded more like an ordinary pathetic dropout teenage boy, one who had moods which lead to ignoring a girl for a month, and who liked to play with bottle tops.

"Well I'm going," she said.

"See you later then," I said without looking up.

I decided to pass the time in my car doing my knitting. I'd been knitting squares for a blanket ever since Emmett had taught me to knit, and if I ever bothered to stitch them together the blanket could now cover the entire town of Forks, but knitting calmed me, and it was creative and distracting, so I knitted.

I'd barely finished the twelfth row when a mental commotion dragged me from my woollen reverie and out of my car. Something was happening in Mr. Banner's biology class, and it involved Bella. I tried searching the thoughts of the students in her class but they all seemed to involve blood dripping out of fingers, so I quickly snapped my attention away again. The loudest mind – as usual – was Mike Newton's, and it was filled with delight at getting Bella to himself for a few minutes, and determination to show such manly concern and strength that she would melt into his arms.

It was a good thing vampires can't vomit.

"Bella!" I called, and Mike Newton's thoughts turned to jealous rage. I found him standing impotently over the figure of Bella, curled onto the pavement in an uncomfortable half-sitting, half-lying position. "What's wrong," I demanded. "Is she hurt?"

Mike wasn't really concerned about Bella at all. He was more anxious about himself, about me encroaching on his knight-in-shining armour routine. "I think she's fainted. I don't know what happened, she didn't even stick her finger."

Too late I remembered that if there was a risk that Bella was bleeding I should have kept my distance. It seemed I had lucked out again. I bent down. "Bella, can you hear me?"

"No," she groaned. "Go away."

Mike was blathering on about how he was taking her to the nurse, and it was his job, and he was supposed to do it, but Bella lying on the pavement was evidence enough of how he had failed at that simple task. Ignoring her protests – and Mike's – I scooped her up in my arms and carried her through the school office to the nurse's room.

"There's always one," the elderly nurse said when I explained what had happened, and we shared a chuckle. Then to Bella she suggested, "Just lie down for a minute, honey; it'll pass."

When the nurse suggested I return to class I borrowed Mike Newton's line and said that I was supposed to stay with her. This time it worked.

"You were right," Bella moaned when the nurse left the room to get some ice.

"I usually am—but about what in particular this time?"

"Ditching is healthy."

"You scared me for a minute there. I thought Newton was dragging your dead body off to bury it in the woods. Honestly—I've seen corpses with better colour. I was concerned that I might have to avenge your murder." It was quite a novel thought: that someone *else* might have killed Bella.

"Poor Mike. I bet he's mad." She understood then, perfectly, what that kid was up to.

He was on his way. Even now, he wasn't giving up. Fuelled by determination to win Bella for himself, and his hatred of me, he was going to make a last ditch effort to be the bold and strong man who saves the fair maiden. "He absolutely loathes me," I told her. I rather liked that about Mike. His jealousy of me was his best quality.

"You can't know that—" she began, then seemed to hesitate. I wondered whether she was wondering. I had, after all, frequently told her what others thought or felt. Yet another clue that I wasn't quite human.

"I saw his face—I could tell," I lied.

"How did you see me? I thought you were ditching."

"I was in my car, listening to a CD," I lied again.

Mrs Hammond bustled back in at that point, but Bella pushed away the ice pack protesting that she felt much better.

I smelled the blood at the same time as I heard Mike Newton's thoughts. Fury, and hope that Bella was still in the room. He was dragging Lee Stevens, who looked as pale as Bella had but had, in fact, actually stuck the needle in his finger, rather than just fainting at the thought of it. Mike had evidently designated himself the "Remove Sick Kids from Classroom Monitor" of the day.

I urged Bella out, partly because the sight of Lee's blood was like to make her faint again, partly because the room was small with only one bed and now Lee needed it, but mostly because I didn't trust myself to be around Lee while blood was dripping from his finger. This was *exactly* why I'd absented myself from Mr. Banner's class – now it seemed that half the class was coming to me.

"You actually listened to me," I observed in surprise when we were safely back in the school office.

"I smelled the blood," she replied.

Er… "People can't smell blood." Well, not *normal* people.

"Well, I can—that's what makes me sick."

I was dubious. I mentally challenged, *Oh yeah? What does it smell like, then?*

"It smells like rust … and salt."

She was correct. Of course, the rust was more to do with the iron, and sometimes it smelled quite sweet too, but—

"What?" she asked. I must have been staring at her. For a change.

Mike Newton's loud and annoying mental grumbling came through the door a minute before he did. "You look better," he said to Bella. He hadn't meant to sound as though he was accusing her; his anger towards me was spilling over into his voice.

"Just keep your hand in your pocket," Bella said.

"It's not bleeding anymore," he protested, then asked, "Are you going back to class?"

For the umpteenth time I wished I could read Bella's mind. She must have been thinking, *Duh!* But all she said was, "Are you kidding? I'd just have to turn around and come back."

Mike Newton remembered his hero act as he half-carried, half-wrestled Bella to the school office, and despite having made rather a fist of it the first time was keen for a repeat performance. Luckily he came to his senses and bit back his suggestion that it was important to her education that she at least try to be in the class again. Instead he changed the subject. "So, are you going this weekend? To the beach?"

I stifled a smile as he shot a glance to me which said, as clearly as his thoughts, *Cullen is* not *going to be there.*

"Sure, I said I was in," Bella replied lightly, and agreed to the arrangements Mike outlined as I kept my distance, exerting all my mental energy to not killing him. I wanted to tell him to keep his filthy thoughts to himself, but as far as he was aware, he was.

I used my vampire charm on Mrs Cope, pleading Bella's weak and feeble state to get her out of gym class, partly because it was evident that she didn't want to go—someone who could barely stand upright without tripping over her own feet had no business trying to do exercise—but mostly so that I could use the free period to quiz her about her plans with Newton.

They were going to La Push. I didn't remember much from my brief human years, but I remembered enough to know that a beach in Washington in March sounded about as much fun as trekking through Siberia wearing nothing but a meat bikini. Which was, in fact, something Rosalie had done—she had a taste for polar bears—and quite enjoyed, but I was going for the human perspective.

Anyway, it wasn't an option for me. The treaty prevented us from going onto reservation land. Without knowing it, Mike Newton was taking Bella to the one place I couldn't follow. But I had her *now*. I grabbed her jacket as we walked across the parking lot together and brushed away her declarations that she wanted to drive herself home with some feeble excuse about having promised to look after her.

"What about my truck?" she protested.

"I'll have Alice drop it off after school," I promised, still half-dragging, half-carrying her to my car, ignoring her objections. She could have yelled, *"Help, I'm being kidnapped!"* and no onlookers would have believed any differently. When I threatened to drag her back to my car if she made a bolt for her truck, she finally climbed into my superb, stunning, shiny, spacious, speedy, silver Volvo.

As we left the parking lot she seemed to accept that she had been successfully abducted and there was little point in complaining any more. Or maybe the music calmed her down. "Clair de Lune?" she noted.

"You know Debussy?" Not the way Carlisle had known Debussy, of course. Debussy sucked at Canasta.

"Not well. My mother plays a lot of classical music around the house. I only know my favourites."

"It's one of my favourites too," I told her, wondering how much more this girl and I could have in common. It was becoming rather clichéd.

I was driving far too fast, as usual, trying to impress Bella, and succeeding only in slightly terrifying her, judging from the smell of adrenaline which laced her blood. Ironic, that my driving—which was perfectly safe—scared her, but I didn't.

"What's your mother like?" I knew that Charlie's thoughts were partly obscured from me; I wondered whether knowing a little more about Bella's mother might help piece together the jigsaw pieces of this strange girl who was at the same time closed to me, an irresistible drug to me, and remarkably perceptive. I studied her carefully as I spoke. I should probably have been watching the road in case I wrapped us around a tree or an oncoming car.

"She looks a lot like me, but she's prettier." I found that hard to believe. "I have too much Charlie in me. She's more outgoing than I am, and braver. She's irresponsible, slightly eccentric, and a very unpredictable cook. She's my best friend."

What Bella's mother looked like, and her cooking style, was going to give me no clues whatsoever.

We'd arrived at the Swan house, so I stopped the car, pleased that I could now stare at her with a clear conscience, knowing that I wasn't a menace on the road. "How old are you, Bella?" I asked.

"I'm seventeen."

"You don't seem seventeen." Like me, she seemed much older than her chronological age. Others might have referred to her as an *old soul,* except that I was a real old soul, so that rang a little hollow. She laughed, and for a moment I worried that *she* could read *my* mind. "What?" I asked.

"My mom always says I was born thirty-five years old and that I get more middle-aged every year." She laughed again. "Well someone has to be the adult. You don't seem much like a junior in high school yourself."

I changed the subject quickly. "So why did your mother marry Phil?"

She paused, perhaps thinking what a stupid question that was—after all, why did anyone ever marry anyone?

"My mother … she's very young for her age. I think Phil makes her feel even younger. At any rate, she's crazy about him."

"Do you approve?" I asked. Having an irresponsible and eccentric mother marry a man who made her even more scatty and vague sounded like a recipe for disaster.

"Does it matter? I want her to be happy … and he is who she wants."

"That's very generous … I wonder—"

"What?" she interrupted.

"Would she extend the same courtesy to you, do you think? No matter who your choice was?" I stared intently at her.

"I-I think so. But she's the parent after all. It's a little bit different."

"No one too scary then."

"What do you mean by scary? Multiple facial piercings and extensive tattoos?"

"That's one definition, I suppose."

"What's your definition?"

She evidently hadn't been listening the multiple times I had told her that *I* was my definition of scary. "Do you think that I could be scary?"

She considered this. "Hmmm … I think you *could* be, if you wanted to."

"Are you frightened of me now?" I stopped smiling and tried to look severe and terrifying, which is difficult when you're devastatingly handsome.

"No," she said, immediately. "So, now are you going to tell me about your family? It's got to be a much more interesting story than mine."

It was, of course, but I gave her the Carlisle-approved edited version, then wished her well for her rainy day at the beach. She wanted to know what I was up to, of course, so I gave her the sanitised version of that too. It wasn't good to start telling the truth this early in a relationship.

"Will you do something for me this weekend," I asked, suddenly struck by the realisation that I had to be away from her for two whole days. I had been watching her closely for the last few days, monitoring her whereabouts, tracking what others were thinking about her, and what they saw when they looked at her, and even watching her sleep. But this weekend she was going somewhere I couldn't go, and I was going somewhere she couldn't go. We would be apart for the first time since I had discovered how very special she was.

Not only that but she would be with Mike Newton, Tyler Crowley, and several others who I knew secretly lusted after her. Also, she was a complete klutz who smelled like filet mignon.

"Don't be offended, but you seem like one of those people who just attract accidents like a magnet. So … try not to fall into the ocean or get run over or anything, all right?"

The problem with starting a sentence with "Don't be offended but" or "No offense but" is that the statement that follows it is invariably offensive, but now it's the recipient of the offensive statement who is to blame for any affront felt. Since I was over one hundred years old I really should have known better than to say that. She stared angrily at me, snapped that she'd see what she could do, and jumped out of the car, slamming the door behind her.

Chapter Seven

"You kidnapped Bella?" Alice said accusingly. Her tone was questioning, but she knew exactly what I'd done. She'd seen it the moment I decided to do it.

"Er… I don't think she minded, much."

"You made her get into your car when she didn't want to. You drove her home under protest. Honestly, Edward, with the way you ignore this girl for weeks, then tell her you're dangerous, then stalk her and kidnap her, it's a miracle she's going to fall in love with you. What she should actually do is report you to her father and get you put on some course about respecting women. It's not 1935 anymore, you know."

"She's going to fall in love with me?"

"Of course she is. Have you looked in a mirror lately?"

I had, because contrary to popular opinion vampires can do that, and looking the way I did I liked to do it often. Sometimes, like a precocious twelve-year-old, I'd even pretend to shave, lathering up my face before blunting the razor on my skin. It seemed rather cruel that I'd only just started shaving, and enjoying some of the other trappings of adult maleness, before I'd had to stop again.

Anyway, Alice was right. I was devilishly handsome, and most of the girls in school were in love with me. Why should Bella be any different?

But Bella *was* different, in so many ways. That was what made her so intriguing.

"So, what did you want to ask me, Edward?"

Oh. Yes. "Bella's truck… it's still in the school parking lot. I wondered whether you could take it to her house."

"Sure." Alice stuck out her hand. "Key, please."

"Er… I might have forgotten to ask Bella for the key."

Alice rolled her eyes. "So go back to her house and ask her for the key."

"No, I don't want to do that. For the same reason that I don't want to take her truck back there myself."

"And what reason could that be?"

I wasn't sure. I didn't really have a good reason. It was odd, really, that I generally didn't need any excuse at all to go to Bella's house, yet on this one occasion I'd randomly decided that Alice would be the one to take Bella's truck back to her. I shrugged and tried to smile winningly at my sister. She was usually immune to my charms, but this time she sighed heavily. "Okay, I'll carry it back once it gets dark."

Chapter Eight

I spent most of the weekend far from home doing my level best to quench my endless thirst, ready for the time when I would be in Bella's presence again, hypnotised by her alluring scent, and only slightly more by my overwhelming love for her. Bear blood wasn't anything like as good as human blood, and the coarse fur tended to get stuck in my teeth, but it would suffice to take the edge off my desire for Bella. Well, one of my desires for Bella.

I kept away from my family, too. I could hear their curiosity, their questions, and I wasn't ready to answer those questions yet, not least because I didn't know the answers myself. I knew that I was in love with Bella to the point of obsession, but I hadn't appreciated before how all-consuming love could be, how distracting, how terrifying.

I wasn't ready to discuss it with anyone, or to justify it to anyone.

I ran home to change late Sunday evening, avoiding seeing my family directly. They would know I was home by my scent; I didn't need to greet them all personally. The questions about Bella had got a bit much recently, and I wasn't prepared to answer questions I didn't really know the answers to myself.

As I leapt through the window I heard Esme, always sensitive to my moods, caution Carlisle and Rosalie to leave me alone, and I was grateful to her.

"For now," Carlisle agreed. He knew I could hear his thoughts, and added, *Edward, we need to talk.*

So much for leaving me alone. It was those interfering little father-son chats that had once driven me away from Carlisle, and my heart dropped into my stomach at the prospect of this one.

Rosalie was disappointed by Esme and Carlisle's edict, too. She was enjoying teasing me, and Emmett, baffled by my interest in a particularly pathetic and vulnerable human, let her do it. I'd actually have rather faced Rosalie's scorn than Carlisle's well-meant but high-handed advice. Alice was on my side, thanks to her remarkable gift, and Jasper would side with Alice. Alice didn't fear letting my relationship with Bella play out, because among the many probabilities she had seen for it were some she liked very much.

Once I had washed off the drying bear blood, plucked the hair from my teeth, and put on fresh clothes I headed back out to Bella's home, climbed in through the window as usual, and drank deeply of that delicious scent. I felt the relief at being once more in her presence, and at seeing her alone in her bed. After her weekend in the company of testosterone-fuelled teenagers I had half expected to see Mike Newton spooning with her. I'd have killed him on the spot if I had.

My phone rang, filling the stillness of the room with the tinny but cheerful chimes of *Calypso*. I fumbled for my Blackberry, stabbed clumsily at the tiny keys, and cursed Esme for calling when she knew I was with Bella. Vampire or not, answering a ringing phone quickly enough not to wake anyone sleeping was next to impossible.

"Edward, you need to get out of there," Esme said calmly before I'd even said a word.

"I do *now*," I hissed back, watching as Bella moaned, grunted and rolled over in bed. "You woke her up!"

"Alice has seen what happens if you stay, and it's not pretty. Get out of there and come home."

"But I don't *wanna—*"

"You do as I say, young man!"

"But *Mooom...*" With a deep rumbling sigh, Bella seemed to have settled back to sleep. I didn't need to leave. I could have another hour in her presence before she woke for school.

"And stop by the store for some laundry detergent on your way back, will you? There's a good lad."

I slammed the detergent on the kitchen counter when I returned to the house and the box crumpled and split under the force of my ire. Powder flew everywhere, covering me from head to foot. Alice, broom already in hand, laughed.

"What did you see?" I asked her sullenly. "Why did I have to come home?"

"Bella waking up," Alice said simply.

Big deal. She did that every morning. "And?"

"You watching from the tree outside her window."

"You said it wasn't a pretty sight!"

"Oh, it wasn't. She had terrible bed hair, and all this crusty stuff round her mouth where she'd drooled in her sleep."

I tried to swish laundry powder over Alice, but she had already seen it coming and dodged away. It's no fun squabbling with someone who can see into the future.

"Edward," Carlisle said. "We need to have that talk."

"Do we? *Now?*" I was still trying to brush laundry detergent off my clothing, and I smelled like a Women's Institute flower festival with a slight edge of bleach.

"We've been talking, and we all feel—"

Alice coughed quietly.

"—*most* of us feel that your feelings for Bella are developing dangerously quickly. We need to take some time to think about the implications of this. No vampire I know has ever had a successful relationship with a human before. This is new ground, and it affects us all."

"Great. Take all the time you need. I have to get changed for school."

"I don't think you should go to school today. I think you should keep your distance from Bella for a while."

I shook my head. I had already tried that. Running away was the first thing I had tried. Ignoring her for a month was the second. Neither had worked.

Esme was suddenly at Carlisle's side. Rosalie and Emmett were suddenly on the sofa. Jasper was suddenly on his knees sweeping laundry powder into a little dustpan.

"We all feel that you should stay home from school for a while."

"But the education authority will issue you with a fine and send out a stern letter," I protested.

"That only happens in England," Jasper said.

"Then my grades will suffer."

Rosalie laughed. "I don't think any teacher at the school will be in the slightest bit worried about your grades, Edward."

"How will I explain my absence?"

"You're sick. I'll write you a doctor's note. You have been looking a bit pale…"

"We should all stay away," Alice said firmly. "It's going to be very sunny for a few days. We need to take another spontaneous family vacation."

My heart sank. I might have been able to talk Carlisle and Esme into letting me go to school, but even I couldn't argue with unfettered sunshine.

Chapter Nine

I had promised my family I wouldn't go to classes, but I hadn't said anything about staying in the house. I spent the next few days watching Bella from afar. I watched as she awoke suddenly from a nightmare, crying "No!" into the empty night as I stared through the slats of her closet. I watched from the trees as she trudged through the forest, deep in thought and wrapped in an oversized green raincoat. I watched from afar as she sat at a picnic bench outside the school on the first sunny day of the year, going over an assignment and doodling in the margins. When Mike Newton appeared and dared to tuck a lock of Bella's hair behind her ear, I almost flew from my hiding place to seize and kill him, but only minutes later Bella had turned his thoughts toward Jessica and I was placated.

I couldn't watch her in school, but I could follow the minds of the people near her, see her in their thoughts. I saw her look towards our table at the cafeteria, and heard Angela wonder why Bella seemed so crestfallen that our family was absent. After school I followed her home and waited outside her house, then climbed a tree again to watch as she read a few pages from a succession of books, seeming to become frustrated by each one. I wondered what there could possibly be in those classic novels that was annoying her. Maybe she'd come across an archaic word she didn't fully understand. I could probably have helped with that.

I continued to stare at her as she dozed on that blanket on the grass.

Was this normal or acceptable behaviour, I wondered. Did typical teenage boys stalk the objects of their lust the way I was stalking Bella? I was pursuing her as though she were my prey, lurking in the shadows, prowling round her, refusing to allow her any privacy or solitude, and doing so without her knowledge. My behaviour, while not quite illegal, was probably immoral. And yet I couldn't leave her alone. I continued to watch her through the night, getting my highest score on Angry Birds in the process. If Bella ever found out I had stalked her for a full twenty-four hours, she'd probably be quite an angry bird herself.

Of course, it was easier for me than it would be for anyone else. Being able to read people's minds meant that I had largely forgotten about the concept of privacy. There could be no secrets from me for anyone in my vicinity. I knew every insecurity, every uncertainty, every skeleton in the closet of every high school student in the town, and many of their parents. Even my own family were not immune from my eavesdropping; there was no keeping anything from me.

So perhaps it was only natural that, when faced with this mysterious girl who *could,* somehow, keep her thoughts, fears and insecurities from me, I would obsessively stalk her, watch her through the minds of others, glean every possible clue about her, from her nocturnal muttering to her notebook doodles, trying to unravel the person she was. She was an enigma, and I wasn't used to those.

That's the excuse I gave myself for my behaviour. That I was too used to knowing everything about everyone, and had to watch every breath she took, every move she made, in order to fill in the uncomfortable gap in my knowledge. Not a good excuse, but it served a purpose.

She had made plans to go to Port Angeles with Jessica and Angela to help them choose dresses for the dance she wasn't planning to go to.

Typical self-sacrificing behaviour, I thought. Not being able to read her mind I couldn't be sure, but Bella didn't strike me as the type of girl who enjoyed dress shopping.

I allowed them a good head start, lest my superb, stunning, shiny, spacious, speedy, sleek, silver Volvo be spotted in their rear-view mirror. The sun was so bright that I was very glad of the tinted windows; it wouldn't do to dazzle other drivers and cause accidents with my glare. Once in the quaint town I parked far enough away to be out of sight, but close enough to see occasional glimpses of Bella through Angela and Jessica's thoughts.

I heard Bella tell Jessica that she'd never had a boyfriend. That surprised and pleased me; if there had been a boy in Arizona who had despoiled my girl I'd have had to kill him. Jessica pointed out that several boys had asked Bella to go to the dance with them and she'd turned them all down. I heard, and enjoyed, the anger in Bella's response when Angela informed her that Tyler was claiming to be taking Bella to the prom. The only person who would be taking Bella to any dance, ever, was me.

Bella's tone was friendly and interested as she commented on the dresses her friends tried on, but I felt I knew her well enough to detect an edge to her voice, which suggested that she was just being polite. Angela certainly seemed to think so. She felt some strange pity for Bella.

There was a rap on the window of my superb, stunning, shiny, spacious, speedy, sleek, sexy, silver Volvo. I rolled down the window, just the smallest crack, and peered out. It was a Washington State Police Department cop, his hand on his useless gun, a tired expression on his lined face.

"Sir, are you aware that your vehicle is illegally parked?"

I wasn't. That was quite an exciting novelty. Part of being a vampire was heightened senses and a brain with greater processing abilities, which meant I was usually aware of everything, all the time. I scanned the officer's mind, and behind a complex algorithm assessing the relative merits and qualities of Dunkin' Donuts, Krispy Kreme and Top Pot Donuts, I found the image of the fire hydrant a foot from my rear fender.

His partner, a trigger-happy young rookie, was itching for this teenage playboy to make something of it. He wanted a confrontation. He wanted the car to have been stolen. He was *bored*.

Well, I could soon fix that.

I feigned astonishment. "I'm so sorry Officer, I had no idea! What is—oh, I see it. Hey, I'm real sorry, I'll move right away, please don't give me a ticket, my dad'll kill me." I paused, looked past the older cop towards the rookie. "Hey—hey, Marco, is that you?"

The rookie looked alarmed at hearing this unknown felon address him by name. I saw him focus on what little he could see of my face – eyes, brows, gleaming forehead – and try to figure out who I was. He cast through faces, memories and occasions in his mind, furiously trying to place me as his partner took a step back to allow him to approach.

"You remember me, Marco, right? Hey, you were pretty wasted the last time I saw you though, that was some pretty hardcore stuff you'd taken. I'm surprised you could even stand up. I had no idea you were a cop, dude. I guess access to the good stuff is one of the perks of the job, eh?"

Marco was white and wide-eyed with alarm. In his mind he cycled through his favourite expletives, but ended with the horrific realisation, *this guy must have been at Joey's that night!*

"You remember me, don't you?" I said again. "From Joey's."

"Oh, hey, yeah…" Marco said hesitantly. "But, you know, that was such a long time ago, it's hard to remember names, especially when you're coming down with some virus and not feeling too good…"

This was too much fun. I turned my attention to his older partner. "I think I know you too," I said, fishing around in his mind. "I've seen you before somewhere… hmm… where was it now..?"

Not Sarah's, not Sarah's, not Sarah's chanted the cop's mind in consternation.

"That's it! I remember now. You were at Sarah's!" I glanced down at the left hand resting on his belt, and shook my head. "Tsk, and you a married man too."

The officers glanced at each other nervously, and then at me.

"If you could just move along away from the hydrant we'll let this go," the older officer said, his voice shaking. Marco, his face a mask of quiet despair, nodded emphatically.

I nodded politely to them, smiled, and pulled away. Sometimes being able to read minds was awesome.

I turned my attention back to Angela's, and found myself tapping my foot to her earworm. Usually the music in people's heads was annoying, but Angela was internally humming *Eat the Rich* by Aerosmith. What she wasn't doing was talking to Bella, which was frustrating. After a couple of minutes, and against my better judgement, I switched to Jessica.

A bookstore! Jessica was thinking. *All these gorgeous gowns and Bella wants to go off looking for a bookstore.*

Gadsbudlikins, she wasn't with them! Zounds and gadzooks! I floored the gas pedal and hurtled down the street towards the only bookshop in Port Angeles. I was going way over the speed limit, but had nothing to fear from Marco and Officer Bennett, after all, and everything to fear for Bella. As I drove I scanned the streets with my eyes and the thoughts of passers-by with my mind, looking for any clue, any memory, which suggested that Bella might not be far away.

With a scent so strong and potent, you'd have thought I'd have been able to smell her from miles away, but even sniffing like a truffle-pig with hay fever I could detect no trace of her. At least it was starting to get overcast and a little dark; before long I could continue the search on foot. She hadn't been into the bookshop; her scent wasn't there.

I backtracked, rounded a corner, and caught the briefest whiff of her aroma. At the same time I stumbled into the minds of four men, and recoiled at their thoughts.

I had long held that being able to read minds was a curse, one reserved for me as punishment for the evil in my vampire nature. It seemed fitting, somehow. Due to my murderous and literal bloodthirsty character I was forced to hear the thoughts of my prey, to understand their feelings, their hopes, their desires, and their fears. Even worse, I was forced to hear the trite, dull minutiae of their every waking minute: their vanities, their petty asides, their recited shopping lists. It was torture.

Most tortuous of all, especially given the human pleasures that my vampire nature denied me, were the thoughts of red-blooded young men. I had discovered early in my new life that men–even in the nineteen-twenties—had one-track minds. Their thoughts, while straying occasionally to higher and nobler planes, invariably returned regularly and frequently to that basest of desires, that appetite which seemed, especially in the young, never to be quite sated. I was eternally condemned to listen to those yearnings, which made the male mind even more unpleasant to peer into than it was when it was filled with thoughts of cars, sports or *Halo.*

These men were no different. Horrified, I tracked their thoughts as I sped towards the industrial district where they stalked Bella. Her scent grew stronger in my nostrils as their nauseating fantasies involving Bella did in my mind.

I could see her now, through the mind of the eldest of the group. His mind was unsteady, rambling. He'd been drinking. If anything, it made his urge keener, more acute.

As I raced toward him, snarling and drooling venom in my need to hunt this prey, I heard their terrible thoughts.

"I could murder a cheeseburger. Hey, there's a pretty girl, I wonder whether she knows where I could get a cheeseburger."

"What I wouldn't do for a chilli dog. That girl looks a bit like a chilli dog, with her brown hair all tumbling down like that."

"Mmm, donuts! I need a donut! Perhaps that girl has a donut in her bag."

"I am hungry, man! I hope momma's saved me some of her mean casserole."

"There you are!" I heard one of the men call out as he spotted his friend. I could hear his words reverberating in his mind and in the air. I was close now.

"Yeah," his friend replied. "We just took a little detour."

I heard Bella's voice, rather higher than usual. "Stay away from me."

"Don't be like that," the first man said, his mind still firmly in his stomach, and added hopefully, "Sugar?"

The others bayed in appreciation. Did Bella have any sugar with her? Just some forgotten candy, maybe, in the purse she held tightly in one hand?

And then I could see her, standing in the centre of the road, the men approaching her from three different angles. I pulled on the handbrake and executed a perfect handbrake turn, sliding effortlessly in a screech of tyres to end up exactly beside Bella. I leaned over and popped open the passenger door. "Get in!" I yelled, and floored the accelerator as soon as she was safely inside.

Those men would have to cook their own dinners.

"Put on your seatbelt," I ordered, and mentally added *so we can be safe*. Of course, if I'd really wanted her to be safe I could have driven more slowly, maybe even below the speed limit, maybe without hurtling round corners so fast the car almost rolled. Realising this, eventually, I pulled to a stop along a stretch of deserted road.

She hadn't yet said anything. Hadn't asked where I'd appeared from so suddenly when she hadn't seen me in days; hadn't thanked me for rescuing her. Maybe she was waiting for me to talk first.

"Bella?"

"Yes?"

"Are you alright?"

"Yes."

I was somewhat embarrassed to have asked such a stupid question. All her limbs remained fully attached, she was breathing at—almost— normal rate, and she wasn't screaming like a banshee.

"Distract me, please," I asked, mortified at my own teenage idiot boy-ness.

"I'm sorry, what?"

"Just prattle about something unimportant until I calm down." Humiliated at how stupid I always seemed when I spoke to her, I closed my eyes and pinched the bridge of my nose with my thumb and forefinger, stopping just short of shaking my head from side to side and moaning, *why?*

"Um, I'm going to run over Tyler Crowley tomorrow before school," she said.

That sounded fun. "Why?"

"He's telling everyone that he's taking me to prom—either he's insane or he's still trying to make up for almost killing me last … well, you remember it, and he thinks *prom* is somehow the correct way to do this. So I figure if I endanger his life, then we're even, and he can't keep trying to make amends. I don't need enemies and maybe Lauren would back off if he left me alone. I might have to total his Sentra, though. If he doesn't have a ride, he can't take anyone to prom."

Halleluiah, another teenage boy was even stupider than I was. I looked positively good and normal compared to Tyler Crowley, even if I was an obsessed emo-psycho stalker.

"I heard a bit about that," I told her.

"You did? If he's paralysed from the neck down he can't go to prom either."

I could arrange that, but I suspected she didn't really want that for Tyler. I sighed and opened my eyes.

"Better?" She asked.

"Not really." Any minute now she would ask me what I was doing in Port Angeles, and I would open my mouth and put my foot in it. Again.

"What's wrong?" she whispered.

Where did I start? Despite my warning to take care of herself she'd ended up being stalked by four men. In fact, technically she'd been stalked by five men, because I was stalking her too. And given what he'd been saying, probably Tyler Crowley would be soon, too. She was like the Pied Piper.

"Sometimes I have a problem with my temper, Bella," I said. "But it *wouldn't* be helpful for me to turn around and hunt down those…" I couldn't figure out what to call them. "At least, that's what I'm trying to convince myself."

Oops. I'd just told her that I, a seventeen-year-old guy, could "hunt" four hungry grown men. Clue Six, unless she assumed I was some kind of ninja.

After a while she said, "Jessica and Angela will be worried. I was supposed to meet them."

Without a word I started the engine and drove back into town, pulling up outside La Bella Italia. Jessica and Angela had given up waiting for Bella and were wandering off down the street.

"How did you know where..?" Bella began, and I got out of the car hurriedly so that I wouldn't have to answer the question I guessed was forming. Oops again. *Clue Seven.* "What are you doing?" she asked.

"Taking you to dinner," I said, suddenly deciding that I was. "Go stop Jessica and Angela before I have to track them down, too. I don't think I could restrain myself if I ran into your other friends again." *Such* a drama king.

Bella hailed her friends, and filled with relief at hearing her voice they turned back and demanded to know where she'd been.

"I got lost," she told them. "And then I ran into Edward."

Actually, I'd run into her. Very deliberately, but only metaphorically. Not in a Tyler Crowley way. "Would it be all right if I joined you?" I asked.

"Er…sure," Jessica said.

I was confused. I had already read the contentment of full stomachs in their minds. Jessica, apparently, was so keen to spend time with me that she'd force down another meal.

"Um, actually, Bella, we already ate while we were waiting—sorry," Angela admitted. Jessica was relieved and annoyed at the same time.

"That's fine—I'm not hungry," Bella said.

I didn't believe that for one moment. She was just being polite to her friends. "I think you should eat something," I insisted, and asked Jessica, "Do you mind if I drive Bella home tonight? That way you won't have to wait while she eats."

"Uh, no problem, I guess," Jessica said. Through her eyes I saw Bella wink at her. I tried not to laugh.

Angela understood too. "Okay, see you tomorrow, Bella … Edward." She grabbed Jessica's hand and pulled her back towards the car. Bella waved at them as they drove away in a car filled with curiosity.

"Honestly, I'm not hungry," she said to me.

She was skinny enough that it might have been true. Maybe she wasn't someone who ate regularly, or sufficiently. But I thought a few curves would suit her. "Humour me." I opened the door of the restaurant and ushered her in.

"Hubba hubba," thought the hostess as she assessed me, but she only smiled a welcome.

"Table for two?" I asked.

The hostess looked at Bella, her emotions a mixture of disappointment and envy. Still, even if I seemed to have a girlfriend—*a girlfriend! Bella was my girlfriend!*—she could nevertheless get some mileage from making me a centrepiece and showing me off to the kitchen staff. When she tried to sit us in the very centre of the room I slipped her a twenty and demanded a more private table. She reluctantly led us to a booth.

"You really shouldn't do that to people," Bella said once we were seated. "It's hardly fair."

I shouldn't tip her generously? I shouldn't ask for a better table in a restaurant? It had been a while—okay, some decades—since I'd been into a restaurant, but I imagined that tipping was still appropriate. "Do what?" I asked.

"Dazzle them like that—she's probably hyperventilating in the kitchen right now."

I checked. Bella was correct.

"Oh come *on*," she added. "You *have* to know the effect you have on people."

"I dazzle people?" And I thought I'd kept out of sunlight.

"You haven't noticed? Do you think everybody gets their way so easily?"

Everybody equipped with a twenty-dollar bill finding themselves in an almost-empty restaurant, for sure. "Do I dazzle *you?*" I asked.

"Frequently," she said.

The servers had finished squabbling over which of them got to serve me, and Amber had won after some hair pulling and blackmail. I ordered two cokes—both for Bella, of course, although she didn't know that—and then turned my attention back to her. "How are you feeling?"

"I'm fine," she said.

"You don't feel dizzy, sick, cold..?"

"Should I?"

"Well, I'm actually waiting for you to go into shock," I admitted with a chuckle. After all, that was the appropriate reaction to my insanely fast driving.

"I don't think that will happen, I've always been good at repressing unpleasant things."

"Just the same, I'll feel better when you have some sugar and food in you."

Amber appeared astonishingly quickly at that point with our drinks and a basket of breadsticks. Table four really wanted her attention—they'd been waiting ten minutes for her to clear away their places—but in her mind she was saying, *"Yeah, yeah, granddad, I'll get to you when I've served pretty boy."*

"Are you ready to order?"

Bella hadn't even looked at the menu at that point, which was maybe why she asked for mushroom ravioli. I'd never eaten pasta—it hadn't really started appearing on menus when I was human—but judging from the smell it's pretty bland, and mushrooms have to be the most disgusting vegetable.

"Nothing for me," I said.

"Are you kidding me?" thought Amber. *"You're going to sit there and watch your girlfriend eat?"*

"Drink," I demanded, once Amber had stalked off, and Bella obediently downed the entire glass of coke. I pushed the second one towards her, and noticed that she was shivering. "Are you cold?"

"It's just the coke."

"Don't you have a jacket?"

"Yes. Oh—I left it in Jessica's car."

She'd gone walking around the streets of Port Angeles in April, with the temperature barely fifty degrees, without her jacket, but now in the

69

warmth of the restaurant she was cold. I took off my beige leather jacket, trying to ignore Amber's behind-the-scenes cries to her colleagues, ("Oh my *goodness,* comes and see, he's *stripping!"),* and passed it to Bella who sniffed suspiciously at it as she put it on. If anything she looked colder now that she was wearing it. Of course—any normal human's jacket would be warm after they took it off.

"That colour blue looks lovely with your skin," I tried to joke, pushing the bread-basket towards her.

"Really, I'm not going into shock," she said.

"You should be—a *normal* person would be. You don't even look shaken."

"I feel very safe with you," she said.

She was less safe with me than she had been with four guys who wanted her to cook their dinner. "This is more complicated than I'd planned," I said mysteriously.

She nibbled on a breadstick and spat crumbs across the table when she replied. "Usually you're in a better mood when your eyes are so light."

A klaxon sounded in my head and red lights started flashing. "What?"

"You're always crabbier when your eyes are black—I expect it then. I have a theory about that."

"More theories?"

"Mm-hm. "

I could almost hear Carlisle berating me for giving away so many clues. "I hope you were more creative this time … or are you still stealing from comic books?" I tried to smile patronisingly, but she had the upper hand and I guessed she knew it.

"Well, no, I didn't get it from a comic book, but I didn't come up with it on my own either."

Amber interrupted us, bringing the fastest-cooked mushroom ravioli in the history of mushroom ravioli. "Did you change your mind?" She asked me. "Isn't there anything I can get you?" In her mind she was draped naked across the table before me, artistically drizzled with ranch dressing.

"No, thank you, but more soda would be nice." Bella had drained the second glass too. "You were saying?" I prompted once Amber had left with the glasses.

"I'll tell you about it in the car. If..."

"There are conditions?"

"I have a few questions, of course."

"Of course."

Amber was lightning fast tonight, possibly because she was ignoring all her other tables. She set down the cokes and left, disappointed that I hadn't even acknowledged or thanked her.

"Well, go ahead," I prompted.

"Why are you in Port Angeles?"

As questions went it wasn't the most difficult she could have asked, but it was still pretty squirm-inducing. I decided to pass. "Next."

"But that was the easiest one."

"Next," I insisted.

She finally started eating her ravioli, chewing thoughtfully as she composed her question. "Okay then, let's say, hypothetically of course, that ... someone ... could know what people are thinking, read minds, you know—with a few exceptions."

"Just *one* exception," I corrected. *Edward, you are* so *busted!*

"All right, with one exception, then. How does that work? What are the limitations? How would … that someone … find someone else at exactly the right time? How would he know she's in trouble?"

"Hypothetically?" I clarified.

"Sure."

"Well, if that someone…"

"Let's call him Joe," she offered.

"Joe, then. If Joe had been paying attention, the timing wouldn't have needed to be quite so exact. Only *you* could get into trouble in a town this small. You would have devastated their crime statistics for a decade, you know."

"We were speaking of a hypothetical case," she reminded me.

"Yes, we were. Shall we call you Jane?"

"How did you know?" she asked, leaning towards me.

Hold on a minute, wasn't she the one who had insisted on the hypothetical names? Shouldn't the question have been 'How did Joe know that Jane was in trouble?'

"You can trust me, you know," she insisted, reaching for my hand. I pulled it away lest she should discover how cold I was from a source other than my jacket.

"I don't know if I have a choice anymore," I admitted. "I was wrong—you're much more observant than I gave you credit for."

"I thought you were always right."

"I used to be. I was wrong about you on one other thing as well. You're not a magnet for accidents—that's not a broad enough classification. You are a magnet for *trouble*. If there's anything dangerous within a ten-mile radius it will invariably find you."

"And you put yourself in that category," she said. From her tone it sounded like she thought I was some sort of pretentious self-aggrandising emo.

"Unequivocally," I said firmly. Obviously I *was* a pretentious self-aggrandising emo, but I was also a vampire and those are dangerous.

As though to test her theory, she reached across the table to touch my hand. I pulled it back slightly, as though to indicate that she shouldn't, but she ignored the action and brushed her fingertips against the back of my hand anyway. Her fingers were warm and soft.

"Thank you. That's twice now," she observed.

"Let's not try for three, agreed?"

She nodded, although her expression suggested she was annoyed at being asked.

"I followed you to Port Angeles," I admitted. "I've never tried to keep a specific person alive before, and it's much more troublesome than I would have believed. But that's probably just because it's you. Ordinary people seem to make it through the day without so many catastrophes."

She was smiling, a smile of victory. It was, I supposed, the first time I had spoken to openly, so freely, about my nature.

"Did you ever think," she asked, "that maybe my number was up the first time, with the van, and that you've been interfering with fate?"

"That wasn't the first time," I replied quietly. "Your number was up the first time I met you.

I saw the spark of memory, of recognition, as she remembered that first day in the biology classroom, and the pieces clicked into place. "You remember?"

"Yes," she said.

"And yet here you sit."

"Yes, here I sit … because of you. Because somehow you knew how to find me today?" There was a pleading, questioning edge to her voice. I had opened up, but she wanted more. She wanted all the answers.

"You eat, I'll talk," I bargained. Her ravioli was going cold. She ate a piece, which I took to be acceptance of the deal. "It's harder than it should be—keeping track of you. Usually I can find someone very easily once I've heard their mind before."

As Bella put away the ravioli, I outlined how I had lost her, searched for her, found her, and just in case she wasn't quite scared enough of me, lingered over the part where I really wanted to kill the men I had discovered her among, and could have done, very easily.

"Are you ready to go home?" I asked when I'd finished.

"I'm ready to leave," she agreed. I noticed the subtle difference. She wanted to be out of the restaurant, maybe so that we could talk more quietly, but she wasn't ready to be back at home with Charlie just yet.

Amber appeared and addressed me again: she'd steadfastly ignored Bella—the only actual diner in our party—throughout the entire meal. "How are we doing?"

"We're ready for the check, thank you." I scanned her mind as she pulled it from her apron, suddenly worried she'd been eavesdropping on us. I'd deliberately spoken as quietly as possible, but wouldn't put it past Amber to have been sitting in the next booth, pretending to fold napkins into swans or fans as she listened. Her thoughts, however, were all along the lines of *OMG he's so hot! Is he really leaving already?* I slipped a twenty dollar bill straight into the leather folder and handed it right back. "No change."

She thanked me and wished me a nice evening as Bella and I stood to leave. She didn't mean it. She was seething with jealousy.

We got into the car and I turned on the heater, aware that Bella was probably still cold. "Now it's your turn," I told her as we pulled out and headed towards the freeway.

Chapter Ten

"Can I ask just one more?" she wheedled.

"One," I agreed, wondering what I was letting myself in for.

"Well … you said you knew I hadn't gone into the bookstore, and that I had gone south. I was just wondering how you knew that." When I hesitated and looked away she said "I thought we were past all the evasiveness." Probably she should have asked why I was looking at her, and then staring off to one side, when I should have been watching the road. But then, I had agreed to answer only one question, so maybe she didn't want to waste it.

"Fine, then. I followed your scent." We really were opening up, now.

"And then you didn't answer one of my first questions."

"Which one?" That was cheating, claiming another question as an earlier question. This girl was crafty.

"How does it work—the mind reading thing? Can you read anybody's mind, anywhere? How do you do it? Can the rest of your family..?"

"That's more than one," I complained, but she sat waiting patiently for my answer. "No, it's just me. And I can't hear anyone, anywhere. I have to be fairly close. The more familiar someone's … 'voice' is, the father away I can hear them. But still, no more than a few miles. It's a little like being in a huge hall filled with people, everyone talking at once. It's just a hum—a buzzing of voices in the background. Until I focus on one voice, and then what they're thinking is clear.

"Most of the time I tune it all out—it can be very distracting. And then it's easier to seem *normal* when I'm not accidentally answering their thoughts instead of their words." If we had more time I could have told her some great funny stories about *that*.

"Why do you think you can't hear me?" she asked.

I'd wondered that often before. "I don't know. The only guess I have is that maybe your mind doesn't work the same way the rest of theirs do. Like your thoughts are on the AM frequency, and I'm only getting FM."

"My mind doesn't work right? I'm a freak?"

Typical Bella, making it all about her. "I hear voices in my mind and you're worried that *you're* the freak?" I laughed. "Don't worry, it's just a theory… which brings us back to you." When she sighed I reminded her, "Aren't we past all the evasions now?"

Apparently not. Having extracted all the answers from me she was going to get, Bella suddenly became completely obsessed with the speed I was driving. Despite my assurances that I always drove fast, and that my vampire reflexes meant we were perfectly safe, Bella insisted that I slow down. Eventually, recognising that I'd get nothing but little girl shrieks and interesting epithets (who says *"holy crow"* these days? Not even me, and I say *gadsbudlikins*) I slowed to around eighty miles per hour. "Enough commentary on my driving," I said once we were cruising at this new painfully slow 'speed'. "I'm still waiting for your latest theory. I won't laugh."

"I'm more afraid you'll be angry with me."

"Is it that bad?"

"Pretty much, yeah?"

78

In which case, I guessed, it was probably the truth. "Go ahead."

It seemed that Bella had flirted and tricked her way into getting some Quileute boy to confess his silly superstition about the Cullen family. Far from being angry with Bella I was furious with Jacob Black. I hoped, for his sake, that I never came face-to-face with him, or had anything else to resent him for.

"What did you do then?" I asked, once she had admitted to what had been said at the beach.

"I did some research on the internet."

"And did that convince you?" I tried to sound nonchalant.

"No. Nothing fit. Most of it was kind of silly. And then…"

"What?"

"I decided it didn't matter?"

I was incredulous. "It didn't *matter?*"

"No. It doesn't matter to me what you are."

"You don't care if I'm a monster? If I'm not *human?*"

"No."

Well, this was new. I could never have predicted this. Much screaming, for sure. Running away too, probably. But not really caring?

"You're angry," she guessed, wrongly. "I shouldn't have said anything."

"No. I'd rather know what you're thinking—even if what you're thinking is insane."

"So I'm wrong again?"

"That's not what I was referring to. 'It doesn't matter'!" Crazy, crazy woman.

"I'm right!" she gasped, and I was alarmed. Could it be that it hadn't mattered because she didn't entirely believe it? Had I just confirmed her suspicions?

"Does it *matter?*" Maybe it did, now.

"Not really," she said. "But I am curious."

"What are you curious about?"

"How old are you?"

I said "Seventeen" quickly and automatically, with the practiced ease of someone who had given that answer many, many times over the years.

"And how long have you been seventeen?"

I tried not to laugh. "A while."

"Okay." She seemed to accept that vague answer. "Don't laugh, but how can you come out in the daytime?"

I did laugh, despite her entreaty. "Myth."

"Burned by the sun?"

"Myth."

"Sleeping in coffins?"

"Myth," I said automatically, but because I wanted her to feel the agony that was my existence I added, "I can't sleep."

She hesitated. "At all?"

"Never," I said quietly. That was my tragedy. Well, one of them. As though living forever wasn't enough, I didn't get to escape the interminability of it, not even temporarily, in dreams. Which reminded me of something else dreadful and ghastly about me. "You haven't asked me the most important question yet."

She blinked at me, confused. "Which one is that?"

"You aren't concerned about my diet?"

"Oh, that," she said, apparently not concerned.

"Yes, that. Don't you want to know if I drink blood?"

"Well, Jacob said something about that."

Jacob. She was on friendly terms with the boy who had betrayed our decades-old family secret. I *really* didn't like this guy. "What did Jacob say?"

"He said you didn't…hunt people. He said your family wasn't supposed to be dangerous because you only hunted animals."

"He said we weren't dangerous?" What an affront to the good name of Cullen!

"Not exactly. He said you weren't *supposed* to be dangerous. But the Quileutes still didn't want you on their land, just in case."

How much could we be insulted in one sentence? Not only were we not dangerous, but we weren't to be trusted to obey the treaty or keep our own promises.

"So was he right? About not hunting people?"

He was, but I already hated Jacob Black enough that I couldn't even bring myself to admit that he had been correct in what he had told Bella. "The Quileutes have a long memory," I said. "Don't let that make you complacent, though. They're right to keep their distance from us. We are still dangerous." How dare the Quileutes besmirch our family. I hoped I had put that right, in Bella's mind at least—and her mind was really all that mattered.

"I don't understand."

"We try," I explained. "We're usually very good at what we do. Sometimes we make mistakes. Me, for example, allowing myself to be alone with you."

"This is a mistake?"

"A very dangerous one."

We drove in silence for a while. I hoped my words were sinking in. I wondered whether, now that she knew more, it might finally *matter* what I was.

"Tell me more," she asked after a while.

"What more do you want to know?"

"Tell me why you hunt animals instead of people."

She seemed to be trying to stifle tears. Her eyes were wet and I could smell the salt. Maybe it *did* matter now.

"I don't *want* to be a monster," I told her.

"But animals aren't enough?"

Not for the first time, I wondered whether she could read *my* mind. I explained how animals didn't really cut it in the fully varied, healthy diet stakes. I expected her to show revulsion, but when she commented on how my eye colour changed depending on whether or not I was thirsty, I realised just how different, how observant, she was.

"Were you hunting this weekend, with Emmett?" she asked.

"Yes. I didn't want to leave, but it was necessary. It's a bit easier to be around you when I'm not thirsty."

"Why didn't you want to leave?"

"It makes me … anxious … to be away from you. I wasn't joking when I asked you to try not to fall in the ocean or get run over last Thursday. I was distracted all weekend worrying about you. And after what happened tonight, I'm surprised that you did make it through a whole weekend unscathed. Well, not totally unscathed."

"What?"

"Your hands," I noted.

She looked at them and seemed to notice the grazes for the first time. "I fell."

"That's what I thought. I suppose, being you, it could have been much worse—and that possibility tormented me the entire time I was away. It was a really long three days. I really got on Emmett's nerves."

"Three days? Didn't you just get back today?"

"No, we got back on Sunday."

"Then why weren't any of you in school?" she demanded.

"Well, you asked if the sun hurt me, and it doesn't. But I can't go out in the sunlight—at least, not where anyone can see me."

"Why?"

It would sound too silly and comic if I told her that I was glittery, like a fairy, so I simply said, "I'll show you some time."

"You might have called me," Bella said.

"But I knew you were safe," I said, puzzled.

"But *I* didn't know where *you* were. I—" She hesitated.

Carlisle had warned me that women could be controlling. They liked to know where you were and what you were doing all the time. Bella and I weren't even officially an item yet, and here she was saying that I should have called her as soon as I got home from hunting.

"What?"

"I didn't like it. Not seeing you. It makes me anxious, too."

She was turning my words back against me. "Ah!" I groaned. "This is wrong."

"What did I say?" she asked.

"Don't you see, Bella? It's one thing for me to make myself miserable, but a wholly other thing for you to be so involved. I don't want to hear that you feel that way. It's wrong. It's not safe. I'm dangerous, Bella—please grasp that."

"No," she said, rebelliously.

"I'm serious."

"So am I. I told you, it doesn't matter what you are. It's too late."

I had known for some time that it was too late for me, but I despaired to hear that she had reached that point too. She needed to have a normal life, without any more danger in it than her own clumsiness created. I couldn't allow her to think that she was irrevocably tied to me in some way, or that she had to throw away her future to be with me. Vehemently, I chided her, "Never say that."

She seemed hurt by my words. She bit her lip and stared out at the road flashing past. I smelled the wet salt again, stronger this time.

"What are you thinking? Are you crying?"

"No," she lied, her voice breaking.

I melted. "I'm sorry." Sorry for everything. Sorry for my hurtful words, sorry for my nature which meant that we could never be together.

"Tell me something," I said after a while.

"Yes?"

"What were you thinking tonight, just before I came around the corner? I couldn't understand your expression—you didn't look that scared, you looked like you were concentrating very hard on something."

"I was trying to remember how to incapacitate an attacker—you know, self-defence. I was going to smash his nose into his brain."

I tried not to laugh at the petite girl attempting to overpower the large hungry man. "You were going to fight them? Didn't you think about running?"

"I fall down a lot when I run," she said, and I had to admit that was true.

"What about screaming for help?"

"I was getting to that part."

"You were right—I'm definitely fighting fate trying to keep you alive."

She sighed. "Will I see you tomorrow?"

"Yes—I have a paper due too." Oops—I might have just given her a clue that I'd been stalking her, watching her work on her paper for English. "I'll save you a seat at lunch," I added, hoping she hadn't noticed my admission.

We were at the Swan residence. I should have driven slower after all. Reluctantly I turned off the engine.

"Do you *promise* to be there tomorrow?"

"I promise," I said, hoping it wouldn't be sunny. As she started to pull off my jacket I added, "You can keep it—you don't have a jacket for tomorrow."

She handed it back to me anyway. "I don't want to have to explain it to Charlie."

"Oh, right." Now I hoped it *would* be sunny tomorrow, so that Bella didn't get too cold. "Bella?"

"Yes?"

"Will you promise me something?"

"Yes," she agreed, a little too quickly.

"Don't go into the woods alone" Might as well admit properly that I'd been following her.

"Why?" She seemed perplexed.

"I'm not always the most dangerous thing out there. Let's leave it at that." Good work, Cullen. Spend half the evening trying to persuade Bella that you're some dangerous, terrifying creature, and then tell her that there are worse things than you in the woods. Of course, I had no idea where those wolves were these days.

"Whatever you say."

"I'll see you tomorrow," I said.

"Tomorrow, then." She opened the car door.

"Bella?" I said again. I was making a habit of interrupting her exit. I wondered whether she might retort "What now?" but she simply looked expectantly at me. "Sleep well."

Looking slightly unsteady, she staggered out of the car. I watched her open the front door, then floored the gas and sped away.

Chapter Eleven

The word *routine* in the past had implied dull, boring, pedestrian. It had meant endless monotony. My days in purgatory—the time before Bella—were identical and interminable, an endless cycle of attending the same lessons in different schools, graduating wearing different colours, maybe going to college or taking up a job or, if I was lucky, neither. Then, when I could no longer pass for the age I was claiming to be—and twenty-three seemed to be the point where people would frown in suspicion or exclaim in surprise—the cycle would begin again. It was the same old same old. Sometimes the lessons might have changed as new discoveries were made, new learning technologies invented, new education policies formulated, but it was still day after day of school with no hope on the horizon that the endless routine would end.

But *routine* no longer meant that to me. I was creating a new routine, a daily routine, one which I planned to follow for weeks and months, for as long as I could. One I wished would never end, although I knew that it inevitably must.

I decided that each night, once I'd done arguing with Rosalie, I would head to the Swan residence and listen outside for a while for the even breathing which told me that Bella was asleep. Then I would climb the tree, leap into her room, and watch in wonderment as she slept. There was nothing dull or boring about that; just being in her presence filled me with a light and a joy I had never imagined might be mine. I had already made that part of each night my routine, and I saw no reason ever to change it, though I did wonder, once or twice, if it might be prudent to bring a gas mask.

As the sun rose I'd reluctantly leave that sacred space, run home and change my clothes, collect my special, superb, stunning, shiny, spacious, speedy, sleek, sexy, silver Volvo, and arrive at her home seconds after Charlie had left.

She'd accept the ride to school and we'd talk, asking each other questions, reacting to the answers, getting to know each other the way couples just starting out in relationships did. That first day Bella surprised me by accepting each new revelation about my nature with much more equanimity than she did my attempts to shield and protect her from myself and from everything else in the world, which seemed to be out to get her. I suspected that pattern might continue in the many days ahead that we would question, respond, and share.

We'd eat lunch together in the cafeteria; that is, she'd eat a lunch I chose for her, and I'd watch her eat it.

Whenever I wasn't with her I would observe her in the minds of others. Perhaps sometimes I'd share with Bella—as appropriate—what I'd read in those minds. After school I would drive her home again, maybe we'd hang out and do some homework, or maybe we'd go on a date. Then I'd head home, and the glorious daily cycle would begin once more.

That first day of my new forever routine Bella was quizzed thoroughly by Jessica, and I witnessed the whole thing with much amusement, and teased my own related answers from Bella over lunch. As might be expected when she was eating and I wasn't, she took an interest in my dietary habits, and we speculated about the reasons behind my preference for mountain lion, and Emmett's for grizzly bear.

To those watching—and there were many—we might have been like any other teenage couple in the early throes of infatuation, except that my girlfriend was asking to see me hunt and kill a predator with my bare hands and teeth, and wasn't happy that I wouldn't let her. It was a fair bet, I thought, that *that* particular conversation hadn't been had in this cafeteria before.

I dropped her back home after school just as any other boyfriend would. We made plans for the weekend, just as any other couple would. This *routine* stuff I could really get used to. It made me feel almost normal.

"Oh, Bella," I called after her as she staggered back to her house.

She turned back. "Yes?"

"Tomorrow it's my turn."

"Your turn to what?"

I smiled. "Ask the questions."

Esme was waiting for me in the garage when I arrived – Alice must have tipped her off. I grimaced, but very attractively. I wasn't in the mood for a heart-to-heart.

"It's serious, then," she said gravely. Despite her tone, there was no hiding from me the fact that she was happy for me. I wondered why anyone ever bothered to talk to me when they knew I could read their minds.

Serious didn't begin to cover it. As though she were a black hole, Bella's gravity drew me inexorably toward her, and she seemed oblivious to the danger.

"It's so *dangerous,"* she reminded me.

"For Bella? Or for us?"

Both, her thoughts told me. She was fiercely protective of her adopted family, but she was worried about what might happen to Bella if she was brought into our world.

"How? The Volturi aren't a serious threat. Their biggest law is that children can't be turned into vampires, but with the exception of you, every vampire Carlisle has made has been under the legal age of adulthood, and they've never so much as sent a stern letter."

"That's not what I meant, Edward." I shuddered as I saw the horrors she laid out for me. Rosalie's seething resentment at no longer being the prettiest, Jasper trailing round after Bella perpetually salivating—much like every teenage boy at school already did.

"It's too late," I told her. "I've tried being aloof and obnoxious to try to scare her off. I've tried bravely running away. I've tried keeping away from Bella. I've tried warning her of the danger."

"Try a cold shower."

On impulse I hugged Esme, and she squeezed me warmly in return. We walked together into the house. She busied herself in the kitchen with pointless minutiae as only Esme could. Since we didn't eat normal food, shed skin cells, make our clothes dirty with assorted bodily secretions, or drop anything, it was tough to know what cooking or cleaning Esme could find to do, yet she bustled about anyway, flicking a duster here, straightening a picture there, throwing on a load of laundry which didn't need to be done.

I settled myself at the piano to pass the interminable hours before I could make my nocturnal visit to the Swan house. I played a more complex and upbeat melody than I had for some time and, buoyed by my unusually light mood, extemporised a little with my left hand, filling in some intricate harmonies as Esme sang along in her mind. It was almost … *fun,* and it would be a nice theme for Bella in the movie.

I hadn't always been good at the piano, of course. For decades, my family had been subjected to *Chopsticks* and *Für Elise.* Things had been thrown at me. It had got ugly. But with precious little else to do as I waited for the Xbox One to be invented I'd plinked away all through the night, year after year, so that by the time I met Bella I could be incredibly accomplished at playing my instrument.

I slammed the lid down and ran out of the house as soon as there was any hope that Bella was asleep, ignoring Esme's protest at my inadvertently destroying yet another perfectly good piano.

Asleep was a relative term. Even with all my keen senses fully tuned to the harmonious rhythm of her breathing, her pulsating heart and that great void which should have been her thoughts, I found it difficult to tell when she was just murmuring and muttering or twitching and turning in her sleep, and when she was waking up. It was lucky that she snored like a pig and drooled like a faucet, or I might have been caught out once or twice.

I darted into the closet several times that night as Bella awoke suddenly, her deep brown eyes taking in the darkness in confusion and disappointment as though dragged from a delicious dream. After all, it wouldn't do to have her waking up and seeing a creepy stalker guy in her bedroom, even a good-looking one. That was just not healthy or acceptable behaviour.

It might be true to say that it was more interesting than most of the nights I had watched her sleep. It was more eventful, certainly, but hours of silent stillness in Bella's presence, just tasting her aroma and indulging my desire for her presence, could never be monotonous. At least, not as monotonous as high school. I left, reluctantly as usual, as dawn broke. Two hours, I figured, of Emmett's teasing and Rosalie's disapproval, and then I could go back.

I timed it just right again; I waited off-road for less than a minute before I heard Charlie approaching in his cruiser. He was thinking about a conversation he'd had with Bella that morning, wondering why she wasn't going to the dance, but it was difficult to pick out specifics from Charlie's strangely opaque thoughts. I smiled to myself all the same. *I* knew why Bella wasn't going to the dance: because she was a klutz with two left feet.

"Good morning," I said gently as she got into my car. "How are you today?" She was wearing a brown turtleneck, which perfectly accented her eyes, but made her look like someone's grandma because, seriously, who wears brown turtlenecks this decade? She looked as might be expected after such a poor night's sleep: beautiful, but in an endearingly dishevelled way.

"Good, thank you."

"You look tired."

"I couldn't sleep," she replied as she brushed her hair forward to frame her face. In doing so she wafted that excruciatingly mesmerising scent right at me, and I stiffened as I felt the venom flow. I couldn't relax my guard just yet. Would I ever be safe around her? Would *she* ever be safe around *me?* Why was I so attracted to the smell of pomegranate and peach shampoo when I couldn't eat either fruit?

"Neither could I," I said, trying to make a joke of it and distract myself from that tantalising taste. It was more polite than saying *liar, liar, pants on fire* anyway. I started the engine. Anything to take my mind off the temptation. Unfortunately, my mind had plenty of capacity for making jokes, driving, and still thinking about killing Bella.

"I guess that's right. I'll wager I slept just a little bit more than you did."

It amazed me again how nonchalantly she could remark about my vampire nature. "I'll wager you did." *Who, apart from me, says* wager *these days?*

"So what did you do last night?"

Watched you sleep, as I do every night. "Not a chance. It's my day to ask questions."

She frowned a little, as though surprised there was anything interesting about her. Another thing I loved about her, I reflected: her natural unassuming modesty. She was beautiful, and smart, and insightful, and generous, and she really had no idea. Of course, the falling over all the time and barely being able to string together a coherent sentence might have been the basis of her humility. "Oh, that's right. What do you want to know?"

"What's your favourite colour?" I wanted to know *everything,* but I had to start with the easy questions.

Not so easy, it seemed. "It changes from day to day."

"What is your favourite colour today?"

"Probably brown."

"Brown?" I had expected blue for the sky, or yellow for the sun, or pink just because girls seem to like pink. Yet another thing I loved about her - her ability to surprise me with every word. Obviously she'd chosen brown because of chocolate. Girls like chocolate.

"Sure. Brown is warm. I *miss* brown. Everything that's supposed to be brown – tree trunks, rocks, dirt – is all covered up with squashy green stuff here."

Arizona, I remembered. I had been there, long ago. Not the most vampire-friendly state. I looked carefully at her – the lustrous hair, the deep chocolate-coloured eyes, and the sweater which so perfectly accentuated her flawless figure. I loved brown too, at that moment. I expressed my agreement and, finding that I could no longer fight the urge to touch her, played it safe by brushing back her glorious brown hair so that I could more fully appreciate her face.

We had reached the school. Time for another question. The CD player in my car provided the inspiration. "What music is in your CD player right now?" I was surprised at how important the question was to me. I already knew she liked Debussy, but music mattered in my life, and I needed her to recognise good music too. I needed it to be something we could share. So, not Nickelback. That would be a deal breaker.

She blushed very slightly, but seemed not to have trouble remembering. "The new Linkin Park album."

If we were not already bonded as soul mates, at that moment she became the most perfect part of creation to me. I reached across and flipped open the CD storage, pulling out the CD she had mentioned. As she took it, I noticed that her hands were shaking slightly. "Debussy to this?" I asked. Did she realise how different the two genres were?

She blushed slightly and replaced the CD in its holder. Maybe she'd always thought her eclectic tastes were yet another thing which made her different from everyone else. Maybe, in my inability to see into her thoughts, I was reading too much into her reactions.

We got out of the car and started walking to her first class. "Favourite movie?" I asked, thinking I was still on safe ground. She frowned as though again the question was difficult. "It depends what mood I'm in. Sometimes I like a light comedy, and sometimes I like something more cerebral. And even movies I think are my favourite, often it's because I have good memories of seeing them with my Mom on my birthday."

Young Bella, going to watch a Disney cartoon with her mother. I wished I could have known her then. I wished I hadn't missed seventeen years of her life. But then, maybe it was for the best that I had. She probably had no desire to be part of a horror movie. Although Bambi…

"Do you always go to the movies with your Mom on your birthday?"

"No."

"Do you read the book first before you see a movie?"

"I like to read the book, if there is one."

"Do you prefer books or movies?"

"Books, mostly." She'd stopped walking. We were outside her classroom. "Uh, this is me."

"Can I meet you after class?"

She blushed. "For more questions?"

"It's my right today."

A barely perceptible nod, and then she looked thoughtfully at me, holding my eyes for a few long moments as though she were trying to read me, rather than the other way around. And then she pushed open the door and in a sudden waft of that heady scent, she was gone.

When you've had the same lesson more times than you can count there's not much you can do to alleviate the crushing boredom of it, but I discovered that formulating questions for Bella, and anticipating answers, made those long hours somehow tolerable. And when I met her outside her Spanish class I was ready to hit her with those questions before she had time to protest.

Favourite book, favourite food, place you would most like to visit, place you most enjoyed visiting… She fielded my questions as quickly as I fired them, occasionally seeming flustered as she picked answers from the air.

"Favourite gemstone?" Two girls nearby overheard. Both thought *diamond* and one pictured the ring she'd like me to present her with. I shut them out to concentrate on Bella's reply. Unlike me, it got old pretty quickly being irresistibly gorgeous.

"Topaz," she said, flushing a deep ruby.

Not the reply I'd expected, especially given what the two eavesdroppers had responded with. "Why topaz?" She shook her head and looked away. "That's an odd choice, why did you pick topaz?" I liked to repeat things. It was going to be a feature of our relationship, I guessed, repeating things. Repetitively going over the same thing over and over again, as though just to increase the word count.

Bella quickened her pace along the corridor but I grabbed her arm gently. "Tell me."

She started fiddling with a piece of her hair, the way she always did when she was nervous, and sighed in resignation. "It's the colour of your eyes today. I suppose if you asked me in two weeks I'd say onyx."

My heart might have started again, so strongly did it seem to lurch in my chest. Not only did the colour of my eyes dictate her preferences, but she had noticed the changes wrought by my diet. I didn't know whether to be thrilled at this suggestion of affection for me, or terrified of what her keen observation would mean for her.

But, she was right, it didn't matter either way, because I was already in too deep.

"What kinds of flowers do you prefer?" I asked hastily to cover my confusion.

In biology we watched a film I had seen a thousand times before. That is, Bella watched the film and I watched Bella, drinking in her aroma as though it alone could slake my thirst, instead of cruelly heightening it. This girl was going to wreck my diet.

After walking her to her gym class I selfishly indulged my longing by gently touching her face, stroking it slowly with the back of my hand, revelling in its warmth and exulting in my newfound ability to do so without imagining following its path with my teeth.

After school we sat on the step outside her home as I relentlessly pestered her with yet more questions, probing deeper this time, needing to fill in all the details I couldn't pluck out of her mind. Her answers were more considered now, verging on the poetic as she spoke of things which were beautiful and meaningful to her, from the proud silhouette of the saguaro against the expanse of red rocks, to the sweetness of her favourite prickly pear jelly. I tried to picture the scenes she painted, to feel the awe and longing she did for her home, but my attempts at empathy were swamped by my feelings for Bella, and my overwhelming gladness that she was not in Arizona now. That she was here, in Forks, with me.

I wondered whether she wished I could read her mind so that I wouldn't have to keep asking these inane questions.

I became aware of a dim haze of fuzzy, stressed thoughts. Police procedures and puzzles, minor irritations and challenges. A bladder nearly full to bursting. Charlie was almost home.

"How late is it?" she asked as I informed her that it was time we parted. I could see perfectly in any light, of course, but her pupils were full and dark, almost covering the brown of her eyes.

"It's twilight." We had been together all day. And I would leave her only briefly soon. I wished I never had to leave her, and yet at the same time I wished I could. I wished I could go far away, somewhere she'd never find me, and thus keep her safe and perfect, just as she was now. Maybe I'd do that in the next book.

She was looking at me quizzically. "The safest time of day for us," I explained. "The easiest time. But also the saddest, in a way … the end of another day, the return of the night." It was those long, sleepless nights which most reminded me how different I was. I could watch the day die, wait through the interminable hours of the night, knowing that darkness would follow day forever, and I would always be there to see it. "Darkness is so predictable, don't you think?" I was settling well into the angst-ridden teenager role in her company.

"I like the night," she said. Something else I loved about her. She surprised me so often with her thoughts. "Without the dark we'd never see the stars. Not that you see them here much."

There was something very profound in that. I laughed. She was as emo as me. It was as though we had both swallowed the complete works of Shelley.

We stood and started towards the front door. Bella thought that I would allow her to ask the questions the next day but I disabused her of that notion quickly. I still needed to know more about her.

As I reached for the door handle I became aware that I wasn't the only person whose mind was full of Bella. Someone else was nearby, someone whose thoughts were wild and earthy and entirely consumed by her. His mind was strangely naïve and yet passionate at the same time, and I was roused immediately to the most insane jealousy. I struggled to contain the surge of feeling; it wouldn't do to allow myself to lose control around Bella.

"Not good."

"What is it?" She asked.

"Another complication." Even I wasn't entirely certain what it might be, but I was comforted to know that Charlie Swan wasn't far away, and reminded Bella of the fact as I got into my car.

There were actually two people I realised as the headlights approached, reflected in the raindrops, but the mind of the second was placid and resolute, quietly mulling over pleasurable plans for the evening, entirely unaware of the exhilaration of the other.

As the car's occupants saw me, however, everything changed. The young one seemed to siphon my jealousy into himself; the elder, *Billy Black*, became filled with anger and some strange primal protective instinct. He hated me with such fierceness that, whilst I knew he was no threat to me, I was more glad to get away from that place than I would have thought possible, given that it was where Bella was.

Did he really remember us, Billy Black? He had been a child the last time I had encountered him, swaddled on the back of a mother with a fierce, hostile and weathered face despite her youth. A mother who had seen too much, knew too much, but was still filled with pride and determination to stand up to the evil threat. Had the tales really been passed down so thoroughly and effectively? Were the Quileutes, even now, ready to enforce the decades old treaty?

100

Chapter Twelve

"Honestly Edward," Alice sang as she stood on the second floor balcony and watched me fly up the stairs of the house, "I don't know why you bother to come home at all."

Because I have to go somewhere, I thought. Somehow I had to while away the hours without Bella. The Sudoku app just wasn't cutting it any more.

"You need to hunt," Alice told me when I came up behind her.

"Do I?"

"Saturday's a big day for you, isn't it?" She spun on her heel to look at me. "Believe me, you don't want anything to go awry."

I made every effort not to pick the pictures from her head. I had seen Bella die in enough ways already.

"Let's hunt tomorrow afternoon," I suggested. Jasper, reading a magazine in the next room, agreed as swiftly as Alice.

"Do you think you can find something to fill the time until then?" Alice smiled at me coquettishly, before throwing herself onto Jasper's lap and nuzzling into his neck. *Ugh, not fair. Get a room.*

Time had been something which had been a heavy burden when I had first entered this new life. The endlessness of it, minute after minute, hour after hour, with no respite and the crystal clear knowledge that this was my lot and there would be an eternity of ... *pointlessness.* At first I fought against it, denied it, tried to pretend that season after season somehow represented progression and movement. After a couple of decades I knew I was doomed to be this forever, and considered forcing the issue, ending it, probably in Italy.

Seeing Alice and Jasper, Rosalie and Emmett, and especially Carlisle and Esme, I had realised that there might be some better escape. I had learned that for our kind happiness lies only in finding that fierce and true love which defines us. Monsters that we are, the only true redeeming quality we possess is our ability to love. Because, you know, nothing eases the pain of being eaten by a terrifying monster more than knowing it loves its wife.

I hadn't known whether I would ever be able to find that all-consuming passion, that love that made time a pleasure, not a curse, until now. That Sudoku app really was great. And Bella was pretty diverting, too.

Now the hours I spent in Bella's company, even waiting to be in Bella's company, were sacred and precious. I paced, I played the piano, I scribbled out some homework, I played Minecraft on the Xbox One, but it was all just to fill the empty hours before I could return to Bella. And as soon as I thought she was likely to be asleep I was in the woods behind Chief Swan's house, smiling at the hazy and surreal dream images in Charlie's mind and listening to Bella's even breathing, waiting for it to turn into the raucous guttural snores that would indicate that she was asleep.

As I watched her sleep, long dark lashes brushing porcelain skin, lips slightly parted, one hand on the pillow tangled in her glorious hair, I knew that this was what my hitherto pointless and endless half-life was for. This soul-creating love was what made life worthwhile. Well, that and re-runs of Downton Abbey.

"How did you sleep?" I asked as she climbed awkwardly into my car the next morning.

"Fine. How was your night?"

She had barely stirred. I had been watching her every minute. I smiled at the memory and the irony.

"Pleasant."

"Can I ask what you did?"

Was she merely curious as to how I whiled away the hours while the world slept, or did she have some inkling that I was standing guard over her during the night? I dodged the question by going back to quizzing her. Today I was steeled and ready to know about her romantic history. A little fearful though, not only of discovering that she had a boyfriend back in Arizona, but of learning that some cruel cad had broken her heart and having to fight the urge to kill him.

I was in luck; there was nothing and no one. Were the guys in Arizona so blinded by the sun that they couldn't see what was right in front of them? Or were they too smitten with tanned and skinny girls who could remain upright for hours at a time?

At lunchtime I remembered that Alice and I had plans to go hunting and Bella's truck was back at the Swan residence. "We'll go get your truck and leave it here for you," I told her when she threatened to walk home.

"I don't have my key with me."

A challenge. Alice, sitting on the other side of the cafeteria, had heard it too, and her thoughts laughed merrily as a vision of Bella's truck in front of the school floated into view. "Your truck will be here and the key will be in the ignition," I promised confidently. For any other car, leaving the key in the ignition might be an invitation to a thief, but Bella's truck had a foolproof anti-theft system: nobody would want it.

"Where are you going?" she asked.

The question brought to my mind the reason *why* Alice and I were going hunting today in the form of a mental image of Bella, cold and still, her face pale and forever frozen in a mask of agony, lying on a nest of weeping wildflowers in the secret meadow on the mountain. This time it wasn't my predator's mind planning the kill as it had been when I first met Bella. It was something Alice had seen, very briefly, during one of my many weak moments. It was a real risk.

"If I'm going to be alone with you tomorrow," I explained, "I need to take whatever precautions I can." I hoped she didn't think I meant I was going shopping for condoms. Trying to slake my thirst, just a little, could make all the difference. I hoped. Part of me still drank in her aroma and laughed at the futility of trying to resist it.

I tried to change the subject again, this time to the arrangements for tomorrow, but as ever Bella seemed fascinated by me, my family, our lifestyle and behaviour and most of all what they thought of *her*. I began to understand where the phrase "morbid fascination" might have come from. She didn't need to know these things; they might be disturbing for her, especially knowing that Rosalie was convinced that Bella wouldn't survive our little outing.

Thinking about that, hearing Rosalie crow her disparagement and seeing her visualise the ways in which I would destroy Bella, I knew I had to leave sooner rather than later. And so did Alice, who was at my side as quickly as was humanly possible.

"Can I meet my best friend now?" Alice thought to me, lightening the tension as always. I made the introductions, but barely a word was exchanged between Alice and Bella before I knew that I had to go, right now, before Bella's blood became too real to me.

All the same, the goodbye was difficult and I lingered dangerously long.

"So where would Bella have left her key?" Alice asked me as we drove out of the school parking lot.

"You tell me. You're the one with the visions."

"Of the *future*," she reminded me.

"Can't you just look for a vision of us finding the key?"

She sighed needlessly - her thoughts told me she was exasperated with me. But she also understood how much fun it was for me to show off to Bella, to show her what we could do, even in little things like this. Just like all the other pathetic teenage boys who fawned over girls out of their league, I was trying to win her admiration.

"What sort of key is it?" Alice asked.

I thought back to the time I had caught it, glad of the perfect memory which came with the perfect vampire senses. "Nickel-plated brass with a rubber grip on a leather fob with the Arizona Diamondbacks logo."

"Easy," Alice concluded, and I agreed. "How do we get into the house?"

There was a key under the eaves, but it was better for us to avoid being seen at the front of the house. Besides, that was too easy and less fun. "The window in the laundry room has a faulty catch. Charlie's been thinking about fixing it. You could get through it without doing any damage to the frame." There were advantages to being small.

Vampire speed and stealth had us at the back of the house and Alice into the laundry room in a matter of seconds. I watched through the window as she tasted the air, and then laughed. Somehow over the stench of

Charlie's dirty underwear she had smelled the combination of nickel, brass, rubber and leather right away, and it was in that very room. Getting Bella's truck to school was going to be easier than she could imagine. Leaving the school, where the beautiful and delectable Bella was surrounded by lascivious adolescent boys, was going to be much harder, even if it *was* to save her life.

My hunt had more purpose that afternoon than it had ever had. Now as I sensed, stalked and slayed my prey it was a thing of urgency, of greater need even than I had known as a newborn so long ago. I needed to quench my thirst for the sake of my own strength and sanity as ever, of course, but more than that I needed to sate my desire for Bella's enthralling blood. I continued to bring down forest dwelling carnivores (and the odd fluffy bunny) long after Alice had grown bored and returned home. Her reassurances that the horrific images of Bella were fading were not enough to dissuade me; I needed to be sure that I could trust myself. If I ever could around her.

"You really think that could make a difference?" Rosalie said scornfully as I arrived back at the house. Her sneer made it clear that she was convinced that it couldn't. "You have no idea just how dangerous your stupid little infatuation is, Edward. It's all going to go horribly wrong."

"I'd leave the predictions to Alice," I replied, trying to remain aloof, despite the fact that Alice had shown me, many times, just how horribly wrong it could go.

"You *told her about us!*" Rosalie hissed. "Just that's enough to get us summoned to Italy. And when you did, did you make it clear that we're dangerous, evil, vicious monsters? Did you *show* her?"

"I didn't tell her, she guessed. One of the Quileutes tipped her off." And when I met him I was going to get really angry and jealous, especially if he turned out to be much buffer than me with his shirt off.

Alice and Jasper appeared in the room at that moment, quickly followed by Esme and Carlisle. It appeared my disagreement with Rosalie had reached the level of a full-scale family discussion.

"Never heard of plausible deniability?"

"I've had enough of this from you over the last couple of days. Could you give it a rest?" I took my seat at the piano and started to play *The Entertainer* gently. Music always calmed me.

"You know your selfishness is going to destroy what we've spent decades building here," Rosalie replied. *It's not surprising I go on about your stupidity all the time, when it's going to wreck all of our lives!*

"I know," I agreed. "I'm sorry. I didn't choose this any more than you chose Emmett."

I could usually count on mention of Emmett to placate my adopted sister, but Rosalie was angrier than I had ever known her, and that was saying something when bitterness was pretty much her default state. We'd barely exchanged a civil word since Bella had arrived in Forks. If it weren't for Carlisle's watchfulness and firm hand, she might have been at my throat literally as well as verbally.

"Promise me you'll tell her how dangerous it is. How dangerous *you* are? Make it really, really clear that if she values her life she'll get as far away from us as possible."

I had the feeling Bella knew how dangerous we were, and my protestations weren't going to change anything. She'd wanted to watch me hunt, after all. And when she had first heard me confirm my nature, she'd said 'I don't care'.

"I was planning to. Today, in fact." At really, great length. I was going to labour the point to the point of tedium, in fact.

To help motivate me, Rosalie conjured up images of some of the worst vampire atrocities we had encountered over the decades. I scowled at her.

"Is Bella going to become part of our family?" Jasper asked in his southern drawl.

"I hope so," I responded blithely, ignoring the real meaning behind his words.

"I mean, are you going to make her one of us?"

I played louder, ignoring the question. *Answer him, Edward,* Carlisle demanded.

I stopped, turned around, looked at my expectant family.

"No. I can't."

Rosalie was alone in being happy about my answer. Esme and Alice were particularly disappointed by my response, and demanded an explanation.

"She is perfect just as she is. I don't want to change her in any way. I can't rob her of her unique quirkiness, her innocence, and I certainly can't rob her of her soul. It just feels so wrong, so *selfish,* even to think of putting her through that…*torment and horror*…just so that I can keep her to myself.

"I want her to have a life. I want her to grow up and grow old, to experience all the wonders of human life. I don't want her to become jaded and empty, a stone shell of the living, breathing person she is now."

"You want her to *die?*" Alice said. "Because she will, eventually, and you'll have to go through the rest of eternity without her."

I wouldn't, but Alice didn't need to know that detail.

"I agree with Edward," Rosalie said, suddenly on my side. "Human beings are meant to grow and change and develop and learn and experience. It's the natural order of things. And they are meant to achieve their own immortality by reproducing, making little versions of themselves that also grow and change. They're not meant to get stuck in some stagnant, stinking shape forever. We're unnatural. We're *wrong.*"

"You don't stink that much," Emmett reassured her.

"Rose is right," I said. "I can't let her be changed. I'm not going to do it, and neither are any of you. It's my choice, and I've made it. I'd ask you all to respect it."

"I think you'll find it's *Bella's* choice," Alice said triumphantly, looking directly at me, challenging me to see what she saw.

In Alice's mind I saw Bella, even more breathtakingly beautiful and pale than ever, a confident smile on her face, running blithely through the forest wearing a blue dress, her glossy brown hair streaming out behind her, the trees blurring around her, her irises blood-red.

And then she tripped over her own feet, and plunged headlong into a tree which split down the middle at the impact, and knocked out the two trees beside it. Bella, the champion klutz, could do untold damage as a vampire.

The image was brief and hazy; only a possible future. But Bella had looked barely older than she was now. I stared back at Alice in disbelief.

"It's not definite," I said at last.

"*I'd leave the predictions to Alice,*" she quoted.

I slunk quickly to my room to change, my mood sombre as I considered Rosalie's terrible predictions, and Alice's. As though to lighten my disposition I selected a long, light tan sweater over a crisp white shirt and my favourite stonewashed jeans. Yet I was still mulling over the words of my sisters when I arrived at Bella's home.

The wan sun had risen and it weak rays were struggling to pierce the ominous dark clouds. A fresh morning mist filtered through the tree branches and descended to mix with the green ground haze. Light struggled to overcome darkness and cold in this place, and the fragrant vapour was the result. There was a metaphor in there, somewhere, and I wondered where Bella and I fitted into it.

It took just a single look at her face to raise my mood, and to reassure me. It *could* be okay. It *had* to be okay. And I was the master of my own choices so I would *make it* okay.

"We match," I pointed out when Bella asked why I was laughing. She had on a light tan sweater and blue jeans too. Way to make a statement. I only wished we were going to school today, instead of somewhere no one would see us. Still, since we were going in her rusty old truck maybe it was better this way. The part of me that was still a seventeen-year-old boy would have been mortified to be spotted in a 1950s Chevy truck when there was a sparkling, special, superb, stunning, shiny, spacious, speedy, sleek, sexy, silver Volvo parked in my garage.

She was as nervous as I was. My vampire senses couldn't help but pick up the racing of her heart and the slight trembling of her hands as she fastened her seatbelt at my insistence. I outlined my plans for a hike, directed her north and we drove painfully slowly in disquieting silence but for the strained roar of the ancient engine.

It frustrated me in the extreme that I couldn't know what she was thinking. Was she angry with me about my plans for the day? Was she thinking about the danger she was in right at this moment? When I could bear it no more, I asked her.

"Just wondering where we're going," she replied. She was new to the area, I remembered.

"It's a place I like to go when the weather is nice," I told her. The weather manifestly was not nice. But had she really been whiling away the last ten minutes wondering where the road would take us?

"Charlie said it would be warm today," she said. Thoughtful of her to affirm me like that.

"And did you tell Charlie what you were up to?"

"Nope."

That was bad. "But Jessica thinks we're going to Seattle together?" At least if one person knew Bella was with me today it could help with my self-control, even if it was an annoying, petulant blonde girl. Because obviously girls are entirely responsible for the self-control of men.

"No – I told her you cancelled on me."

I could hardly believe what I was hearing. Even if I hadn't been the most dangerous predator on the planet, it was entirely inappropriate for her to be alone with me if no one knew we were together.

"No one knows you're with me?" I clarified.

"That depends…I assume you told Alice?" Alice, no doubt, had just discovered that the only thing preserving Bella from a painful and swift death was my tenuous grip on my visceral nature. I wondered what kind of graphic vision she had had. Maybe it was one of me, standing majestically over Bella's crumpled body, in that glorious flower-filled meadow.

"Are you so depressed by Forks that it's made you suicidal?"

She was almost apologetic. "You said it might cause trouble for you…us being together publicly."

I had thought she understood. Rose was right; I was going to have to spell it out much more clearly. "So you're worried about the trouble it might cause *me*—if *you* don't come *home?"* When she nodded, I muttered, "Typical warped thinking." When we fell back into uncomfortable silence for the rest of the drive, I was relieved.

The road ended where the trail began and we got out of the car. It was, as Charlie had predicted, unseasonably warm. I took off my sweater when I saw Bella do the same, and stood there before her in my half-naked vampire glory. I'd prepped for this; I'd borrowed some of Rosalie's make-up and body-sculpted some fake abs with subtle shading, but now I wished I'd worn my string vest instead. What if my "abs" were the only bit of me that didn't sparkle in the sunshine?

"This way," I said, reassuring her when she wondered why we weren't taking the marked trail. All the same she seemed wrong-footed, disturbed by something. At last. Maybe, finally, it was dawning on her how wrong this was, that she should be here, with me. "Do you want to go home?" I asked her, gently.

"No." She stepped up boldly beside me. Not that, then.

"What's wrong?"

"I'm not a good hiker, you'll have to be very patient."

Was that all? If she could only understand how patient I could be. Walking at human pace, even a very slow human pace, was something I had practised daily for decades. I did my best to reassure her, wishing for the millionth time that I could understand what was going on inside her perplexing head. Reading the minds of others had always seemed like a curse, but I would have given anything, everything, to be able to fathom the depths of this one mind.

"If you want me to hack five miles through the jungle before sundown, you'd better start leading the way," she said, an irritated note in her voice which I struggled to understand. Did she really hate hiking that much? I did as she suggested, clearing a path through the ferns and branches where necessary, helping her across obstacles and asking more questions to distract her from the onerous task of following me through this inhospitable forest.

As the sun's rays began to pierce the green canopy ahead, transforming the spectrum into one of luminescence and bright hues, her mood seemed to lift. I could smell the flowers of the meadow, see the glistening motes of pollen circling in the shining beams like millions of little fairies, and see the vapour rising from the leaves as they were bathed in the warmth. I drew Bella's attention to the change in the atmosphere, but it was a few more yards before she was able to see the difference.

I let Bella take the lead as we approached the edge of the line of trees, where the carpet of colourful flowers was laid out just for her. As I hung back in the safe shadows I felt, rather than saw, her joy and wonder at the place. I saw her posture straighten as she exulted in the warm sun. I saw her head sweep around her as she drank in the beautiful meadow. I saw her fingers stretch and reach to brush against the tall grasses as she walked slowly through the field. And then I saw her stop, frown in puzzlement, and look around for me.

When she saw me she smiled, heart-meltingly, and beckoned for me to come out. I hesitated, knowing that there was no going back after this, knowing that she had to be shocked and horrified. And then I stepped forward into the bright glow of the midday sun.

Chapter Thirteen

I stood still, and let her stare. To comfort myself I sang *Hungry like the Wolf* quietly. I gave her time to come to terms with what she was seeing. At last I felt her gently touch the back of my hand, as though checking that I was real. I opened my eyes, and saw those deep brown eyes looking at mine curiously, my dazzling reflection in their irises.

"Please stop singing, Edward. Your singing voice is the only thing about you I find scary."

"I don't scare you?"

"No more than usual."

Despite myself, I smiled, and let her touch my arm nervously, her fingers light and warm as they traced the contours of my skin, every part of my heightened vampire senses focussed on those small points of contact. I closed my eyes so that at least my sight would not be filled with her, yet her touch was still mesmerising, her delicious aroma assailed my mind, and it took more self-control than I had ever had to exercise before to fight back all my urges, monster and human.

Even so I forgot myself and moved too quickly as she examined my hand, alarming her. "Sorry," I muttered. "It's too easy to be myself with you." And I *was* being myself. Not my predatory vampire self controlled by my carnivorous instincts, but Edward, the person I was, the man I had been before Carlisle had brought me immortality at the price of my soul. When I was with Bella, I could almost believe that I still *had* a soul.

I asked her what she was thinking, because it was infuriating not knowing.

"I was wishing that I could believe that you were real. And I was wishing that I wasn't afraid."

Ironic. I felt more real, more alive, when I was with her than I had for many decades. Ironic too that *at last* she understood that she needed to be afraid of me.

"I don't want you to be afraid," I admitted.

"Well, that's not exactly the fear I meant, though that's certainly something to think about."

I moved closer, wondering what she could mean. It was intensely frustrating that, not only could I not read her mind, but I couldn't even begin to guess at her perceptions of the world, so strangely mixed-up did they seem. I looked hard into her eyes as though that might help me fathom the thought processes going on behind them. "What are you afraid of, then?"

She didn't answer. Instead she moved nearer to me. The venom flowed.

I fled, back to the shadows where I belonged, where the heady aroma was less strong, less tempting. It didn't stop the sight of her beautiful rueful face assailing my senses, or my own mortification at destroying a perfect moment stabbing at my dead heart. I had overestimated my self-control. Rosalie was right, and I hadn't yet made clear to Bella just how much she was risking by being here with me.

"I'm the world's best predator," I told her as I tentatively returned to her, my apologies fresh on my lips. "Everything about me invites you in— my voice, my face, even my *smell.* As if I need any of that!"

What was the point of luring my prey, like an angler fish or some pheromone-laced insect, when I was fifty times faster, stronger and more agile than any human being? I demonstrated my strength and speed, and she watched me, wide-eyed, still and silent. I could smell the adrenaline which laced her heady scent, and hear the racing of her heart. She was frightened of me. And not just because of my tuneless warbling of *I am a cannibal* by Ke$ha.

I was immediately remorseful, and anxious to make amends. I had intended her to show what a danger I was to her, but I didn't want her to be distressed. "Don't be afraid," I crooned, approaching her as one might a frightened baby deer. "I promise, I *swear* not to hurt you. Please forgive me, I *can* control myself." All these promises, these reassurances, were like a mantra to me as much as an oath to her. It was as though by saying it I could make it true, strengthen myself where I needed to be strong. How cruel it was that I was so strong physically, and yet the strength I needed most now was mental. But I had only to remind myself of the visions seen by Alice, and the scenarios imagined by Rosalie to know that if anything were to happen to Bella, whether by my hand or any other, the hurt it would cause me would be unendurable.

"I'm not thirsty today, honestly." I winked at her. She laughed uncertainly. "Are you alright?"

In answer she resumed her examination of my hand, tracing her warm fingertips across the smooth skin, tracing my lifeline and loveline, feeling the difference between my cold porcelain palm and her rough warm peach skin.

117

"So where were we, before I behaved so rudely?" I asked. Of course I remembered, and when she claimed that she didn't I prompted, "You were talking about why you were afraid, besides the obvious reason."

She evidently didn't want to tell me. Seconds ticked by and she said nothing, merely continued her aimless examination of the fascinating artefact that was my hand. I prompted her again.

"I was afraid...because, for, well, obvious reasons, I can't *stay* with you. And I'm afraid that I'd like to stay with you, much more than I should."

"Yes," I agreed. "That is something to be afraid of. Wanting to be with me. That's really not in your best interest." She was right. I had to leave her and never see her again. "I should have left long ago. I should leave now." *I should never have come back from Alaska.* And yet the thought of parting from her forever filled me with despair and alarm. I couldn't do it. I couldn't bear not to be near her. "I don't know if I can."

"I don't want you to leave," she admitted, and with those words the seal was set. There was no way I could leave her. *At least, not until the next book.*

"Which is exactly why I should. But don't worry. I'm essentially a selfish creature. I crave your company too much to do what I should."

"I'm glad."

"Don't be! It's not only your company I crave! Never forget that! Never forget I am more dangerous to you that I am to anyone else." Because when Bella was near I almost failed to notice anyone else. Her blood, and hers alone, was so perfectly attuned to my desires that it filled my mind and blotted out almost everything else. Almost everything. Everything but my undeniable love for her.

118

"I don't think I understand exactly what you mean—by that last part anyway."

I tried to explain, tried to put into words just how much my vampire essence desired her life blood, but there was just no analogy strong enough to convey it. Humans have addictions, cravings, desperate desires, but nothing as urgent, as overruling, as vampire thirst. I drew on the experiences of my adopted brothers; Jasper, who still struggled to be around humans at all, and Emmett who had shown me, graphically, what had happened when he had come across someone whose blood called to him the way Bella's did to me. That, at least, unsettled her.

"Even the strongest of us fall off the wagon, don't we?" Emmett was very strong. I wanted Bella to compare us, to see that I was less strong than he was. If Emmett could fail…

"What are you asking? My permission?" she snapped. "I mean, is there no hope, then?"

"No, no!" I backtracked quickly. "Of course there's hope! I mean, of course I won't…" I couldn't bring myself to say it. Things were different for Emmett. He wasn't *in love* with those strangers. I tried to explain it to her without actually using those words, *in love,* because I'd scared her enough already.

"So if we'd met …oh, in a dark alley or something…"

"It took everything I had not to jump up in the middle of that class full of children and—" Again, I couldn't say what we both knew I meant. "When you walked past me, I could have ruined everything Carlisle has built for us, right then and there. If I hadn't been denying my thirst for the last, well, too many years, I wouldn't have been able to stop myself. You must have thought I was possessed."

"I couldn't understand why," she admitted. "How you could hate me so quickly."

Hate her? It was quite the opposite, even then. "To me, it was like you were some kind of demon, summoned straight from my own personal hell to ruin me. The fragrance coming off your skin… I thought it would make me deranged that first day." *Maybe it had.* "In that one hour, I thought of a hundred different ways to lure you from the room with me, to get you alone."

I saw her shudder, very slightly, a tiny tremor that no human would have noticed. I wondered whether she was reflecting that I had finally succeeded.

"And I fought them each back," I reassured her, "thinking of my family, what it could do to them. I had to run out, to get away before I could speak the words that would make you follow. You would have come."

"Without a doubt," she assured me.

"And then, as I tried to rearrange my schedule in a pointless attempt to avoid you, you were there—in that close, warm little room, the scent was maddening. I so very nearly took you then. There was only one other frail human there—so easily dealt with."

I saw her shudder again, as well she might.

"But I resisted. I don't know how. I forced myself *not* to wait for you, *not* to follow you from the school. It was easier outside, when I couldn't smell you anymore, to think clearly, to make the right decision. I left the others near home—I was too ashamed to tell them how weak I was, they only knew something was very wrong—and then I went straight to Carlisle, at the hospital, to tell him I was leaving."

As she stared at me in surprise, I related to her the circumstances around my cowardly flight to Alaska, my reflections there, and my arrogant decision to return. Without shame I described my fascination with her shrouded mind, how I had been forced to resort to seeing her through the mind of airhead Jessica, and others, and how even her very gestures and expressions had pulled me deeper into my morbid fascination with her.

I explained why I had been compelled to save her from that car, and described the fights that had ensued as my family had finally become aware of my dangerous obsession with the fragile little girl from Arizona and my irrational and foolish behaviour. I even admitted that my life might have been easier if I had succumbed to that instinct on that first day. At least now I wouldn't have to endure this torture, the censure of half my family, the tearing of my instinctive vampire side against my human side, which needed, at all costs, to protect her.

"Isabella," I said gravely, using her full name so that she knew I was serious, "I couldn't live with myself if I ever hurt you. You don't know how it's tortured me, the thought of you, still, white, cold…to never see you blush scarlet again, to never see that flash of intuition in your eyes when you see through my pretences…it would be unendurable." As I stared deep into those eyes I saw understanding, composure, despite the catch in her throat as she breathed. "You are the most important thing to me now. The most important thing to me ever."

I had said enough. I had explained it all. Now it was her turn, but she waited an agonisingly long time, maybe processing all that I had said, maybe wondering how to respond.

"You already know how I feel, of course," she said. I laughed inwardly, because I really, really didn't. I *hoped,* of course, but for the first time I needed more than anything to hear a human tell me verbally how she felt. "I'm here…which, roughly translated, means I would rather die than stay away from you."

The exultant thrill which filled me was greater than any I'd experienced hunting or running, or in any other part of my life, vampire or human. We laughed together at her idiocy, and then I encapsulated our declarations. "And so the lion fell in love with the lamb."

"What a stupid lamb," she mused.

"What a sick, masochistic lion."

In my childhood, my *human* childhood, I had attended church with my mother, and I knew the Bible spoke of a time when predators and prey would live together, tranquil and safe, a great symbol of future peace. "The wolf also shall dwell with the lamb, and the leopard shall lie down with the kid; and the calf and the young lion together." I had chosen deliberately the noble lion to represent myself, and the innocent and endearing lamb for Bella. The wolf was not my favourite creature, especially not when it came to being in company with my precious lamb.

"What *exactly* did I do wrong before?" she asked me. When I had run suddenly, presumably. "This, for example, seems to be all right." She stroked my hand, as she had before.

"You didn't do anything wrong, Bella. It was my fault."

"But I want to help, if I can, to not make this harder for you."

It thrilled me that by "this" she meant being close, being together, touching each other. Thrilled and terrified me. We had to be so careful.

"Well, it was just how close you were. Most humans instinctively shy away from us, are repelled by our alienness." Oops, better get my story straight. Hadn't I said, just a few pages ago, "Everything about me invites you in—my voice, my face, even my *smell*"? But then, Bella was different from most humans in so many ways, and not just in that I couldn't read her mind. "I wasn't expecting you to come so close. And the smell of your *throat,"* I didn't dare go on; I didn't want to frighten her.

"Okay then," she dipped her chin down comically. "No throat exposure."

I laughed. As if anything she might do could mask the enticing scent, or hide the alluring expanse of white skin from my vampire senses. "No, really, it was more the surprise than anything else." I was assuring myself as much as her, but if we were going to be together – and I wanted us to be together more than anything else – then we needed at least to try to be a normal couple.

I put my hand gently on the side of her neck. I could feel that thick, delicious blood pulsing through the arteries and coursing back through the veins. "You see," I assured us both, "perfectly fine."

She blushed. She was like a delicate china doll with rosy cheeks, and I marvelled that I could be here with her and not break her. I moved my other hand to her face as though to protect it. "Be very still," I said. She understood, and obeyed.

I moved my face close to her neck first, slowly and deliberately, testing each movement, each moment, looking for any wavering in my resolve. Each time I felt the venom flowing, or the urgent thirst overwhelming me, I stopped, made my breathing shallower, reminded myself of her worth to me, her perfection, until I was again in control.

I moved my head across her throat, and laid it against her chest. This was the hardest test of all, being this close to a thudding human heart, drinking in her heady aroma, yet remaining composed and mastering the urges which beat deep within me. Yet master them I did.

"It won't be so hard again," I said in triumph.

"Was that very hard for you?"

"Not nearly as bad as I imagined it would be. And you?"

"No, it wasn't bad…for me."

I smiled. "You know what I mean." But she had a point. Maybe it was her turn. "Here." I gently placed her hand against my cheek. We were like reptiles; naturally cold, but warmed by our environment, and it was sunny in the meadow.

"Don't move," she said, just as I had. I closed my eyes and obeyed.

Her soft, warm fingertips caressed my cheek, feeling the smooth coldness of my dead skin. From there they travelled gently to my eyes, my nose, my lips. It was a moment of pure wonder and magic as I forced my predatory nature into abeyance, and allowed myself to be what Bella needed me to be. For the briefest of moments I was truly myself, a seventeen-year-old boy falling in love with a girl, rather than a vampire with its prey. And that meant quite a different type of desperate compulsion, one which rivalled the urge to hunt.

She dropped her hand away and I opened my eyes. "I wish...I wish you could feel the...complexity...the confusion...I feel. That you could understand."

"Tell me," she said.

"I don't think I can. I've told you, on the one hand, the hunger—the thirst—that, deplorable creature that I am, I feel for you. And I think you can understand that, to an extent. But there are other hungers. Hungers I don't even understand, that are foreign to me."

"I may understand *that* better than you think."

"I'm not used to feeling so human. Is it always like this?"

"For me? No, never. Never before this."

Unable to read her mind, I was reduced to reading between the lines, searching for the meaning behind what she said. I hoped this meant she had never felt about anyone else that way she did for me, that there had never been any other boys—men—in her life. I was strangely jealous and possessive. Had Bella admitted even to a previous crush, I might have felt the need to hunt him down.

"I don't know how to be close to you," I admitted. "I don't know if I can." I had only just learned to master one primeval urge, I didn't know whether I could handle another.

Her eyes met mine, firm and determined. Her expression said *you must.* Slowly she moved her head and pressed her cheek against my chest. A test, of sorts.

"This is enough," I admitted. Her closeness now was balm to what was left of my soul. It was more than I had ever hoped for.

"You're better at this than you give yourself credit for," she allowed.

"I have human instincts—they may be buried deep, but they're there."

We rested like that for some time, watching the shadows lengthen, the sun make its meandering course downward, neither of us really wanting to admit that our time together, here, had to end. Real life had to come rushing back in. Probably a good thing, too. This scene in the meadow had dragged on for page after page, and the *"be careful, I'm dangerous"*, *"I don't care"* thing was getting old.

"You have to go," I sighed.

"I thought you couldn't read my mind."

"It's getting clearer." I was getting better at thinking the way she did, or maybe at guessing. I calculated how long it would take us to get back to Bella's truck, and then back to Forks, and knew we had stayed too long.

"Can I show you something?" I asked her.

"Show me what?"

"I'll show you how *I* travel in the forest." She looked uncertain. "Don't worry, you'll be very safe, and we'll get to your truck much faster."

125

She looked dubious, uncertain. "Will you turn into a bat?"

I laughed loudly at that. "Like I haven't heard that one before!"

"Right, I'm sure you get that all the time."

Yes, obviously, from all the people I tell I'm a vampire. I knew a delaying tactic when I saw one. "Come on, little coward, climb on my back."

When she hesitated, I reached for her, wrapping my arm around her waist and lifting her easily onto my back. Her legs wrapped securely around me, her arms locked together around my shoulders. There was no need for her to cling so tightly; there was no way I was going to let her fall. But I didn't mind.

She made some comment about being heavier than the average backpack, at which I laughed, and then we set off.

I loved running, and running through dense forest was even more exciting than running on the flat. It required me to anticipate obstacles, dodge or leap them, weave between trees and clear paths where there were none before. As I ran I was careful to allow a little more space between me and the undergrowth so that Bella would not be whipped by foliage or impaled by twigs, and I paid careful attention to her movements, alert to any shifting of her weight or loosening of her grip, but she remained still throughout but for her laboured breathing and pounding heart, her head tucked down behind mine.

She was closer than she'd ever been; her scent, as much as her weight and her presence, assailed my keen senses, and yet I felt nothing but joy, wonder and elation. There was only one thing I could think of which could possibly bring me more bliss than I felt at that moment, and that also involved Bella being wrapped around me, but this time with our faces close together, my lips on hers…

Much of what I dreamed would have to remain forever a dream, but maybe, just maybe, there was *something*...

We reached the truck too soon. "Exhilarating, isn't it?" I said.

She didn't move, her feet still clamped tightly together at my waist, her fingernails digging into her wrists. There was a stench of gall and stomach acid almost masking her usual heady aroma.

"Bella?"

"I think I need to lie down," she gasped.

Immediately remorseful, I helped her back to her feet. "How do you feel?"

Unfocussed, she replied, "Dizzy, I think."

I hadn't factored in her fragile human nature. That was probably the fastest she'd ever travelled. It might have been quite a white-knuckle ride, as her white knuckles seemed to testify.

"Put your head between your knees," I suggested.

She did so, and I waited quietly for her to recover her equilibrium. "I guess that wasn't the best idea," I apologised.

"No, it was very interesting."

It was kind of her to make me feel better, but I didn't believe her. "You're as white as a ghost—no, you're as white as *me!*"

"I think I should have closed my eyes."

"Remember that next time."

She groaned. "Next time!"

I laughed. I preferred the quicker method of travel to the long hike of that morning. "I was thinking while I was running…"

"About not hitting the trees I hope."

"Silly Bella, running is second nature to me. It's not something I have to thinking about. No, I was thinking there was something I wanted to try."

I reached out and cupped her beautiful face in my hands, then paused to check that I really was fully in command of *both* my urges. I felt, and smelled, her hot breath, her pounding heart, and then I leaned in and touched my lips to her warm and soft and yielding ones.

There's nothing more attractive or appealing than a woman who's feeling faint and trying not to vomit, and any man would naturally be overcome by the desire to kiss her.

Almost immediately Bella responded, pressing urgently into my embrace, grasping my hair and pulling me closer, gasping through parted lips in her urgent need for me. Recognising that she was subject to the same desires as I was, I snapped back immediately. I was working so hard to control myself, and yet the irony seemed to be that it wasn't *me* that had the self-control issues.

"Oops," she said, contrite.

"That's an understatement." Did she have any clue just how dangerous that sort of behaviour could be?

She started to move back, but I reassured her. *I* was still in control, at least, and that was encouraging. "I'm stronger than I thought. It's nice to know."

"I wish I could say the same. I'm sorry."

"You *are* only human, after all."

"Thanks so much," she said caustically.

I stood, and held out my hand to raise her to her feet. She was still a little unsteady. "Are you still faint from the run? Or was it my kissing expertise?"

She laughed. "I can't be sure. I'm still woozy. I think it's some of both, though."

"Maybe you should let me drive."

She wasn't keen on that idea, and as we disputed and debated the merits of letting me take the wheel versus her concern for her truck, I realised that I had never felt freer, happier or more human. Not even, as best I could remember, when I *was* human.

"Friends don't let friends drive drunk," I laughed. "You're intoxicated by my very presence."

I had won the argument, and she reluctantly dropped the key into my hands with a warning. "Take it easy—my truck is a senior citizen."

"Very sensible," I said, glad that reason had won out in the end.

"Are you not affected at all by my presence?" she asked.

If only she knew just how much her presence had changed me already, in those few days. How she filled my thoughts, my senses, the tattered fragments of my soul. How nothing that had been before Bella had any significance any more, and the world was shaped and interpreted entirely in light of how it related to her. I loved Arizona because it had given me Bella, hated Alaska because it was where I had been apart from her. Those interminable hour-long lessons now filled me with excitement because I would be with Bella there, and even the colour brown had a new magic because it was the colour of her eyes and hair. She was everything. She was my world.

Filled with my new-found self-possession, I kissed her chin, her angular jawline, up to her ear, and then back again, listening to her shallow breathing, her pounding heart, and enjoying the way her skin trembled beneath my touch.

"Regardless," I whispered, "I have better reflexes."

Chapter Fourteen

I turned on the radio in the truck, about the only thing in it that still worked properly, and sang along to *Pledging my Love*. Such a tragedy that Johnny Ace had died in a stupid accident. I remembered it as though it were yesterday.

"You like fifties music?" Bella asked.

"Music in the fifties was good. Much better than the sixties, or the seventies, ugh! The eighties were bearable."

"Are you ever going to tell me how old you are?"

I really didn't want to put her off. Finding out that your boyfriend was old enough to be your great, great grandfather had the potential to destroy any relationship. "Does it matter much?"

"No, but I still wonder."

"I wonder if it will upset you." We were from such different worlds.

"Try me."

I sighed, and looked into her eyes to make sure she was serious. She met my gaze with steadfast resolve. She wasn't like other women, I remembered. Maybe she really did want to know all about my past. Maybe, for some perverse and unfathomable reason, my vampire nature and history intrigued her, when it should have terrified and alienated her.

"I was born in Chicago in 1901," I began, watching her in my peripheral vision as I spoke to check her reaction. She was unfazed.

"Carlisle found me in a hospital in the summer of 1918. I was seventeen and dying of the Spanish influenza."

When she gasped, I reassured her. "I don't remember it well—it was a very long time ago, and human memories fade." Actually that wasn't entirely true. Most of my human memories had faded, but *that* I remembered. At the time it had seemed the most wretched, the most unpleasant experience. I had longed for death. That was, until death—or whatever *this* was—had come along, and I had realised that, as unpleasant experiences went, influenza was a picnic in the park on a sunny day. "I do remember how I felt, when Carlisle saved me. It's not an easy thing, not something you could forget."

"Your parents?"

"They had already died from the disease. I was alone. That was why he chose me. In all the chaos of the epidemic, no one would ever realise I was gone." I left out the part where my dying mother had pleaded with Carlisle to save me, to make me what he was. She had known, somehow. I wondered how. I wondered, to this day, whether she might also have had this gift that I had, or something like it.

"How did he…save you?"

I paused, thinking about what it entailed, marvelling at the strength of my adopted father. "It was difficult. Not many of us have the restraint necessary to accomplish it. But Carlisle has always been the most humane, the most compassionate of us…I don't think you could find his equal throughout all of history." A vampire who chose to work as a doctor among humans, to heal and save them when his nature was about destroying them. A vampire who had not only resolved never to take a human life, but had built up a coven, a *family,* of others with his same commitment. A vampire who, for some bizarre reason, had chosen to surround himself with perpetual teenagers and all the drama and angst that went with them.

"He acted from loneliness," I went on. "That's usually the reason behind the choice. I was the first in Carlisle's family, though he found Esme soon after. She fell from a cliff. They brought her straight to the hospital morgue, though, somehow, her heart was still beating."

Bella understood. "So you must be dying, then, to become..." she didn't seem to be able to say the word, and I was glad.

"No, that's just Carlisle. He would never do that to someone who had another choice."

"And Emmett and Rosalie?"

"Carlisle brought Rosalie to our family next. I didn't realise till much later that he was hoping she would be to me what Esme was to him—he was careful with his thoughts around me." It was clever of him, I had often thought. Another indication of Carlisle's incredible self-control.

Bella looked a little irked. I was quick to reassure her. "But she was never more than a sister. It was only two years later that she found Emmett. She was hunting—we were in Appalachia at the time—and she found a bear about to finish him off. She took him back to Carlisle, more than a hundred miles, afraid she wouldn't be able to do it herself. I'm only beginning to guess how difficult that journey was for her." Could *I* have done it? Could I have carried my precious Bella, near death, to my adopted father?

"But she made it," Bella said.

"Yes. She saw something in his face that made her strong enough, and they've been together ever since. Sometimes they live separately from us, as a married couple. But the younger we pretend to be, the longer we can stay in any given place. Forks seemed perfect, so we all enrolled in high school." I laughed. "I suppose we'll have to go to their wedding in a few years, *again.*"

"Alice and Jasper?"

"Alice and Jasper are two very rare creatures. They both developed a conscience, as we refer to it, with no outside guidance. Jasper belonged to another…family, a very different kind of family. He became depressed, and he wandered off on his own. Alice found him. Like me, she has certain gifts above and beyond the norm for our kind."

"Really? But you said you were the only one who could hear people's thoughts."

"That's true. She knows other things. She *sees* things—things that might happen, things that are coming. But it's very subjective. The future isn't set in stone. Things change." I had often been surprised, when reading Alice's thoughts, at the speed with which a course could be set, snatched away, and then re-established, as the subject dithered over a decision. Possibilities became probabilities, and then certainties, and Alice saw the outcome become clearer, more detailed, as the choice was made and resolved upon.

"What kinds of things does she see?"

"She saw Jasper and knew he was looking for her before he knew it himself. She saw Carlisle and our family, and they came together to find us. She's most sensitive to non-humans. She always sees, for example, when another group of our kind is coming near. And any threat they may pose." We had relied heavily on Alice over the last few decades. I wondered whether I had thanked her enough.

"Are there are lot…of your kind?"

She was scared. As well she should be. "No, not many. Most won't settle in any one place. Only those, like us, who've given up hunting you people can live together with humans for any length of time." I wondered whether she understood the reasons, the implications. That too many deaths in one area drew attention and suspicion. That the drifters travelled in order to give themselves the largest possible hunting ground without doing too much damage to the local *herd.* "We've only found one family like ours, in a small village in Alaska. We lived together for a time, but there were so many of us that we became too noticeable." *As though the impossibly beautiful, white-skinned family of seven, where the parents were barely five years older than the children, passed entirely unnoticed in Forks.*

"And the others?"

"Nomads, for the most part. We've all lived that way at times. It gets tedious, like anything else. But we run across the others now and then, because most of us prefer the North."

"Why is that?"

We had arrived at her house. Part of me was glad that this unhealthy line of questioning would have to end soon. I didn't like highlighting what made me so very different from Bella, so *alien,* and I worried that the more she learned about me, about my nature, the more appalled and repelled she would be. And yet the larger part of me didn't want this time together, speaking honestly, ever to end. Charlie wasn't yet home; we might have a little more time.

"Did you have your eyes open this afternoon? Do you think I could walk down the street in the sunlight without causing traffic accidents? There's a reason why we chose the Olympic Peninsula, one of the most sunless places in the world. It's nice to be able to go outside in the day. You wouldn't believe how tired you get of night-time in eighty-odd years."

"So that's where the legends came from?"

"Probably."

"And Alice came from another family, like Jasper?"

"No, and that is a mystery. Alice doesn't remember her human life at all. And she doesn't know who created her. She awoke alone. Whoever made her walked away, and none of us understand why, or how, he could. If she hadn't had that other sense, if she hadn't seen Jasper and Carlisle and known that she would someday become one of us, she probably would have turned into a total savage." It didn't bear thinking about. Alice was very dear to me.

Bella's stomach growled and I realised, with a shock, that I'd taken her away from her home all day without thought about food for her. "I'm sorry, I'm keeping you from dinner."

"I'm fine, really."

"I've never spent much time around anyone who eats food. I forget."

"I want to stay with you," she said quietly, blushing. She must have thought that I couldn't see her unease in the dark, or hear the quickening of her heart. If anything were ever to have made my dead one leap to life, that confession from Bella would have been it.

"Can't I come in?"

"Would you like to?"

"Yes, if it's all right." I opened the car door for her, before she could realise what a bad idea that was, and we walked together up the pathway to the house. The scent of brass and nickel reminded me about the key under the eaves, and I opened the door for her. When she asked me how I'd known about the key, I confessed, "I was curious about you," hoping that, however vague, that answer might satisfy her.

"You spied on me?"

Not so much, then. "What else is there to do at night?"

136

She led the way to the kitchen, where I sat on the rickety kitchen chair, and she took a very pungent dish from the fridge and put it in the microwave. The smell almost overpowered Bella's. Almost.

"How often?" she asked, without taking her eyes off her cooking food.

"Hmmm?" I tried my best to pretend I didn't know what she was referring to. For *once* I knew what was in her mind.

"How often did you come here."

We were being honest with each other. "I come here almost every night." Well, maybe the *almost* wasn't that honest.

She turned round to look at me. I studied her face. Was she angry? Shocked? Anxious? "Why?"

"You're interesting when you sleep." I tried to elaborate. "You talk." Actually, that was the least interesting part. She was mostly interesting because she was Bella: beautiful, quiet, still and mesmerising.

"No!" she gasped, blushing again and clutching at the kitchen counter.

"Are you very angry with me?"

"That depends!"

"On?"

"On what you heard!"

I stood and took her hands, wanting to reassure her. "Don't be upset."

She tried to look away. She was still mortified. It was worth going for broke; showing her just what wonderful things her spirit had communicated to me as she slept.

"You miss your mother," I said, reverentially. "You worry about her. And when it rains, the sound makes you restless. You used to talk about home a lot, but it's less often now. Once you said 'It's too *green.*'"

137

"Anything else?" she pouted, not mollified in the least by the benign nature of her unconscious confessions.

"You did say my name," I told her, trying hard not to smile at the memory.

"A lot?"

"How much do you mean by 'a lot', exactly?"

"Oh no!" she seemed more embarrassed than ever. I pulled her gently to me in a reassuring hug.

"Don't be self-conscious," I said. "If I could dream at all, it would be about you." She took up all my waking thoughts; I had no doubt that my sleeping ones would follow the same pattern.

I had been distracted. The obscure jumble of Charlie's thoughts came to me at the same time as the sound of tyres on the driveway. "Should your father know I'm here?" I asked.

"I'm not sure…"

That was enough. I left, laughing as I heard her hiss my name when she found her arms empty.

I didn't go far. I waited near the big tree outside the house, listening to the amusing exchange between Bella and Charlie. He was quizzing her on possible romantic interests within the teenage male population of Forks High School. I wondered whether she might say that they were all too immature, that she liked men who were older than she was. Maybe almost a century older. I smiled to myself.

And then Mike Newton's name was mentioned as a possible suitor, and I felt a flare of jealous resentment. I tried to swish the pooling venom away with my tongue. *I know where he lives… it would be quick, and then I'd never have to hear his name paired with hers again.* I steeled myself, challenging the animal instincts. *Mind over matter.*

I waited until I heard the tired, heavy tread of Bella's feet on the stairs, then sprang up to the window, let myself in, and waited near the closet. I watched, amused, as Bella slammed the door behind her, sprinted to the window, threw up the sash and looked eagerly for me below, where I had been standing only seconds ago. I lay on the bed in an attitude of complete relaxation and repose, as though I had been there all along.

"Edward?" she hissed into the night.

"Yes?" I said, stifling a laugh.

She whirled around, and sank to the floor in shock when she saw me. I'd startled her.

"I'm sorry."

"Just give me a minute to restart my heart."

I sat up slowly and reached out to help her back to her feet. "Why don't you sit with me?" She settled unsteadily on the bed beside me. "How's the heart?"

"You tell me—I'm sure you hear it better than I do."

It was racing, but then, it usually was. I tried hard not to laugh, and failed.

"Can I have a minute to be human?" She asked.

"Certainly," I agreed, and gestured towards the bathroom. I had forgotten that she needed food today; I was going to have to remember that she had other needs to attend to.

"Stay," she demanded, and I obediently stilled completely.

I tried very hard not to listen to the sounds coming from the bathroom, and associate them with images. Bella cleaning her teeth was one thing; Bella in the shower was not something I had any business picturing, either as a vampire or as a seventeen-year-old guy. And no one, vampire or human, wanted to picture their loved-one on the toilet.

She ran down the stairs before she came back to me, saying goodnight to Charlie. Insurance, I guessed. Not that it would stop him checking on her. He did every night. It wasn't that he doubted that she was indeed safely tucked up in bed as she should be, but because Charlie was still overwhelmingly happy, and a little surprised, that she was actually living with him, and liked to look in at her as he made his own way to bed. "Making up for lost time" was one of the few thoughts I had been able to discern clearly in his mind as I waited in the closet one night near the beginning. It was unbearably sad: the loving father who had longed to tuck his daughter into bed each night, maybe read her a story and kiss her goodnight, for so many years. Now that she was, at last, living with him she was too old for all those things.

Did everyone who loved Bella like to watch her sleep? I couldn't help but like Charlie. He loved Bella and wanted to protect her, and that made him a great ally in my book.

When Bella came back in I complimented her on her eclectic nightwear—grey sweatpants and a faded t-shirt—and asked why she had gone down to see her father.

"Charlie thinks I'm sneaking out."

Wasn't I the one who could read minds? I certainly hadn't detected that suspicion in Chief Swan, although his mind was tough to penetrate. "Oh. Why?"

"Apparently I look a little overexcited."

I studied her face. She was certainly flushed (when wasn't she?) but with her hair damp and tousled and her extremely casual attire, it was difficult to picture someone less likely to escape through the window for a night on the town.

She smelled even more delicious than ever. The various mixed florals of her shower gel and shampoo, the mint of her toothpaste, served only to provide a contrasting and enriching base to Bella's own unique and intoxicating aroma. I pressed my cheek against hers, breathing that mesmerising scent, revelling in it.

"It seems to be ... much easier for you now, to be close to me."

"Does it seem that way to you?" I brushed back her hair and kissed her neck gently, just below her ear. In one way, maybe. In another, not at all.

"So I was wondering," she went on, "Why is that, do you think?"

Lost in the moment I murmured, "Mind over matter".

She pulled back at that second, and I froze, holding my breath in a futile attempt to try not to taste that potent fragrance.

"Did I do something wrong?" I asked her.

"No—the opposite. You're driving me crazy."

That was an interesting thought; that even as I gloried in my closeness to her, she too had been fighting desires, urges, which threatened to overpower her; that although I had been acting instinctively as I revelled in the warm softness of her skin, it had brought about an all-too-human reaction. She, too, had been invigorated by my nearness.

"Really?" I smiled.

"Would you like a round of applause?"

"I'm just pleasantly surprised. In the last hundred years or so I never imagined anything like this." *Understatement of the century. Literally.* "I didn't believe I would ever find someone I wanted to be with...in another way than my brothers and sisters. And then to find, even though it's all new to me, that I'm good at it...at being with you..."

"You're good at everything," she pointed out, and we laughed together quietly.

"But how can it be so easy now?" She wondered.

"It's not *easy,*" I clarified. "But this afternoon, I was still…" I reached for the right word. What *had* changed since we walked into the meadow? I had realised that destroying Bella would also destroy me. "I was undecided," I concluded. I watched her face carefully for any sign that she understood just how much danger she had been in. "I am sorry about that, it was unforgivable for me to behave so."

"Not unforgivable," she said. I felt sure she hadn't understood what I was telling her. How could she forgive me when I had lured her to a flower-filled meadow without being completely certain that I wouldn't kill her there? And really, after I'd laboured the point for hours, and hours, and tedious hours, how did she still not get the "I might kill you" thing?

"Thank you," I said lamely, and smiled. "You see, I wasn't sure if I was strong enough. And while there was a possibility that I might be overcome…" I was holding her hand, as I did so often now. As I spoke I lifted it, and drank deep the fragrance from the pulse point of her wrist. "I was…susceptible. Until I made up my mind that I *was* strong enough, that there was no possibility at all that I would…that I ever could…" And now I couldn't even bring myself to say it.

"So there's no possibility now?" she confirmed.

"Mind over matter," I reassured her again.

"Wow, that was easy."

I laughed. *If only she knew!* "Easy for *you!*" and I touched her adorable nose with my fingertip. But she needed to know. "I'm trying. If it gets to be…too much, I'm fairly sure I'll be able to leave. And it will be harder tomorrow. I've had the scent of you in my head all day, and I've grown amazingly desensitized. If I'm away from you for any length of time, I'll have to start again. Not quite from scratch, though, I think."

"Don't go away then," she suggested.

"That suits me," I replied. "Bring on the shackles—I'm your prisoner." This was all becoming a bit too *Fifty Shades.* Although – wasn't that us, too? Very confusing.

"You seem more…optimistic than usual," she observed. "I haven't seen you like this before."

"Isn't it supposed to be like this?" I said. "The glory of first love, and all that. It's incredible, isn't it? The difference between reading about something, seeing it in the pictures, and experiencing it?" I might have added that it was different, too, seeing it in someone else's mind. I had experienced my family's love for their spouses, but it felt so much more intense now that I was swept up in my own passion.

"Very different," she agreed. "More forceful than I'd imagined."

"For example," I went on, "the emotion of jealousy. I've read about it a hundred thousand times, seen actors portray it in a thousand different plays and movies. I believed I understood that one pretty clearly. But it shocked me…" I grimaced as I remembered. "Do you remember the day that Mike asked you to the dance?"

She nodded. "The day you started talking to me again."

"I was surprised by the flare of resentment, almost fury, that I felt—I didn't recognize what it was at first. I was even more aggravated than usual that I couldn't know what you were thinking, why you refused him. Was it simply for your friend's sake? Was there someone else? I knew I had no right to care either way. I *tried* not to care. And then the line started forming." I recounted how anxious I had been when it seemed that every guy in the school was going to ask Bella to the dance, how I had wrestled

143

with the choice before me: whether to ignore her and carry on, let her fall in love with Mike Newton or some other guy, or to act on what I wanted. I told her how I had heard her mumble my name in her sleep, and had been stunned and elated, and had made the decision. "I'm new at this," I concluded. "You're resurrecting the human in me, and everything feels stronger because it's fresh."

"But honestly," she said, "for that to bother you after I hear that Rosalie—Rosalie the incarnation of pure beauty, *Rosalie*—was meant for you, Emmett or no Emmett, how can I compete with that?"

"There's no competition," I assured her, pulling her close to me. Rosalie may have been the world's idea of beauty, all long legs and blonde curls, but she paled against Bella.

"I *know* there's no competition," she muttered. "That's the problem."

She had misunderstood. "Of course Rosalie is beautiful in her way, but even if she wasn't like a sister to me, even if Emmett didn't belong with her, she could never have one tenth, no, one hundredth of the attraction you hold for me. For almost ninety years I've walked among my kind, and yours, all the time thinking I was complete in myself, not realizing what I was seeking. And not finding anything, because you weren't alive yet."

"It hardly seems fair," she said. "I haven't had to wait at all. Why should I get off so easily?"

"You're right. I should make this harder for you, definitely." Waiting for her this long only meant I appreciated the wonder of knowing her all the more, and was even more keenly aware of what our relationship really was. "You only have to risk your life every second you spend with me, that's surely not much. You only have to turn your back on nature, on humanity. What's that worth?"

"Very little—I don't feel deprived of anything."

"Not yet." Some day she would want a boyfriend she could have a real life with.

A sound, a scent, and then a thought. "Lie down!" I hissed at her, retreating instantly to the closet. Bella pulled the quilt over herself the moment before the door cracked open and Charlie peered in. Bella tried to keep her breathing even and deep, her face still and serene, but no one who'd spent time studying her while she slept would be fooled. Luckily most people, including Charlie, aren't that creepy.

When Charlie had left, satisfied that his daughter was where she was supposed to be, I broke the bad news to Bella. "You are a terrible actress— I'd say that career path is out for you."

"Darn it," she said, laughing.

She looked comfortable. Peaceful. She needed to sleep. I started to hum the song I had composed for her. "Should I sing you to sleep?" I checked.

She laughed. "Like I could sleep with you here!"

"You do it all the time."

"But I didn't *know* you were here," she replied.

"So if you don't want to sleep..." I teased.

"If I don't want to sleep...?"

I laughed nervously. "What do you want to do then?"

She paused, as uncertain as I was. "I'm not sure," she said at last.

"Tell me when you finally decide." We were passing the buck, both—I guessed—keenly aware that we were two people in love alone in a bedroom. I moved close to her, my face brushing against hers as I inhaled the intoxicating sweet scent between her neck and the curtain of glossy hair. I probably wasn't helping.

"I thought you were desensitized," she commented.

145

"Just because I'm resisting the wine doesn't mean I can't appreciate the bouquet. You have a very floral smell, like lavender...or freesia. It's mouthwatering."

"Yeah, it's an off day when I don't get *somebody* telling me how edible I smell."

I laughed at that, but drew back, recognizing that I was about to cross a line.

"I've decided what I want to do," she declared. "I want to hear more about you."

"Ask me anything," I said, accepting that this was probably the best decision for both of us, given the circumstances.

"Why do you do it?" she began. "I still don't understand how you can work so hard to resist what you...*are*. Please don't misunderstand; of course I'm glad that you do. I just don't see why you would bother in the first place."

Did she understand what she was saying? Bella never ceased to surprise me. All the same... "That's a good question, and you are not the first one to ask it. The others—the majority of our kind who are quite content with our lot—they, too, wonder at how we live. But you see, just because we've been dealt a certain hand...it doesn't mean that we can't choose to rise above—to conquer the boundaries of a destiny none of us wanted. To try to retain whatever essential humanity we can."

Carlisle had once told me, "A creature is not evil until it does evil." We could choose to rise above our carnal and monstrous natures. Carlisle had made that choice from the very beginning, as difficult as it was. The rest of us had, at various times and in varying degrees, come to realise that we could be noble, strong, honourable. That it was the better way, if we wanted to live true to whatever was left of our human souls, spirits, consciences.

Bella hadn't said anything. "Did you fall asleep?" I asked.

"No."

"Is that all you were curious about?"

"Not quite."

Of course not. "What else do you want to know?"

"Why can you read minds—why only you? And Alice, seeing the future...why does that happen?"

"We don't really know. Carlisle has a theory...he believes that we all bring something of our strongest human traits with us into the next life, where they are intensified—like our minds, and our senses. He thinks that I must have already been very sensitive to the thoughts of those around me. And that Alice had some precognition, wherever she was."

I remembered little of my human life, but I had known, when my human mother told me that we were both going to recover and that it was going to be alright, that she had been lying.

"What did he bring into the next life, and the others?"

"Carlisle brought his compassion, Esme brought her ability to love passionately. Emmett brought his strength, Rosalie her...tenacity. Or you could call it pig-headedness. Jasper is very interesting. He was quite charismatic in his first life, able to influence those around him to see things his way. Now he is able to manipulate the emotions of those around him— calm down a room of angry people, for example, or excite a lethargic crowd, conversely. It's a very subtle gift."

"So where did it all start? I mean, Carlisle changed you, and then someone must have changed him, and so on..."

147

"Well, where did you come from? Evolution? Creation? Couldn't we all have evolved in the same way as other species, predator and prey? Or, if you don't believe that this world could have just happened on its own, which is hard for me to accept myself, is it so hard to believe that the same force that created the delicate angelfish with the shark, the baby seal and the killer whale, could create both our kinds together?"

"Let me get this straight—I'm the baby seal, right?"

"Right." I laughed, and kissed her hair. She was much cuter and more vulnerable than a baby seal, and wouldn't make half such a stylish stole. "Are you ready to sleep, or do you have any more questions?"

"Only a million or two."

"We have tomorrow, and the next day, and the next." We had forever. Well, maybe not *forever,* but her forever. Maybe seventy short years. Maybe long enough for me to answer all her questions, because they sure did keep coming.

"Are you sure you won't vanish in the morning? You are mythical, after all."

Her world had been turned upside down today. Everything she thought she knew about what was the truth and what were myths and legends had been swept away. She was handling it remarkably well. "I won't leave you," I vowed.

"One more, then, tonight." She blushed, and fell silent.

"What is it?"

"No, forget it. I changed my mind."

"Bella, you can ask me anything." As though fighting two animal urges wasn't difficult enough, being with Bella added the new frustration of not being able to figure out what was going on in her unique mind. "I keep thinking it will get less frustrating, not hearing your thoughts. But it just gets worse and worse."

"I'm glad you can't read my thoughts. It's bad enough that you eavesdrop on my sleep-talking."

"Please?" I begged. "If you don't tell me, I'll just assume it's something much worse than it is. Please?"

"Well," she hesitated, still blushing furiously.

"Yes?" I prompted.

"You said that Rosalie and Emmett will get married soon...Is that...marriage...the same as it is for humans?"

I never would have guessed that that was her question. As usual with Bella, it was completely left of field. But I could understand entirely where it was coming from, because my thoughts had naturally turned along similar lines.

"Yes, I suppose it is much the same," I told her. "Most of those human desires are there, just hidden behind more powerful desires." *Not far behind,* I remembered, thinking of Rosalie and Emmett's prolonged and very passionate "honeymoon". There are times when being able to read minds really is a curse, and there were some pictures I really wished I could get out of my head.

"Oh."

"Was there a purpose behind your curiosity?" I hoped there was.

"Well I did wonder...about you and me...someday..."

I pushed away the thrill that coursed through me at her words, and tried to keep the sadness from my voice as I replied, "I don't think that...that...would be possible for us."

"Because it would be too hard for you if I were that...close?"

149

"That's certainly a problem. But that's not what I was thinking of. It's just that you are so soft, so fragile. I have to mind my actions every moment that's we're together so that I don't hurt you. I could kill you quite easily, Bella, simply by accident, if I was too hasty…if for one second I wasn't paying enough attention. I could reach out, meaning to touch your face, and crush your skull by mistake. You don't realise how incredibly *breakable* you are. I can never, never afford to lose any kind of control when I'm with you."

She said nothing. I waited for her response, then when it didn't come I asked, "Are you scared?" My description had maybe been a little too graphic.

"No, I'm fine."

The jealous fury rose in me again when I asked, "I'm curious now, though. Have *you* ever…"

"Of course not," she assured me, and the resentment was quelled. "I told you I've never felt like this about anyone before, not even close."

"I know. It's just that I know other people's thoughts. I know love and lust don't always keep the same company." She could never begin to guess at just how much the minds of the guys at school circulated endlessly, obsessively, around that single topic. Some of the girls were almost as bad. But sitting here with Bella, endearingly tired and dishevelled she was, I understood those consuming passions better than I ever had before.

"They do for me. Now, anyway, that they exist for me at all."

"That's nice. We have that one thing in common, at least." It seemed the easiest way of reciprocating, of telling her I'd waited for her.

She was surprised. "Your human instincts… Well, do you find me attractive, in *that* way, at all?"

If only she knew! "I may not be a human, but I am a man." When she yawned, I added, "I've answered your questions. Now you should sleep."

"I'm not sure if I can."

"Do you want me to leave?"

"No!"

I laughed at how quickly she said it, then realised that if I started to sing she might pretend to sleep in order to get me to shut up. I began again to hum the lullaby I had composed for her, and watched as she succumbed at last to sleep.

Chapter Fifteen

I passed the hours as Bella slept reflecting on that magical day. As I looked at her chestnut hair spread lightly across the pillow, her soft lips gently parted, her delicate hands spread over the counterpane, I recalled her saying the words which, had I had a soul, might have sent it into heavenly flight.

Blessed with vampire memory I was able to replay each word, envisage each gesture, and picture each scene. As I did so I considered the nuances, the meaning and implications of all that had passed. We had declared ourselves, we had accepted and explored the differences between us, and we had spoken, however tentatively, of our future.

As I processed the events in the meadow, and beyond, I guessed that Bella would be doing the same through her dreams. I knew I had featured in her dreams before. I wondered how my role in them might have changed after the last twenty-four hours.

My question was answered as she started mumbling. At first the words were indistinct or meaningless, related to her surreal and disjointed dreams, I suspected. But then she said my name, twice, and then a deep sigh, and "I love you."

"I love you too," I replied, looking down at her peaceful face. It seemed to me that she smiled, just a little.

I ran home as soon as I could bear to leave her, jumping to the balcony adjoining my bedroom rather than have to talk to any members of my family. I changed at lightning vampire speed, and tossed yesterday's clothes, complete with grass stains from the meadow, into the hamper.

"Edward," Esme said as she knocked politely on the door. She wasn't alone. Several curious minds were crowded around her.

Two seconds earlier and I'd have been naked. Nice timing.

"Come in," I sighed. "All of you."

"Is she here?" Esme asked hopefully as she entered, her face falling as she took in the empty room.

"You'd have smelled her a mile off," Rosalie said acerbically. "She's pretty pungent."

"Pay up," Jasper said from behind her. As Emmett peeled some bills from a wad, he frowned at me. I tried to ignore the fact that he was mentally questioning my masculinity. "She's human," I reminded him. And I wasn't about to disrespect her father when he'd gone to such lengths to make sure his daughter stayed right where he wanted her.

"I told you so," Alice laughed. "He never even considered bringing her here. Oh, but *now* he is."

"She'd be very welcome," Esme smiled. "Anytime, Edward. Really."

"Mmm, yes, really," Jasper's thoughts echoed. "I'll order a nice Chianti and some fava beans."

"I'll ask her. Jasper, will you..."

"We'll all take care of Jasper," Carlise said from his den.

"Then...thank you. Thank you Mom." Esme loved it when we called her 'mom'. "Sorry you lost the bet."

I sprinted back to Bella's bedside. I couldn't bear to miss even five minutes with her. This time I settled into the chair. Dawn was beginning to break, and it might frighten her if she were to wake to find me standing over her.

When she did wake up, she sat up with a start, as though surprised to rediscover real life.

"Your hair looks like a haystack," I observed. "But I like it."

"Edward, you stayed!" Like a perfumed china cannonball she hurled herself across the room into my lap, her arms wrapping round my neck, her soft body pressing thoughtlessly against mine. But I was prepared. I'd been in her company for a long time now, breathing her scent, seeing the blood pulse through blue veins under her peach-soft skin.

"Of course," I laughed. It felt so good to hold her again.

She nestled into my neck. "I was sure it was a dream."

"You're not that creative."

"Charlie!" She jumped up and headed to the door.

"He left an hour ago—after reattaching your battery cables, I might add. I have to admit I was disappointed. Is that really all it would take to stop you, if you were determined to go?"

She stood at the door, uncertain.

"You're not usually this confused in the morning," I said, and held my arms open for her to return.

"I need another human minute," she said.

"I'll wait." I mentally kicked myself for forgetting yet another human need, and reminded myself that she would need to eat soon. She was back in my arms only five minutes later, chiding me for leaving even to change my clothes.

"What did you hear?" she asked when I told her that the talking had been early in the night, before she was in the deepest sleep.

"You said you loved me."

155

"You knew that already." She tucked her head back into my shoulder.

Guessed rather than knew. "It was nice to hear, just the same."

"I love you," she repeated.

I had read in many sources the received wisdom that the only correct response to "I love you" is "I love you too". Not "Ditto", "I know" or "Thank you" or, indeed, anything else.

I ignored all that. "You are my life now," I replied.

We sat, quiet and still, just being together, enjoying the nearness and the peace. Or maybe after all that tedious gabbing yesterday we'd run out of things to say, and now we were at the awkward stage.

"Breakfast time," I said eventually. She clutched at her throat in alarm, then laughed at my shocked reaction. "That wasn't funny!"

"It was very funny, and you know it."

"Shall I rephrase? Breakfast time for the human." To pay her back for the tasteless joke about my breakfast I slung her over my shoulders and ignored her protests as I carried her down the stairs, placing her in a chair at the kitchen table. When I didn't also produce a plateful of pancakes and bacon for her, she fetched herself a bowl of cereal.

"Can I get you anything?" she asked a little awkwardly. Human social convention, I remembered, to want to share the experience of eating with others. I waved away her offer, and watched her eat just as I had watched her sleep.

"So what's on the agenda for today?" she asked.

"Hmmm… What would you say to meeting my family?"

She gulped. Nervous, as well she should be.

"Are you afraid now?" Maybe, finally, she was understanding just what she was involved with. I must have laboured the point enough yesterday after all.

"Yes."

I remembered Carlisle's promise. Jasper was still struggling with his new diet, and the temptation to break it. "Don't worry, I'll protect you."

"I'm not afraid *of* them, " she said. "I'm afraid they won't...like me. Won't they be, well, surprised that you would bring someone...like me...home to meet them? Do they know that I know about them?"

"Oh, they already know everything." I explained about the bets they'd placed that night. I was pleased that she seemed to have understood what I'd told her about our gifts, and how they fitted into the family dynamic.

"So did Alice see me coming?" she wanted to know.

Alice had seen many things relating to Bella. Some I couldn't bear to think about. "Something like that," I fumbled, and changed the subject to her soggy cereal. "Is that any good? Honestly, it doesn't look very appetizing."

"Well, it's no irritable grizzly..." she muttered. I didn't like it when she joked about such things, made light of our destructive nature. I worried that she didn't fully understand just how dangerous it was for her to be around me, or that she didn't realise just how much the impossibility of a natural relationship between predator and prey could make both our lives into tragedies to rival Romeo and Juliet, Cleopatra and Mark Anthony, Cathy and Heathcliff, or, even worse, Kim and Kanye.

Rosalie was right. *This couldn't end well.* Bella's death was inevitable. Either I would kill her in a moment of weakness or passion, or both, or she would die after just a few short decades of a chaste relationship blighted by the fundamental differences between us. And for as long as it lasted, there could be no romantic dinners, because I didn't eat; no drifting off in each other's arms, because I couldn't sleep; no growing old together, because I didn't grow old.

As Bella ate I stared through the window, thinking that I had never been happier, and yet at the same time I had never felt more hopeless or despairing.

Bella deserved better.

But Bella didn't want better. Bella wanted me. She *needed* me. Apart from whatever feelings she had for me, she needed me to protect her from everything that was out to get her, from Tyler Crowley's car to nomadic vampires to uneven paving stones.

And so I resolved that I would always be there for her, for as long as she wanted me, and that I would do everything in my power to enjoy whatever time I had with Bella, and to make our love as normal and natural as possible. Because Bella deserved that, at least.

I turned back to her and smiled. "And I think you should introduce me to your father."

"He already knows you," she replied.

She wasn't getting away with that. "As your boyfriend, I mean."

She frowned at me. "Why?"

"Isn't that customary?" In a *normal* relationship.

"I don't know," she said. "That's not necessary, you know. I don't expect you to…I mean, you don't have to pretend for me."

"I'm not pretending." I wanted this. Because if I were human, surely the time would come when she would introduce me to her father. "Are you going to tell Charlie I'm your boyfriend or not?"

She pulled a face. "Is that what you are?"

"It's a loose interpretation of the word 'boy', I'll admit."

"I was under the impression that you were something more, actually."

"Well, I don't know if we need to give him all the gory details." I hadn't made it clear to her yet that no one else could know what we are. Maybe because I couldn't bring myself to tell her that I had put her at risk by allowing her to find out. As though she needed to be in any more danger than she already was. "But he will need some explanation for why I'm around here so much. I don't want Chief Swan getting a restraining order put on me."

"Will you be?" she asked. "Will you really be here?"

"As long as you want me," I promised her, just as I had promised myself.

"I'll always want you," she declared. "Forever."

Her forever was so very much shorter than mine. I reached out my fingertips and gently stroked her cheek. The time would come, very, very quickly, when that flawless porcelain skin was dry and wrinkled, when her deep brown eyes grew hooded and cloudy, when her lush, kissable lips were thin and pale.

"Does that make you sad?" she asked me.

Rather than answer, I drank in the beauty of the young, fresh Bella, the gawky, clumsy, endearing teenager who mattered more to me than anything or anyone ever had.

"Are you finished?" I asked when I could no longer bear to dwell on the brevity of this time.

"Yes." She stood up.

"Get dressed—I'll wait here."

While Bella was gone, I called Esme. Doubtless Alice had seen a future suddenly appear in which Bella was in our home, but it seemed the polite thing to do. Esme was as delighted at the news as I had known she would be. As I ended the call I heard her call to Carlisle, "We have to go grocery shopping! Right now!"

I wished I could be there to witness Esme and Carlisle in Wal-Mart, trying to figure out how to put together a normal human menu using corn dogs and canned cheese, while distracted by an obese guy in a blue dress riding a mobility shopping cart.

Bella returned just a few minutes later in a knee length khaki skirt and the dark blue blouse I had once admired. Her hair was pulled back into a severe ponytail, but stray wispy hairs framed her hair, catching the light like a halo. She looked demure, but devastating.

"Okay, I'm decent," she said as she bounced into the kitchen.

"Wrong again," I said, catching her and pulling her to me. "You are utterly indecent. No one should look so tempting, it's not fair."

"Tempting how? I can change…"

Bella had looked beautiful and alluring in the grey sweatpants and stained t-shirt. There was nothing she could wear that would make her look any less enticing.

"You are so absurd." I kissed her forehead. "Shall I explain how you are tempting me?" I held her close, letting her feel my cold breath on her neck, my smooth skin against hers. I traced a light, gentle line down her spine, my fingertips delicate but determined, and smiled to myself when I felt the warmth of her blood run up to meet my touch as the nerves fired in frenzy. Then I tilted my head and kissed her, more fervently this time.

I felt her go limp in my arms. "Bella?"

"You…made…me…faint!" she stammered as she regained her feet.

"*What am I going to do with you! Yesterday I kiss you and you attack me! Today you pass out on me! So much for being good at everything.*" *Maybe I just needed more practice.*

"That's the problem," she murmured. "You're too good. Far, far too good."

She was ghostly white, although her cheeks were flushed fiery red. "Do you feel sick?" I asked.

"No—that wasn't the same kind of fainting at all. I don't know what happened. I think I forgot to breathe."

"I can't take you anywhere like this."

"I'm fine. Your family is going to think I'm insane anyway, what's the difference?"

"I'm very partial to that colour on your skin," I murmured.

"Look, I'm trying really hard not to think about what I'm about to do, so can we go already?"

"And you're worried, not because you're headed to meet a houseful of vampires, but because you think those vampires won't approve of you, correct?"

She confirmed that I was right. I shook my head. "You're incredible." But I meant it in a good way. Almost a century of reading minds, and I still couldn't fathom the way Bella thought or viewed the world. It was refreshing.

I drove Bella's truck. I wondered whether her light-headedness was really because I had made her weak at the knees, or whether she was, as she should be, somewhat nervous at the prospect of being the lone, vulnerable human amidst seven bloodthirsty vampires in their own territory. But then knowing the way Bella's brain seemed to work, if she was nervous at all it was probably at the speed with which we had arrived at the stage in our relationship where she was being brought home to meet my parents.

Whatever the cause of her earlier wooziness, I wasn't about to let her drive. I had vowed to keep her safe, and that included behind the wheel.

As we drove, I found that I, too, was nervous. I had reason to be; I knew that Rosalie wouldn't give Bella a friendly or even polite welcome, and Emmett, for all his strength and bluster, always seemed to follow Rosalie's lead. Alice might be delightful and fun, as she always was, but she equally might be tense and edgy as she sensed Jasper's struggle and foresaw the outcomes of it. That left Esme and Carlisle, if they had arrived home from Wal-Mart without incident. With their unfamiliarity with human food, was Bella about to be treated to a lunch of raw cauliflower, frozen lasagne and maple syrup? I listened as hard as I could to get some idea of the mood at home as we drove through the woods.

"Wow," Bella said as we drew up outside the house.

"You like it?" It was important to me, for some reason, that she did.

"It has a certain charm," she said coyly, and I laughed.

"Ready?"

"Not a bit. Let's go."

I opened the door for her, then took her hand as we walked up to the house. I listened carefully for clues about the mood within the walls, scanning my family's thoughts to build up a picture of what we would find. Had they dressed for a special occasion? Was Rosalie going to behave, or would she cause trouble?

Esme was excited and happy, if a little anxious, as much because it she wanted to make a good impression as at the strangeness of having a human in her home.

Rosalie was angry. "It's going to break the up the family," she said, and I felt Esme's mood plummet like a burst balloon. "It's going to destroy us."

When Esme had quelled her anger and mustered the appropriate level of decorum and parental authority, she chided Rose. "Nonsense. It doesn't have to be a problem at all if we all take care."

"It's just so stupid! What is he thinking?"

She knew I could hear her. Surely Bella could too? I rubbed circles on the back of her hand to reassure her.

"We are going to support Edward in this," Esme said with a tone of finality. "This is important to him."

"What about the rest of us?" Rosalie protested.

"It's important to us too," Carlisle said, leaving his study to come to his wife's side. "We've wanted for years to see him happy."

"Emmett and I are already thinking of leaving, if things get to difficult. We want to be far away from here when it all goes wrong. We've even planned where we're going."

I wondered why she bothered to lie when I was around. Not only was there nothing in her mind about possible places they might settle, but all this was news to Emmett. Loyal as ever, he said nothing.

"They're here," Esme said, plastering on her best smile at the instant I opened the door. And there they stood, Carlisle and Esme, as curious to see the human I had fallen in love with as she must be to see them.

I introduced Bella politely, and Carlisle, easy and confident around humans after centuries living among them, stepped forward to shake her hand. Esme followed, a little more cautiously. "It's very nice to know you," she said to Bella.

163

"Thank you," Bella responded, seeming perfectly at ease. "I'm glad to meet you, too."

There was no sign of Rosalie and Emmett, and I couldn't hear them either. I smiled ruefully to myself. *Running away from a human.*

Alice appeared at the top of the stairs just as I was wondering where she was, and flew down in that lightning-speed ballerina way of hers to kiss Bella on the cheek and greet her like a long-lost friend which, from Alice's perspective, was probably what she was. Carlisle and I exchanged glances, nervous at Alice's rash behaviour.

"You do smell nice, I never noticed before," Alice commented, and I groaned inwardly.

Jasper followed behind Alice, waves of wellbeing emanating from him, and calming any residual tension in the room. I caught his eye and nodded my thanks. Jasper greeted Bella, but didn't approach her, and I was relieved.

"It's nice to meet you all—you have a beautiful home," Bella said.

"Thank you," Esme replied. "We're so glad that you came." *And surprised,* she might have added. *And a little worried.*

Edward.

Carlisle's thought tone was urgent, and I dragged my attention away from Bella.

Alice has seen others coming. Nomads. They're near. They know we're here and they're curious about the vegetarian vampires. They're on their way. Stay close to Bella.

I nodded, tersely. As though Bella needed any more danger.

Do you play?" Esme asked Bella, who was studying our Steinway grand piano.

"Not at all. But it's so beautiful. Is it yours?"

Esme laughed as she shook her head. "Edward didn't tell you he was musical?"

"No." She glared at me, and I tried to look innocent. "I should have known, I guess."

Esme didn't understand the allusion.

"Edward can do everything, right?"

Jasper found that hilarious. *She must mean some other Edward.* Esme was concerned that I'd been bragging about my vampire abilities. "I hope you haven't been showing off—it's rude," she scolded.

"Just a bit," I admitted, and laughed. *She's lovely, Edward,* Esme thought to me. *And you're happy at last.*

"He's been too modest, actually." Bella said.

"Well, play for her," Esme said

"You just said showing off was rude," I protested.

You know what I meant. "There are exceptions to every rule."

"I'd like to hear you play," Bella said.

"It's settled then," and Esme steered me towards the piano. I caught Bella's hand and she sat on the bench beside me.

With a look to assure her that I was showing off under protest, I started to play Esme's sonata, losing myself in the gentle notes, the delicate harmonies, the complex chords and the lilting tune, which so reminded me of my sweet and loving adoptive mother. As I reached an eight-bar interlude I looked at Bella, and saw her staring in astonishment, her mouth open.

It felt so good to be appreciated by her. I winked. "Do you like it?"

"You wrote this?" She gasped.

"It's Esme's favourite."

She closed her eyes and shook her head. "I'm feeling extremely insignificant."

She forgot that I had been learning to play the piano for many decades. I had been able to play Mozart's piano concerto number nine before she was born. I had filled the long night hours for many years sitting at this instrument playing, practising, and composing.

I moved my right hand higher along the keyboard, wandering across some pretty notes, gently transposing the key and seguing into Bella's lullaby, a melody as hypnotic and beautiful as she was, as affirming and inspiring, and with undertones of excitement and wonder, representing my love for her.

"You inspired this one," I told her.

She said nothing, caught up in the music.

"They like you, you know," I assured her. "Esme especially."

Bella came back to the present, and noticed that the room was empty. "Where did they go?"

"Very subtly giving us some privacy, I suppose."

She sighed. *"They* like me. But Rosalie and Emmett..."

She'd noticed. Of *course* she'd noticed. How could she not?

"Don't worry about Rosalie. She'll come around."

She didn't look convinced. "Emmett?"

I toyed with telling her that Emmett was following Rosalie's lead, but decided she didn't need another reason to dislike my sister. "Well, he thinks *I'm* a lunatic, it's true, but he doesn't have a problem with you. He's trying to reason with Rosalie."

"What is it that upsets her?"

She really knew how to ask the most difficult questions. It had taken me a while to get to the truth of that, and I could read Rosalie's mind. But it

166

didn't help when Rosalie couldn't admit it to herself. "Rosalie struggles the most with...with what we are. It's hard for her to have someone on the outside know the truth. And she's a little jealous."

"*Rosalie* is jealous of *me?*" she said, incredulous.

"You're human. She wishes that she were, too." Right at that moment I understood and shared Rosalie's jealousy. I also wished I were human, albeit for different reasons.

"Even Jasper, though..."

"That's really my fault," I admitted. "I told you he was the most recent to try our way of life. I warned him to keep his distance."

"Esme and Carlisle?"

"Are happy to see me happy. Actually, Esme wouldn't care if you had a third eye and webbed feet. All this time she's been worried about me, afraid there was something missing from my essential makeup, that I was too young when Carlisle changed me...She's ecstatic. Every time I touch you she just about chokes with satisfaction."

"Alice seems very...enthusiastic."

"Alice has her own way of looking at things." Alice's world was so complex and confusing, with so many possibilities always whirling in her mind, so many outcomes. I remembered what she had most recently warned us of.

"And you're not going to explain that, are you?"

She had noticed my reticence, my tension, and she knew that I was hiding something. She was right. I wasn't going to explain it. She had enough to deal with. My role was to protect her from threats, but not necessarily to spell out all the dangers.

"So what was Carlisle telling you before?"

167

She had a disarming way of getting right to whatever I wanted to hide. "You noticed that, did you?"

She shrugged. "Of course."

"He wanted to tell me some news—he didn't know if it was something I would share with you."

"Will you?"

"I have to, because I'm going to be a little…overbearingly protective over the next few days—or weeks—and I wouldn't want you to think I'm naturally a tyrant." There would be plenty of others who would say I was controlling and obsessive, but I didn't want Bella to be one of them.

"What's wrong?"

"Nothing's wrong, exactly. Alice just sees some visitors coming soon. They know we're here, and they're curious."

"Visitors?"

"Yes…well, they aren't like us of course—in their hunting habits, I mean. They probably won't come into town at all, but I'm certainly not going to let you out of my sight until they're gone." Bella turned a shade paler, and I saw goosebumps on her flesh. "Finally, a rational response. I was beginning to think you had no sense of self-preservation at all."

Bella ignored me archly, and instead looked around the room with interest.

"It's not what you were expecting, is it." I observed.

"No," she admitted.

"No coffins, no piled skulls in the corners; I don't even think we have cobwebs…what a disappointment this must be for you."

She continued steadfastly to ignore me. "It's so light…so open."

That's what I loved about it too. I could be myself at home, in the same way I could be myself with Bella. "It's the one place we never have to hide."

Bella's lullaby was drawing to its close; I played the final bars slowly, not wanting it to end. As the last note died down, Bella thanked me and wiped a tear from the corner of her eye. Slowly, gently, I reached up and did the same, marvelling once more at this manifestation of the difference between us, this drop of moisture that meant my music had moved her.

I studied it, noting the refraction of the light across the taut surface, the salt molecules which hung within it, and then, in a moment of impulsiveness, I tasted it. It tasted like Bella might.

She was watching me, curious, wondering at my strange behaviour. "Do you want to see the rest of the house?" I asked her.

"No coffins?" She asked sarcastically.

"No coffins," I confirmed, wondering at the slight note of nervousness in her voice, and hoping Emmett had hidden his coffin collection.

I led her up the staircase and past some of the bedrooms, but she stopped dead midway along the hall as she saw the huge carved cross hanging on the far wall. I chuckled. I had wondered what she would make of it. She looked perplexed.

"You can laugh," I told her. "It is sort-of ironic."

She reached out to touch the ancient soft wood reverently and respectfully, but then seemed to change her mind. "It must be very old."

"Early sixteen-thirties, more or less."

"Why do you keep this here?" she asked, turning to me.

"Nostalgia. It belonged to Carlisle's father."

"He collected antiques?"

I rather liked that she seemed to have forgotten just how much older we all were than she was. "No. He carved this himself. It hung on the wall above the pulpit in the church where he preached."

Her mouth fell open slightly as she worked out the implications of this statement. She turned back to look at the cross as though to hide her shock. "Are you all right?" I asked.

"How old is Carlisle?" she said quietly. Nearby, Carlisle chuckled too quietly for Bella to hear.

"He just celebrated his three hundred and sixty-second birthday," I told her.

She looked at me more steadfastly now, waiting for the rest of the story.

"Carlisle was born in London in the sixteen-forties, he believes. Time wasn't marked accurately then, for the common people anyway. It was just before Cromwell's reign, though. He was the only son of an Anglican pastor. His mother died giving birth to him. His father was an intolerant man. As the Protestants came into power, he was enthusiastic in his persecution of Roman Catholics and other religions. He also believed very strongly in the reality of evil. He led hunts for witches, werewolves...and vampires.

"They burned a lot of innocent people—of course the real creatures that he sought were not so easy to catch. When the pastor grew old, he placed his obedient son in charge of the raids. At first Carlisle was a disappointment; he was not quick to accuse, to see demons where they did not exist. But he was persistent, and more clever than his father. He actually discovered a coven of true vampires that lived hidden in the sewers of the city, only coming out at night to hunt."

Carlisle had told me that story often, and I'd never questioned it, despite the fact that sewers weren't invented in England until the early nineteenth century.

"In those days, when monsters were not just myths and legends, that was the way many lived. The people gathered their pitchforks and torches of course, and waited where Carlisle had seen the monsters exit into the street. Eventually, one emerged. He must have been ancient and weak with hunger. Carlisle heard him call out in Latin to the others when he caught the scent of the mob. He ran through the streets and Carlisle—he was twenty-three and very fast—was in the lead of the pursuit. The creature could have easily outrun them, but Carlisle thinks he was too hungry, so he turned and attacked.

"He fell on Carlisle first, but the others were close behind, and he turned to defend himself. He killed two men and made off with a third, leaving Carlisle bleeding in the street.

"Carlisle knew what his father would do. The bodies would be burned—anything infected by the monster must be destroyed. Carlisle acted instinctively to save his own life. He crawled away from the alley while the mob followed the fiend and his victim. He hid in a cellar, buried himself in rotting potatoes for three days. It's a miracle he was able to keep silent, to stay undiscovered. It was over then, and he realised what he had become."

Bella had listened, rapt, and I saw tears in her eyes again. "How are you feeling?" I asked.

"I'm fine," she assured me, unconvincingly.

"I expect you have a few more questions for me."

"A few."

I smiled, took her hand, and pulled her along the hall. "Come on then, I'll show you."

Chapter Sixteen

I led Bella to Carlisle's office, but hesitated outside, waiting for Carlisle's confirmation. *You may tell Bella the rest of my story,* he agreed calmly. *I think it will help her to know, and I understand how important she is to you. By the way, I hope you've cleaned your room, because I definitely saw cobwebs there. Can't have Bella seeing a mess.*

"Come in," he said vocally for Bella.

Carlisle was sitting behind his desk, and rose politely as we entered.

"I wanted to show Bella some of our history," I said. "Well, your history, actually." Carlisle already knew that; he'd been able to hear everything I'd said to Bella, but we both felt it important to keep up the human standards of polite behaviour wherever possible, even when we didn't have a human in our home. Decorum and tradition dictated that I ask him permission to share his history, so I did.

"We didn't mean to disturb you," Bella said.

"Not at all. Where are you going to start?"

I considered that question briefly, and concluded "The Waggoner." I turned Bella around gently to see the wall behind us, the one covered with Carlisle's eclectic mix of framed pictures. As I touched her I heard her heart skip and thump, and I smiled to myself. So did Carlisle.

"London in the sixteen-fifties," I said, indicating a faded oil painting in a plain wooden frame.

"The London of my youth," Carlisle said softly. Bella seemed startled. I didn't know whether she hadn't realised that Carlisle was standing behind her, or whether this confirmation of his age and nature was too much for her to process. I squeezed her hand.

"Will *you* tell the story?" I asked Carlisle. I'd told Bella much of it, and it was Carlisle's story. It was only fair that he have the honour of filling in the rest.

"I would," he smiled. "But I'm actually running a bit late. The hospital called this morning—Dr. Snow is taking a sick day. Besides, you know the stories as well as I do." He grinned at me. *Make me sound good. Elaborate plenty. Oh, and leave out that bit about the Irish frat party and the celery.*

"What happened then?" Bella asked over the sound of Carlisle's car pulling out of the driveway. She was looking intently at the painting again. "When he realized what had happened to him?"

I moved her along to the next painting in the sequence; the Yorkshire moors. "When he knew what he had become he rebelled against it. He tried to destroy himself. But that's not easily done."

"How?" she asked.

"He jumped from great heights, he tried to drown himself in the ocean...but he was young to the new life and very strong. It is amazing that he was able to resist...feeding...while he was still so new. The instinct is more powerful then, it takes over everything. But he was so repelled by himself that he had the strength to try to kill himself with starvation."

"Is that possible?" she asked meekly.

"No, there are very few ways we can be killed. So he grew very hungry, and eventually weak. He strayed as far as he could from the human populace, recognizing that his willpower was weakening, too. For months he wandered by night, seeking the loneliest places, loathing himself.

"One night a herd of deer passed his hiding place. He was so wild with thirst that he attacked without a thought. His strength returned and so he realized there was an alternative to being the vile monster he feared. Had he not eaten venison in his former life? Over the next months his new philosophy was born. He could exist without being a demon. He found himself again.

"He began to make better use of his time. He'd always been intelligent, eager to learn. Now he had unlimited time before him. He studied by night, planned by day. He swam to France and—"

"He *swam* to France?" she interrupted.

"People swim the Channel all the time, Bella."

"That's true, I guess. It just sounded funny in that context. Go on."

"Swimming is easy for us—"

"Everything is easy for *you*."

I loved these little ripostes with her. It was so refreshing, so enjoyable, to converse with someone and not be able to hear them composing each sentence before they uttered it.

"I won't interrupt again," she promised.

"Because technically we don't need to breathe," I finished.

She rolled her eyes. "You—"

"No, no, you promised." I put my finger on her lips to quiet her. "Do you want to hear the story or not?"

"You can't spring something like that on me, and then expect me not to say anything," she protested.

I capitulated.

"How long can you go…without *breathing?*"

"Indefinitely, I suppose; I don't know. It gets a bit uncomfortable—being without a sense of smell."

"A bit uncomfortable," she agreed.

From her point of view, I realised, this conversation might seem somewhat surreal. The local doctor had just told her he was over three hundred years old before heading off to his duties at the hospital, and her boyfriend had calmly informed her that he didn't need to breathe. Surely any normal person would have fainted in shock by now? And yet the only thing that had so far made Bella faint had been me touching her tenderly.

She was either remarkably resilient, a little bit out-of-touch with reality, or whatever was going on in that mysteriously shrouded mind of hers really wasn't like that of a normal person.

"What is it?" she asked, touching my face in concern.

"I keep waiting for it to happen," I admitted.

"For what to happen?"

"I know that at some point, something I tell you or something you see is going to be too much. And then you'll run away from me, screaming as you go. I won't stop you. I want this to happen because I want you to be safe. And yet, I want to be with you. The two desires are impossible to reconcile…"

"I'm not running anywhere," she declared.

"We'll see," I smiled. One day, I was sure, she would realise what she was doing, and forbid me ever to come within five miles of her again.

"So go on—Carlisle was swimming to France."

I moved along to the next picture in the haphazard sequence, the largest and most ostentatious, dating from the renaissance.

"Carlisle swam to France, and continued on through Europe, to the universities there. By night he studied music, science, medicine—and found his calling, his penance, in that, in saving human lives." I felt a great deal of awe and admiration for my adopted father, and knew that it showed as I related his history to Bella. "I can't adequately describe the struggle; it took Carlisle two centuries of tortuous effort to perfect his self-control. Now he is all but immune to the scent of human blood, and he is able to do the work he loves without agony. He finds a great deal of peace there, at the hospital…" The irony of that, when I found high school somewhere between hell and purgatory, was something I thought of often. I had to be very careful even visiting Carlisle at the hospital.

"He was studying in Italy when he discovered the others there. They were much more civilized and educated than the wraiths of the London sewers." I indicated the images of the Volturi within the painting, standing on the uppermost balcony, Carlisle among them. "Solimena was greatly inspired by Carlisle's friends. He often painted them as gods." More irony, when Carlisle believed them to be the very opposite. "Aro, Marcus, Caius, night-time patrons of the arts." I indicated them as I spoke their names.

"What happened to them?" Bella asked.

"They're still there, as they have been for who knows how many millennia," I said, as nonchalantly as I could when these three had the power and the precedent to destroy Bella, and all of us, were they ever to find out that she knew what we were. "Carlisle stayed with them only for a short time, just a few decades. He greatly admired their civility, their refinement, but they persisted in trying to cure his aversion to his 'natural food source' as they called it. They tried to persuade him, and he tried to persuade them, to no avail. At that point, Carlisle decided to try the New World. He dreamed of finding others like himself. He was very lonely, you see.

177

"He didn't find anyone for a long time. But as monsters became the stuff of fairy tales he found he could interact with unsuspecting humans as if he were one of them. He began practicing medicine. But the companionship he craved eluded him. He couldn't risk familiarity.

"When the influenza epidemic hit, he was working nights at a hospital in Chicago. He'd been turning over an idea in his mind for several years and he had almost decided to act—since he couldn't find a companion, he would create one.

"He wasn't absolutely sure how his own transformation had occurred, so he was hesitant. And he was loath to steal anyone's life the way his had been stolen. It was in that frame of mind that he found me. There was no hope for me; I was left in a ward with the dying. He had nursed my parents, and knew I was alone. He decided to try…"

At that moment, maybe for the first time in my life, I couldn't regret anything. Had I lived through that illness I would be dead now. I would never have met Bella. I smiled at her as I said, "And so we come full circle."

"Have you always stayed with Carlisle, then?" she asked.

She always knew how to ask the difficult questions. But my answer was truthful. "Almost always."

We had finished Carlisle's story now, and her inquisitiveness was turning in directions I preferred not to go. I steered her away from the wall of pictures, and back into the hallway.

"Almost?"

I sighed. "Well, I had a typical bout of rebellious adolescence—about ten years after I was…born…created, whatever you want to call it. I wasn't sold on his life of abstinence, and I resented him for curbing my appetite. So I went off on my own for a time."

"Really?" She was like a dog with a bone. She was going to drag out all my secrets. But I owed her the truth.

"That doesn't repulse you?" I asked as we headed up the stairs.

"No."

"Why not?"

"I guess…it sounds reasonable."

Most adolescents with appetites who shunned a life of abstinence didn't go on killing sprees. I had dressed up the horror in trite and trivial language, and maybe Bella hadn't fully understood what my little rebellion truly meant. It was time to tell her.

"From the time of my new birth I had the advantage of knowing what everyone around me was thinking, both human and non-human alike. That's why it took me ten years to defy Carlisle—I could read his perfect sincerity, understand exactly why he lived the way he did.

"It took me only a few years to return to Carlisle and recommit to his vision. I thought I would be exempt from the…depression…that accompanies a conscience. Because I knew the thoughts of my prey, I could pass over the innocent and pursue only the evil. If I followed a murderer down a dark alley where he stalked a young girl—if I saved her, then surely I wasn't so terrible.

"But as time went on, I began to see the monster in my eyes. I couldn't escape the debt of so much human life taken, no matter how justified. And I went back to Carlisle and Esme. They welcomed me back like the prodigal. It was more than I deserved."

I didn't tell her that I still remembered the thoughts of the dying, that my conscience still haunted me. If anything, Carlisle and Esme's welcome back into the fold had only added to the sense of guilt. Maybe the interminable, endless pointlessness of my life was my penance, my purgatory. But now that Bella was here, and I was no longer empty and despairing, tortured by the tedium, where did that put me on the scale of reparation?

"My room," I told Bella as we went inside. I hurriedly kicked aside the dirty underwear on the floor.

I watched as she took in the stunning view, the bank of CDs which filled the western wall, the swathes of fabric which draped the walls. "Good acoustics?" she asked.

I nodded, and switched on the music system. Gentle lyrical jazz filled the room, the perfect soundtrack for this perfect moment, with the beautiful, beloved girl in my room, looking through my music collection.

I had never thought it was possible for me to be this happy.

She had asked something. I had almost missed it, so caught up in the wonder of her, here. Something about how my collection was organised.

"Ummm, by year, and then by personal preference within that frame," I told her quietly.

She turned to look at me, and must have noticed that I was distracted. "What?"

"I was prepared to feel…relieved. Having you know about everything, not needing to keep secrets from you. But I didn't expect to feel more than that. I *like* it. It makes me…happy."

"I'm glad," she smiled, and then, when my expression betrayed my fear that, at some point, she would wake up to the danger, she added, "You're still waiting for the running and screaming, aren't you?"

I nodded. Something which seemed too good to be true usually was.

"I hate to burst your bubble, but you're really not as scary as you think you are. I don't find you scary at all, actually."

I didn't believe her, but I still couldn't let that pass. "You *really* shouldn't have said that."

With exaggerated movements, I crouched, growled, and pounced, wrapping her in my arms mid-flight, and landing on the sofa. She gasped and giggled, and struggled to escape my clutches, but I held her tight, close to my chest. She looked at me to check that I was in control. I was.

"You were saying?" I prompted.

"That you are a very, very, terrifying monster," she acquiesced.

"Much better." Not that I thought she actually meant it.

"Um, can I get up now?"

I would have held her like that, close and protected, for longer, but Alice was at the door asking to come in. *What are you doing to that poor girl, Edward?* I unlocked my arms and sat Bella on my lap, and Alice pranced lithely into the room and sat cross-legged on the floor. Jasper, nervous and tentative, waited at the door for a moment longer.

"It sounded like you were having Bella for lunch," Alice joked, "And we came to see if you would share."

Bella seemed to tense somewhat, and I wrapped her tighter in my arms. "Sorry, I don't believe I have enough to spare."

"Actually," Jasper smiled as he walked into the room, "Alice says there's going to be a real storm tonight, and Emmett wants to play ball. Are you game?"

Yes, I was game, as always. But I couldn't be apart from Bella now, not with the nomads nearby.

"Of course you should bring Bella," Alice said. Jasper was uncomfortable with this proposition. He was working hard to restrain his thirst, and concerned that it would be harder to do so when he was engrossed in the game. But Alice's returned glance reassured him that he would be fine. She had seen it.

"Do you want to go?" I asked Bella.

"Sure. Um, where are we going?"

"We have to wait for thunder to play ball—you'll see why."

"Will I need an umbrella?"

Alice had the answer. "The storm will hit over town. It should be dry enough in the clearing."

"Good, then." Jasper was keen, now that he knew he wouldn't accidentally attack Bella while he was running for the ball.

"Let's go and see if Carlisle will come," Alice said. An excuse to get out of the room and give Bella and me some privacy. I was grateful to her.

"Like you don't know," Jasper said, and I was less grateful to him, until he thoughtfully closed the door behind them.

"What will we be playing?" Bella asked.

"*You* will be watching," I insisted. "*We* will be playing baseball."

She rolled her eyes. "Vampires like baseball?"

"It's the American pastime," I reminded her.

Chapter Seventeen

As we neared Bella's house a pungent smell and earthy thoughts warned me that others were there. I had encountered these before: Quileutes, our enemies. Carlisle had told me that their tribal name came from their word for wolf, *Kwoli,* but even disregarding the wolf connection, everything about them warned me to keep away.

These two were Billy Black and his kid, Jacob, the one I was so ... *indebted* ... to for sharing my secret with Bella. The boy had designs on my girlfriend. He was eager and excited to see Bella. He wanted to invite her to a cook out on the reservation. I was so irritated by his licentious thoughts that I almost didn't take in what the father was thinking.

Billy Black was here to warn Bella to keep away from me, and he was going to use Charlie to do it.

"This is crossing the line!" I muttered as I parked the truck. I was furious.

"He came here to warn Charlie?" Bella guessed. I had forgotten how intuitive she was. I nodded.

Billy's gaze was fixed firmly on me, challenging me; his son was looking down awkwardly, trying to work out what to make of my presence in the driving seat of Bella's truck. I saw no way this confrontation could be amicable, and plenty where it ended in bloodshed. Doubtless Alice would appear soon, having seen the outcome.

"Let me deal with this," Bella suggested.

And there was the solution. Bella was friends with these people. She was neutral. I readily agreed. "That's probably best. Be careful, though. The child has no idea."

"Jacob is not much younger than I am," she said abruptly.

"Oh, I know," I smiled. Bella, too, was a child compared to me. But, let's be honest, everyone was. I was 105, for goodness' sake. "Get them inside so I can leave. I'll be back around dusk."

"Do you want my truck?" she asked.

"I could *walk* home faster than this truck moves."

"You don't have to leave." She stuck out her lower lip in an endearing pout.

"Actually I do. After you get rid of *them* you still have to prepare Charlie to meet your new boyfriend." I grinned at the thought.

"Thanks a lot," she intoned.

"I'll be back soon." I kissed her just below her ear, and laughed inwardly as I felt Billy Black's fury and Jacob Black's despondency in response to the gesture.

"*Soon,*" she insisted as she got out of the truck and ran over to the porch to join the Blacks.

I waited behind the house for a while. I had to know what Billy Black was doing; how he was destroying my happiness and poisoning Bella's precious mind against me. I heard them chat meaninglessly about fishing, and smiled to myself when I could tell, despite not being able to read her thoughts, that Bella felt uncomfortable and was trying to get rid of them. I also took pleasure in Billy's growing impatience and frustration, until he sent young Jacob out to the car to fetch a non-existent photograph. And then the serious conversation began.

"Bella, Charlie is one of my best friends."

"Yes."

I noticed you've been spending time with one of the Cullens."

"Yes."

"Maybe it's none of my business, but I don't think that is such a good idea."

"You're right," Bella said coldly. "It *is* none of your business." I silently cheered.

He felt her antipathy but continued resolutely. "You probably don't know this, but the Cullen family has an unpleasant reputation on the reservation."

"Actually, I did know that," she responded, and he was surprised. "But that reputation couldn't be deserved, could it? Because the Cullens never set foot on the reservation, do they?"

He began to suspect that she knew everything about the legends, the treaty. "You seem…well informed about the Cullens. More informed than I expected."

"Maybe even better informed than you are."

"Maybe," he accepted. I clenched my fists and stood rigid to prevent myself bursting into the house as he formed the thought that would become his killer punch. "Is Charlie as well informed?"

"Charlie likes the Cullens a lot," Bella told him.

"It's not my business, but it may be Charlie's."

"Though it would be my business again, whether or not I think that it's Charlie's business, right?"

Are you always this articulate? Her message, while not well phrased, was clear.

"Yes," Billy conceded. "I guess that's your business too."

"Thanks, Billy."

"Just think about what you're doing, Bella."

"Okay."

I was in awe of how skilfully Bella had put Billy in his place, defused a tense situation and still maintained a friendship with the Blacks. The boy went blundering back into the house at that point, complaining that there was no photograph in the car. Confident that Bella could handle everything they could throw at her, I chose that moment to head back home.

Rosalie often spoke about me as though I were not there. I was used to it. But when I could hear everything said anywhere in the house, both audibly and inwardly, it made no difference whether I was in the room or not. There could be no secrets. Especially not when Rose was so very vocal in her scorn. So it was no surprise to arrive back at the house and hear her declaring to the assembled family that their pandering to my romantic whim was foolish and dangerous.

"I thought Bella was delightful," Esme said.

"That's hardly the point," Rosalie retorted, frustrated.

"So what *is* the point, Rose?" I asked her.

"She's *human*."

"Really? I hadn't noticed."

"Has a vampire ever fallen in love with a human before?" Jasper asked quietly. He was doing his best to calm the tension, but Rosalie wasn't easily placated.

All attention turned to Carlisle, who apologized inwardly to me before saying, "Not that I know of. It is, as you all know, the nature of our kind to love devotedly and enduringly. But I'm not aware of any vampire I've met having fallen in love with its prey."

"Never gets the chance," Emmett sniggered. In his head I saw a quick, clean kill. The human never saw the vampire; the vampire never even considered the human as anything worthy of acknowledgement, let alone conversation.

"No vampire has ever lived among them quite as we do," Esme said.

I was feeling uncomfortable, discussing my deepest and most sacred feelings with my family, knowing how much they worried, or feared, or misunderstood. But realisation hit me that really, they *ought* to understand.

"I'm *not* the first vampire to fall in love with a human. Not even *in this family,*" I declared.

They all looked at me, and only Rosalie seemed to have any idea what I was alluding to.

"Rose, when you found Emmett, he was human. When you carried him to Carlisle he was human. You must have loved him then, otherwise why would you have done that? You must have seen something in him that drew you to him."

"That was different," Rosalie pouted. I wondered why she bothered to protest when she knew I could hear her inward capitulation.

"And Carlisle, you treated Esme when she was human. I know that you felt something for her then. And she certainly felt something for you."

"Ah, but everyone in that hospital was in love with Doctor Cullen," Esme joked in an attempt to lighten the mood. But she, too, knew that if it weren't for her husband, the cruel and ill-fated Mr. Evenson, she and Carlisle might have acted on their mutual attraction.

"All the women in the hospital still are in love with Doctor Cullen," Emmett rumbled, grinning.

"*Are* you in love with Bella?" Carlisle asked. *Way to dodge the question.*

187

I was in the unique position of being able to feel and understand how people felt about others. I knew the deep and abiding affection Carlisle and Esme shared; the passion and intensity of Rosalie and Emmett's feelings for each other; the ardour and adoration which overwhelmed Alice and Jasper whenever they were together. My feelings for Bella were in every way as powerful and eternal. But Bella herself was neither of those things. She was delicate and mortal.

"It's like… I finally understand why people refer to each other as 'my other half'. It's as though I've been a shadow for all these decades, a wraith, not really existing. I was incomplete without her. And now that I've found her, I can't bear to be without her."

Carlisle nodded, satisfied with my answer.

"But you will have to be without her," Rosalie said. "Because she's human. And even if you don't kill her, time will." Never mind *time;* Bella was so clumsy she was bound to accidentally kill herself soon enough.

Esme scolded Rose immediately, but the truth was out there, hanging among us, and every one of them inwardly acknowledged it, albeit apologetically and regretfully.

"I'll have to deal with that when the time comes," I said, already knowing what I would do.

"Will you make her one of us?" Emmett asked.

The disgust which filled Rosalie's mind at his comment was only just outweighed by the sense of betrayal she felt toward Emmett for suggesting it. But it was nothing compared to my own abhorrence and horror. Bella was precious, and I was working so hard to control myself around her. There was no way I could destroy her soul. I shook my head.

Rosalie was relieved, although I couldn't tell—maybe she wasn't sure herself—whether it was because she didn't want Bella to be part of our family forever, or because she, like me, felt that Bella's human life was precious. Esme was anxious. Carlisle was uncertain. Alice and Jasper were disappointed for different reasons. Too many emotions coming at me at once.

"I can't hurt her," I explained.

"Then you'll hurt yourself," Alice said. A prophecy, of sorts, but not one of Alice's usual visions. Simply inevitability. I would lose Bella one day. It wasn't pleasant to contemplate that, so soon after I had found her, but it was true.

"You'd better enjoy every minute, then," Emmett said with a playful punch, ignoring Rose's narrowed eyes. "As much as you can, at least, without breaking her."

I agreed.

"So what are you still doing here?" Emmett added.

He had a point. I had said that I would never be far away, that I would protect her. No explanation was needed when I raced up to my room to change, then left the house at a run. I had said that I would give Bella some time, that I would be back at dusk, but I could hang around in the trees behind Bella's house until then.

I did my best to respect Bella's privacy and not listen to her conversation with Charlie, but curiosity got the better of me. I laughed when it became evident that he had confused me with Emmett, and then when he couldn't get my name right. When it seemed like Charlie had come round to the idea I ran back to the jeep which I'd left parked half a mile down the road, and drove to the house as fast as possible.

"Come on in, Edward," Charlie greeted me. I was pleased that he was being friendly.

"Thanks, Chief Swan."

"Go ahead and call me Charlie. Here, I'll take your jacket."

"Thanks, sir." My mother—both my mothers—had taught me how to be respectful and deferential in such circumstances.

"Have a seat there, Edward."

I took the armchair. It didn't seem right to sit beside Bella or Charlie on the sofa, although Bella seemed to disagree.

"So, I hear you're getting my girl to watch baseball."

"Yes, sir, that's the plan."

"Well, more power to you, I guess." We laughed. Charlie was still a little wary and unsure, but mostly because he wasn't entirely happy with the idea of Bella having a boyfriend at all, not because it was me.

"Okay," Bella said. "Enough humour at my expense. Let's go."

"Not too late, Bell," Charlie said as Bella took her jacket from the peg.

"Don't worry, Charlie, I'll have her home early," I assured him.

"You take care of my girl, all right?"

He loved her almost as much as I did. "She'll be safe with me, I promise, sir."

Bella wasn't amused by our chitchat, and stalked out. Laughing again, I followed her.

She hadn't got very far. She was standing in the rain, staring at our transport. Behind me, Charlie let out a low whistle. "Wear your seatbelts," he said in a croaky voice. Obediently, I ensured that Bella put on her harness. When she fumbled with it, I helped her, enjoying having the excuse to brush my fingers against her neck.

"This is a…um…*big* Jeep you have."

"It's Emmett's. I didn't think you'd want to run the whole way."

I waited for her reaction, but it was a while in coming. An idle question about where in the house we might be hiding such a big vehicle, and then, "Run the *whole* way? As in, we're going to run part of the way?"

And there it was. "You're not going to run," I assured her. This was not necessarily the good news.

"*I'm* going to be sick."

"Keep your eyes closed, you'll be fine." I leaned over to kiss the top of her head reassuringly, then paused there, inhaling the delicious scent of Bella seasoned with a smattering of fresh, salty raindrops. "You smell so good in the rain," I groaned.

"In a good way or a bad way?"

"Both. Always both." But I was getting stronger.

My human side came out more in her presence. I enjoyed the drive, relished the Jeep's off-roading capabilities, and marvelled at how much I was behaving like the stereotypical seventeen-year-old; showing off an automobile to my girlfriend, taking her to a ball game, struggling to control my urges, and letting my thoughts run away with me during the long pleasant silence as we drove.

"Sorry, Bella, we have to go on foot from here," I told her gently as we reached the end of the trail. I deliberately left out that word *run* this time.

"You know what? I'll just wait here."

"What happened to all your courage? You were extraordinary this morning." She had fearlessly faced a houseful of vampires, and yet now she wouldn't let me carry her through the forest.

"I haven't forgotten the last time yet."

191

I unbuckled her harness, ignoring her protests, and lifted her out of the Jeep. "I can see I'm going to have to tamper with your memory."

"Tamper with my memory?"

I'd made her lunge at me, and I'd made her faint. Maybe I could make her trust me. I put my hands on the Jeep, either side of her head, and leaned close to her. "Now, what exactly are you worrying about?"

"Well, um, hitting a tree, and dying. And then getting sick." I took a moment to process that. Did she mean that she was worried about getting sick after she'd died, or was getting sick the thing she was worried most about, after dying? She wasn't always the most articulate person.

I looked her right in the eyes and blinked deeply, watching as her pupils widened. Then slowly, gently, I kissed the base of her throat, hearing and feeling her breath catch as I did so.

"Are you still worried now?" I murmured, my lips brushing her smooth skin.

"Yes," she gasped. "About hitting trees and getting sick."

I worked my way gently up her throat until my lips were caressing her jawline. I could feel the heavy thumping of her pulse there. "And now?"

"Trees," she declared weakly. "Motion sickness."

It wasn't working. I kissed her eyelids in turn. "Bella, you don't really think I would hit a tree, do you?"

"No, but I might."

I kissed a tender line down her cheek, stopping at her mouth.

"Would I let a tree hurt you?" I had sworn never to let anything hurt her, not even Bella herself.

"No," she admitted.

I kissed her lips as a reward for her faith in me.

"You see. There's nothing to be afraid of, is there?"

"No," she agreed.

I cupped her face gently in my hands and kissed her in earnest. Without warning, she flung her arms around my neck and tried to pull me down to her, twisting her fingers in my hair and gasping in passion. I pulled back immediately. *Nothing to be afraid of!* What was I imagining? Her boyfriend was a vampire whose every instinct was to kill her, and yet she seemed determined to make him let go of his self-control and succumb to the most natural and base appetites.

"Damn it, Bella, you'll be the death of me, I swear you will."

She looked sheepish. "You're indestructible," she muttered.

"I might have believed that before I met you. Now, let's get out of here before I do something really stupid."

Without waiting for her response I threw her onto my back, and she locked her arms around my neck and her legs around my waist then, at my bidding, tucked her head down and closed her eyes. As I ran I focussed on keeping my stride even and level, my course as straight and clear as possible, and doing all that I could to keep the ride smooth for my precious passenger. But I also ran fast, wanting the journey to be over for her as quickly as possible.

"It's over, Bella," I told her gently when we arrived.

She let go so quickly that she fell onto her backside on the soft, wet ground, and sat there looking indignant. I bellowed with laughter as she picked herself up and dusted herself down, then laughed still harder as she started to stride off the way we had just come.

"Where are you going, Bella?" I asked, looping my arm around her waist.

"To watch a baseball game. You don't seem to be interested in playing anymore, but I'm sure the others will have fun without you."

"You're going the wrong way."

She spun around and simply stalked off in the right direction. I fell into step beside her.

"Don't be mad, I couldn't help myself. You should have seen your face." Remembering it, I chuckled.

"Oh, you're the only one who's allowed to get mad?" she replied archly.

"I wasn't mad at you," I told her.

In reply, she quoted me, even trying to mimic my voice, "Bella, you'll be the death of me."

"*That* was simply a statement of fact."

She tried to turn away from me, but I held her arm.

"You were mad," she insisted.

"Yes."

"But you just said—"

"That I wasn't mad at *you*. Can't you see that, Bella? Don't you understand?"

"See what?"

"I'm never angry with you—how could I be? Brave, trusting…warm as you are."

"Then, why?" she whispered. She really didn't understand. But how could she? She could no more read my mind than I could hers.

I cupped her porcelain face gently in my hands. "I infuriate myself. The way I can't seem to keep from putting you in danger. My very existence puts you at risk. Sometimes I truly hate myself. I should be stronger, I should be able to—"

She put her delicate fingers across my mouth. "Don't."

I moved her hand away, held it to my face. "I love you," I said. "It's a poor excuse for what I'm doing, but it's still true." I bent down to kiss her. "Now, please try to behave yourself." I seemed to have a pretty good grip on my self-control provided Bella stayed completely still, like a little china doll. But she wasn't a china doll, she was a living, breathing, unpredictable woman, and yet more fragile than any antique figurine.

She obeyed.

"You promised Chief Swan that you would have me home early, remember? We'd better get going."

"Yes, ma'am."

I led her by the hand to the mountain field we'd discovered many years ago when we first came to Forks. My family were there, waiting, marking out bases, testing the durability of the ball. I set Bella down near a rock close to Emmett and Esme. While probably not entirely comfortable, it was at least a seat of sorts.

Alice came running towards us. "It's time," she declared, and a dramatic rumble of thunder confirmed her words. Emmett teased Bella about her edginess and winked at her. If it hadn't been for Rosalie watching us from second base, I might have taken issue with my brother for his flirtation. Not that what he'd said was objectionable, but I could see what was in his mind, and it came dangerously close to crossing a line.

Alice stepped in, reaching for Emmett's hand and running with him to his assigned position, first up to bat.

"Are you ready for some ball?" I asked Bella, excited to begin the game. There weren't many good things about being a vampire, but baseball in a thunderstorm was one of them, and I was eager for her to experience it.

"Go team!" she responded with fake enthusiasm.

"Off you go, Edward," Esme thought to me. "I'll look after Bella."

195

Reassured, I stroked her hair and ran to my place in left field. Bella could probably barely see me from where she was sitting. Baseball was dull enough when you *could* see the players. With a field over a mile wide, and most of the action too fast for her to follow, this wasn't really a great first date.

"Batter up," Esme said, and Alice hurled the ball towards Emmett, who swung and missed. Strike. The second time he hit it, and I smiled as I heard the thunderous crack echo round the mountain range. Did Bella understand now why we needed to play during a thunderstorm? I only had time to glance at her before I had to run for the ball, deep into the forest, listening for the swish of the ball through the displaced air. I jumped high to grab it through the branches, enjoying the satisfying *thud* as it smacked into my hand, then sprinted back to the field wishing she could have seen my catch; it's a lot easier to show off your prowess to your girlfriend when she's actually able to see you.

"Out!" Esme called as she saw me. I grinned at the chagrined look on Emmett's face. That would teach him to wink at my girlfriend.

Bella seemed fascinated by the game, and jumped up in concern when Carlisle and Jasper had an impressive collision. After catching my third out I ran back to her to see how she was enjoying it, and maybe just slightly to bask in her admiration. She commented wryly that she would never be able to watch dull old major league baseball again. The Diamondbacks' loss was my gain.

"I am a little disappointed," she said.

"Why?" I asked, worried.

"Well, it would be nice if I could find just one thing you didn't do better than everyone else on the planet."

I grinned. Even for a vampire, I had played well today. I was showing off, I guessed. I may have been past my century, but sometimes I wasn't so different from a teenage boy. It was my turn to bat; I ran back, looking forward to showing off that skill too.

We were only partway through the second half when something significant changed. I caught it the second after Alice did. The nomads were coming to meet us. They had heard our game and they wanted to join in.

We were wary enough of strangers at the best of times. Today, we had a human with us. I ran back to Bella immediately. My family were right behind me.

"Alice?" Esme was tense. She'd known Alice long enough to recognise that expression.

"I didn't see—I couldn't tell," Alice whispered. She felt responsible. She was upset, mortified that she hadn't realised that our game would bring them to us.

"What is it Alice?" Carlisle asked. His voice was calm and authoritative, and I was glad for Bella's sake that he had hidden his own concern.

"They were travelling much quicker than I thought. I can see I had the perspective wrong before," Alice muttered, replaying the images again and again in her mind.

"What changed?" Jasper asked. He was working hard to keep Bella calm. I was grateful to him, too.

"They heard us playing, and it changed their path," Alice said. The nomads had been closer than she had realised. She hadn't known that they would hear us.

"How soon?" Carlisle asked me.

They were at the very edge of my range. I shut out my family and focussed on the minds hurtling towards us. Three of them, exhilarated, excited, anticipating an exciting variation to their empty, dark lives. Two men and a woman.

"Less than five minutes. They're running—they want to play."

"Can you make it?" Carlisle asked me. In his mind he saw me scooping up Bella and running to the safety of the town with her. But it was a long way, and one of the nomads in particular might think it was part of the game.

"No, not carrying—" I thought better of using her name, frightening her. "Besides, the last thing we need is for them to catch the scent and start hunting." The younger male had the keenest hunter senses I had ever encountered. It was his passion and his skill.

"How many?" Emmett asked Alice.

"Three," she answered tersely.

Emmett was overconfident. There were seven of us, and one of us was him. He flexed his muscles. "Three! Let them come!"

Carlisle weighed up the options, of which there were few. Running was not a good idea, and that left only staying and doing our best to avoid a confrontation. *Do they know Bella is with us?* he thought to me. I shook my head. *Not yet.*

"Let's just continue the game," he said finally, his voice cooler and more level than his thoughts. "Alice said they were simply curious." Because when three vampires are coming to kill your girlfriend, playing baseball is a sure-fire way to stop them.

"Are they thirsty?" Esme asked me, sotto voce. I shook my head slightly.

Maybe their curiosity, our scents and the damp weather could combine to mask Bella's presence. As I placed myself squarely in front of her I murmured to Bella to let her hair down. Her scent was strongest around the pulse points in her neck; the mixed fragrances in her shampoo might help obscure it for our visitors.

"The others are coming?" she confirmed as she pulled the band out of her hair and shook it around her shoulders.

"Yes. Stay very still, keep quiet, and don't move from my side, please." Our only hope was that they would overlook her, somehow. Assume, despite all the obvious evidence, that she was one of us. I pulled her hair forward in a desperate and futile attempt to dissipate her delicious odour.

"That won't help," Alice said. "I could smell her across the field."

"I know," I hissed through gritted teeth. Her pessimism didn't help Bella.

"What did Esme ask you?" Bella asked, as we watched my family continue the game with a decidedly marked lack of enthusiasm. Reluctantly I told her. She said nothing, just fixed her eyes on my family, and even managed to grimace at Rosalie's lacklustre batting.

"I'm sorry, Bella," I said, angry with myself. "It was stupid, irresponsible, to expose you like this. I'm so sorry."

She didn't get a chance to reply, because the nomads reached us at that moment.

Chapter Eighteen

They sauntered out of the forest, walking with brash confidence but alert and wary. The darkest and oldest led the way, the woman at his right hand and the younger male, their leader despite his youth, eagerly flanking at his left. I heard them assessing us as they approached, noting Emmett's strength, our numbers, Carlisle's authority. They were in no doubt that this was our territory, but they didn't need to challenge us.

Something changed as they drew closer. The young one, his astonishingly focussed mind roving continually across the terrain, always assessing, weighing, seeking, found something he had been looking for.

I felt him hone in on Alice. Surprise mingled with overwhelming satisfaction. He savoured the moment of discovery.

He knew her, but they were not friends. There was no inkling of recognition from Alice. I wondered whether she had noticed that his attention was completely focussed on her, to the exclusion of everything else. I was perplexed, but relieved. I'd take anything which diverted attention from Bella, even if I didn't understand it.

"We thought we heard a game," the first said, then introduced his group. He was Laurent; the woman, red-haired and cunning, was Victoria. The other was James, Victoria's mate.

Carlisle introduced us in our pairs, showing our strength and numbers, and giving Bella the safety of inclusion.

"Do you have room for a few more players?" Laurent asked. He didn't mean us any harm, but he wasn't just interested in baseball.

"Actually we were just finishing up. But we'd certainly be interested another time. Are you planning on staying in the area for long?"

"We're headed north, in fact, but we were curious to see who was in the neighbourhood. We haven't run into any company in a long time."

"No, this region is usually empty except for us and the occasional visitor, like yourselves."

Jasper was working hard to keep the atmosphere friendly and sociable, and Carlisle was giving wise answers and doing all he could to keep from antagonising them. As Laurent enquired about our hunting range, and was openly curious about our permanence in the area, I began to think that there might be hope. That they might simply ask their questions and pass by, perhaps driven by their leader who was growing impatient with the pointless chit-chat, and was still gazing at Alice as though she were some coveted prize.

I knew that they could sense that there was a human nearby, but they did not yet seem to have connected the scent with Bella herself. It probably helped that she was naturally so pale and beautiful.

And then, just as Carlisle had offered us a means of escape, a cool breeze swept through the clearing from the west, ruffling Bella's hair and carrying her scent directly to the nomads. Just as it had twice already in the story, an inopportune breeze put Bella's life in jeopardy.

James caught the scent immediately and leapt into a crouch, Alice forgotten. I matched his posture, threatening him. His mind was working quickly, all his attention snapping into sharp focus in Bella's direction, his animal instinct taking over. He may not have been as thirsty as usual, but

202

Bella was a particularly delectable treat, and James liked to eat between meals.

I snarled a warning at him when he feinted to one side, trying to get round me to her. I was alarmed to find his mind exultant at seeing my defence of her.

"What's this?" Laurent exclaimed, staring enquiringly at Bella.

"She's with us." Carlisle said firmly.

"You brought a snack?" Laurent said incredulously. He took a step forward to better appraise our pet human, and I snarled at him. He retreated again.

"I said she's with us," Carlisle insisted, all hint of politeness dropped now.

"But she's *human,*" Laurent protested. Emmett moved closer to me to protect Bella from the attentions of the hunter.

"Yes," Carlisle said patiently.

"It appears we have a lot to learn about each other," Laurent admitted, backing down.

"Indeed," Carlisle agreed coolly.

"But we'd like to accept your invitation."

Carlisle had invited these hostile nomads to our home, I remembered. It had been a ploy to lead the nomads away. But now they were not going to be distracted that easily.

"And, of course, we will not harm the human girl," Laurent assured us. He meant it, but James did not. Not only did James lead this coven and find himself under no obligation to obey directives issued by Laurent, the pretender, but James had sensed prey.

Get her away from here, Carlisle thought urgently to me. He called Jasper, Rosalie and Esme to him. They would run with the nomads to the house. Bella and I had Emmett, our strongest, and Alice, with her useful gift, for protection.

"Let's go, Bella."

We walked to the edge of the field, then I scooped Bella onto my back and we ran. Driven by fury and fear, I was grateful for my speed. We needed every advantage we could get.

At the Jeep, Emmett strapped Bella into her harness and I pushed the gas to the floor the whole way. There was nothing to fear from speed. Alice could see potential problems on the road ahead, and I could hear the minds of other drivers long before I saw their vehicles. Emmett was furious too, but not because of the danger Bella was in. He'd wanted to stay and fight. Maybe we should have done. But I couldn't risk it; Bella was too vulnerable to be a spectator at such a battle.

"Where are we going?" Bella asked meekly after a few miles of silence.

I didn't know, so I didn't answer.

"Dammit Edward! Where are you taking me?"

"We have to get away from here—far away—now."

She didn't like that idea and yelled louder than I would have thought she could. "Turn around! You have to take me home!"

She was fiddling with the straps on her harness. We were travelling at over one hundred miles per hour, and she seemed hell bent on jumping out. At a word from me, Emmett had stopped her and pinned her safely to her seat.

"No! Edward! No, you can't do this."

"I have to, Bella, now please be quiet." Like nails down a blackboard, or maybe a crying baby to its mother, Bella's distress pierced me to the core and I couldn't listen to it.

"I won't! You have to take me back—Charlie will call the FBI! They'll be all over your family—Carlisle and Esme! They'll have to leave, to hide forever!"

So what else was new? It would be worth it to know that she was safe. "Calm down, Bella. We've been there before."

"Not over me, you don't! You're not ruining everything over me!"

Alice was feeling conflicted. She may not have been able to read Bella's mind any more that I could, but she saw her distress. "Edward, pull over."

I made it clear from my expression what I thought of that suggestion, and for good measure added, "You don't understand! He's a tracker, Alice, did you *see* that? He's a tracker!"

We'd encountered one before in the sixties. A tracker who had taken exception to our family's ways, thought us arrogant and unnatural. Wanting only peace, we had tried to evade her. She had tracked us across two continents and found us in the isolation, cold and gloom of northern Russia. She had appeared in the snow, clothes torn and eyes bright, half-maddened with the thrill of the pursuit. Alice could not see any future where she would abandon her quest to destroy us, and we had been faced with no alternative but to destroy her. It had not been a pleasant interlude. Emmett and Alice both stiffened as they heard my assessment of James.

"Pull over, Edward," Alice insisted.

"Listen to me, Alice. I saw his mind. Tracking is his passion, his obsession—and he wants her, Alice—*her,* specifically. He begins the hunt tonight." I spoke in a low tone and avoided using Bella's name, hoping vainly that she wouldn't hear me.

"He doesn't know where—"

"How long do you think it will take him to cross her scent in town? His plan was already set before the words were out of Laurent's mouth."

Bella understood the implications and gasped in horror. "Charlie! You can't leave him there! You can't leave him!"

"She's right," Alice said. She was working quickly now, looking for outcomes for us, for Bella, for Charlie. None seemed good. "Let's just look at our options for a minute."

I didn't want to look at my options. I just wanted to get as far away from James as quickly as possible. "There are no options."

"I'm not leaving Charlie!" Bella yelled.

"We have to take her back," Emmett said.

"No."

"He's no match for us, Edward. He won't be able to touch her."

Typical Emmett, always about the strength, the brawn. But the hunter was cunning, too. "He'll wait." Bella would be alone eventually, even if just for a human minute while we were complacent or off our guard. It would be enough.

"I can wait too."

"You don't see—you don't understand. Once he commits to a hunt, he's unshakeable. We'd have to kill him."

Emmett didn't mind that option at all. He alone among us did not think with regret on the day we had killed Jenny in Norilsk. "That's an option."

"And the female. She's with him. If it turns into a fight, the leader will go with them, too."

"There are enough of us." But I wasn't certain. If it were just vampire against vampire, maybe, especially with Emmett and Jasper on our side.

But we had to stay close to Bella, and she was weak and vulnerable. It would take only a momentary lapse for James to—

"There's another option," Alice said.

As Emmett and I argued, Bella had formulated a plan and shared it with Alice. "There—is—no—other—option!" I snarled at Alice.

You don't give Bella enough credit, Alice thought to me. *This is about saving her life, and she had a good idea. You need to listen to it. You need to consider it. For her.*

I knew that Bella was very smart and had an original and unusual way of looking at things. But she was also too important to risk. I had to get her as far away from James and Victoria as possible.

"Doesn't anyone want to hear my plan?" Bella asked.

"No," I said.

She told us anyway. "Listen, you take me back. I tell my dad I want to go home to Phoenix. I pack my bags, we wait until this tracker is watching, and then we run. He'll follow us and leave Charlie alone. Charlie won't call the FBI on your family. Then you can take me any damned place you want."

Smart, original, and extremely self-sacrificing. She would deliberately lure the hunter to her house in order to save her father.

"It's not a bad idea, really," Emmett said.

"It might work—and we simply can't leave her father unprotected. You know that."

Alice was right. All the same, "It's too dangerous—I don't want him within a hundred miles of her."

Emmett was supremely confident. "Edward, he's not getting through us." I managed a wry smile because the words in his mind didn't tally with what he said. What he meant was that James wasn't getting through *him*. It was good to know.

Alice looked through the likely scenarios. "I don't see him attacking. He'll try to wait for us to leave her alone."

"It won't take him long to realise that's not going to happen."

"I *demand* that you take me home," Bella insisted, then added meekly, "please."

I thought the plan through quickly, picking from Alice's mind the least horrifying of the likely endings of each choice. They were hazy and uncertain, but with every other decision I took, Charlie's death was inevitable. It would destroy Bella just as much as James could.

But I had some conditions. "You're leaving tonight, whether the tracker sees or not. You tell Charlie that you can't stand another minute in Forks. Tell him whatever story works. Pack the first things your hands touch, and then get in your truck. I don't care what he says to you. You have fifteen minutes. Do you hear me? Fifteen minutes from the time you cross the doorstep." I swung the Jeep round in a wide U-turn, and headed back to Forks as fast as we'd left it.

When I outlined my plan for how we would play out Bella's escape, Emmett objected. "I'm with you."

"Think it through, Emmett. I don't know how long I'll be gone."

"Until we know how far this is going to go, I'm with you."

"If the tracker is there, we keep driving."

"We're going to make it there before him," Alice informed me confidently, then asked, "What are we going to do with the Jeep?"

"You're driving it home," I told her.

"No, I'm not."

Bella was evidently getting fed up with us ordering each other about when it was her life on the line. "I think you should let me go alone," she said quietly. "Listen, Charlie's not an imbecile. If you're not in town tomorrow, he's going to get suspicious."

"That's irrelevant. We'll make sure he's safe, and that's all that matters."

"Then what about this tracker? He saw the way you acted tonight. He's going to think you're with me, wherever you are."

I'd forgotten how smart she was. Emmett was impressed too. He urged me to consider her point, all the while thinking that we should just have allowed Bella to come up with her own escape plan all along. I might have really appreciated how much Emmett and Alice respected her if I weren't too busy trying to save her life. *Let her go without you,* Emmett's thoughts told me.

"I can't do that," I replied.

"Emmett should stay too, he definitely got an eyeful of Emmett."

"What?" Emmett wasn't so sure.

"You'll get a better crack at him if you stay," Alice said. Emmett liked that idea. Kill the hunter before he even left the area to follow Bella.

"You think I should let her go alone?" I put to Alice tersely.

"Of course not," she replied. "Jasper and I will take her."

I knew that I had reacted instinctively in throwing Bella into the Jeep with no thought but to get as far from James as possible. It took my family—and especially Bella herself—to actually think this through clearly and come up with a workable plan. Even so, "I can't do that."

Bella was evidently still thinking through her strategy. "Hang out here for a week...a few days. Let Charlie see you haven't kidnapped me, and lead this James on a wild-goose chase. Make sure he's completely off my trail. Then come and meet me. Take a roundabout route, of course, and then Jasper and Alice can go home."

She sounded calm, almost hopeful. "Meet you where?"

"Phoenix."

"No, he'll hear that's where you're going." She couldn't go *home,* it was the first place he'd look for her.

"And you'll make it look like that's a ruse, obviously. He'll know that we'll know that he's listening. He'll never believe I'm actually going where I say I'm going."

"She's diabolical," Emmett chuckled.

"And if that doesn't work?"

"There are several million people in Phoenix."

But only one with such a distinctive smell. The tracker had a more finely honed sense of smell than even regular vampires. He would find her there, especially if he had a starting point in the sprawling city. "It's not that hard to find a phone book."

"I won't go home."

"Oh?"

"I'm quite old enough to get my own place."

"Edward, we'll be with her," Alice reminded me.

"What are *you* going to do in *Phoenix?"* I said. Blue skies, long hours of hot, bright sunshine. I'd been there only once. It wasn't very vampire-friendly and I didn't stay long.

"Stay indoors," Alice replied, and mentally added, *as the tracker will have to do if he goes there.*

She was right. It was about the safest place Bella could hide, especially with Alice, with her special ability, looking out for her in more ways than one.

"I kind of like it," Emmett said, still savouring the thought of ripping James apart before the hunt ever started.

"Shut up, Emmett."

"Look, if we try to take him down while she's still around, there's a much better chance that someone will get hurt—she'll get hurt, or you will trying to protect her. Now, if we get him alone…"

I had already considered that, and I knew he was right. Unfortunately Emmett's mental images of James's demise didn't yet tally with what Alice saw. But we were going with Bella's plan, much as it pained me.

"Bella," I said. "If you let anything happen to yourself—anything at all—I'm holding you personally responsible. Do you understand that?"

"Yes," she assured me. Clumsy and careless as she often was, I trusted her to prioritise her own safety now.

"Can Jasper handle this?" I asked Alice.

She was offended that I needed to ask. "Give him some credit, Edward. He's been doing very well, all things considered."

"Can *you* handle this?"

In response her mind hurled a volley of four-letter profanities and personal insults at me, and she pulled back her lips and snarled forcefully, reminding all of us that demure, petite little Alice was also a powerful predator.

"But keep your opinions to yourself," I told her.

Chapter Nineteen

I scanned the area using every one of my enhanced senses as we drew up to the house. There was no trace of the tracker. "He's not here," I said. "Let's go."

Emmett helped Bella out of the harness. "Don't worry Bella, we'll take care of things here quickly." He liked and admired her; I felt a swelling of appreciation for my adopted brother.

At my command, Alice and Emmett took positions in the forest behind the house. I helped Bella out of the Jeep and put a protective arm around her as I walked her towards the house. "Fifteen minutes," I said quietly, as I reluctantly removed my arm from her shoulders.

"I can do this," she assured me in a small voice. She took hold of my face in her light little hands and fixed her red-rimmed eyes directly on mine. Did she finally understand the danger she was in? "I love you," she said. "I will always love you, no matter what happens now."

"Nothing is going to happen to you, Bella," I promised her.

"Just follow the plan, okay? Keep Charlie safe for me. He's not going to like me very much after this, and I want to have the chance to apologize later."

I wondered what she had in mind. But there was no time to ask further. The tracker was within two miles of the house. I had just become aware of his thoughts; focussed, obsessed, fixated on the scent, which led here. "Get inside, Bella. We have to hurry."

"One more thing," she hissed. "Don't listen to another word I say tonight." She stretched up and kissed me firmly and passionately, then turned and kicked open the front door. "Go away, Edward!" she yelled, and the door slammed shut in my face.

I stood there for a few seconds, as though shocked, in case Charlie could see me through the window, then sprinted and jumped up to Bella's room. Bella was giving a stellar performance, every inch the distressed and conflicted teen, but I felt Charlie's concern and heard his confusion, and knew how hard this must be for Bella. The tears, which flowed freely down her face as I joined her in the bedroom, were genuine enough. I didn't have to be able to read her mind to know that she was as upset for Charlie's pain as she was for her own peril.

I helped her stuff clothes into her bag, then sent her back out to face Charlie again, and ran to her truck where I settled into the passenger footwell and listened to what was going on inside the house. Bella had a good ruse going; she didn't want to get stuck in Forks because of me. Charlie was swallowing it all with increasing dismay and shock. In his mind I saw hazy images of a petite blonde woman, eclectically dressed, with a baby on her hip, standing where Bella was standing and saying what Bella was saying. As Bella pulled open the door and shouted to Charlie that she'd call him tomorrow, I saw him fall sideways into the wall, tears shining in his eyes, bereft and horrified at what seemed to just have happened.

James, the hunter, was in the woods behind the house. I could feel the darkness, the intensity of him. It was as though he had tunnel vision, oblivious to anything but his prey, all his senses, all his thoughts, fully focussed on tracking her.

He was processing what he was hearing. He didn't believe her story, but he took from it what we wanted him to: Bella wasn't going home, and Charlie meant little to her. I heard him discount using Charlie as bait, or killing him to unsettle her, at the same time as Alice saw it.

Charlie would live. Bella had, at least, saved him.

As Bella drove her ancient truck away from the house I took her hand. "Pull over." Given that she needed her hand to change gear, steer, and in fact, pull the truck over, taking her hand was probably not the best move I might have made.

"I can drive," she said, through the free-flowing tears.

"You wouldn't be able to find the house," I explained. She'd only been to my home once, after all. I wasn't sure she could see the road clearly either, with her eyes misted with the salt water of her tears.

She acquiesced, and I pulled her easily to the passenger seat and took my place at the wheel as the truck continued to rattle its way along the road. When the Jeep pulled in behind us, Bella was alarmed. "It's just Alice," I reassured her.

"The tracker?" she asked.

"He heard the end of your performance."

"Charlie?"

"The tracker followed us. He's running behind us now."

"Can we outrun him?"

"No." We didn't need to; with three of us near Bella he wouldn't dare attack. But I'd feel safer if we were with the rest of my family. I sped up, and the truck's engine whined in protest.

Emmett leapt into the Jeep, and Bella screamed in alarm. I reassured her that it was only Emmett, but realized that she was on edge, and much more nervous than she wanted to admit to me. I decided to distract her with conversation.

"I didn't realise you were so bored with small-town life. It seemed like you were adjusting fairly well—especially recently. Maybe I was just flattering myself that I was making life more interesting for you."

"I wasn't being nice," she admitted, looking dejected at the reminder. "That was the same thing my mom said when she left him. You could say I was hitting below the belt."

It must have hurt Charlie a great deal; it had certainly hurt Bella. I tried to reassure her. "Don't worry. He'll forgive you."

She didn't believe me. She had a point. How could she make it up to Charlie when the tracker was after her and she might spend the rest of her life—however long it might be—on the run from him?

"Bella, it's going to be all right."

"But it won't be all right when I'm not with you," she whispered in reply.

My heart, dead as it was, leapt. She might be afraid of the tracker, but she was more concerned at our having to part for a while. It bothered me too. I had sworn to stay close to her and protect her from the nomads, and yet for her own safety I had to leave her. I tightened my arm around her. "We'll be together again in a few days. Don't forget that this was your idea."

"It was the best idea—of course it was mine."

I tried to smile at that, but was still struggling with the concept of being apart from Bella while the hunter was after her.

"Why did this happen?" she asked, her voice catching. "Why me?"

216

There was no denying the truth. "It's my fault. I was a fool to expose you like that." I was furious with myself. Knowing the nomads were in the area, I should have kept Bella close to the town and other humans, indoors, away from their field of interest.

"That's not what I meant," she said. "I was there, big deal. It didn't bother the other two. Why did this James decide to kill *me?* There're people all over the place, why me?"

I didn't want to tell her, but I had a feeling that she wouldn't rest until I did. "I got a good look at his mind tonight. I'm not sure if there's anything I could have done to avoid this, once he saw you. It *is* partially your fault. If you didn't smell so appallingly luscious, he might not have bothered. But when I defended you...well, that made it a lot worse. He's not used to being thwarted, no matter how insignificant the object. He thinks of himself as a hunter and nothing else. His existence is consumed with tracking, and a challenge is all he asks of life. Suddenly we've presented him with a beautiful challenge—a large clan of strong fighters all bent on protecting the one vulnerable element. You wouldn't believe how euphoric he is now. It's his favourite game, and we've just made it his most exciting game ever."

Had I done the right thing in defending Bella? If I had been cool and dispassionate, would the hunter have seen her as the prize he now did? I answered my own question out loud. "But if I had stood by, he would have killed you right then."

"I thought...I didn't smell the same to the others...as I do to you," she said.

I had seen their minds. They didn't respond to Bella's scent the way I did. But she was still human. "You don't. But that doesn't mean that you aren't still a temptation to every one of them. If you *had* appealed to the tracker—or any of them—the way you appeal to me, it would have meant a fight right there." Might that have been better? We wouldn't now be undertaking this impossible flight and Bella would not be facing this terrible danger. Probably because she—and some of us—would already be dead.

"I don't think I have any choice but to kill him now," I concluded. "Carlisle won't like it."

"How can you kill a vampire?" she asked.

"The only way to be sure is to tear him to shreds, and then burn the pieces."

"And the other two will fight with him?"

"The woman will. I'm not sure about Laurent. They don't have a very strong bond—he's only with them for convenience. He was embarrassed by James in the meadow…"

"But James and the woman—they'll try to kill you?"

"Bella, don't you *dare* waste time worrying about me. Your only concern is keeping yourself safe, and—please, please—*trying* not to be reckless."

"Is he still following?"

"Yes. He won't attack the house, though. Not tonight." Part of the tracker's skill was stealth, cunning, planning and plotting, laying traps, making strategies. Charging into a house full of vampires wasn't a good strategy and would ruin his game.

Emmett, as the strongest, scooped Bella from the truck and ran her into the house to where the rest of our family were waiting for us with Laurent. I quickly apprised them of the situation. "He's tracking us."

"I was afraid of that," Laurent said.

"What will he do?" Carlisle asked.

"I'm sorry. I was afraid, when your boy there defended her, that it would set him off."

"Can you stop him?"

Laurent shook his head. "Nothing stops James when he gets started."

"We'll stop him," Emmett declared, not only meaning it, but relishing the prospect. Unfortunately I could also catch Laurent's thoughts, both his pained memories of James's past hunts, and his certainty that there was nothing Emmett could do.

"You can't bring him down. I've never seen anything like him in my three hundred years. He's absolutely lethal. That's why I joined his coven."

Carlisle was surprised to learn that James was the leader of their coven. Maybe I should have mentioned it to him before now.

"Are you sure it's worth it?"

I roared in rage, and Laurent cringed, understanding.

"I'm afraid you're going to have to make a choice," Carlisle said gravely.

I knew Laurent's choice. He was a coward. He was scared of James.

"I'm intrigued by the life you've created here. But I won't get in the middle of this. I bear none of you any enmity, but I won't go up against James. I think I will head north—to that clan in Denali." Then came his warning. "Don't underestimate James. He's got a brilliant mind and unparalleled senses. He's every bit as comfortable in the human world as you seem to be, and he won't come at you head on...I'm sorry for what's been unleashed here. Truly sorry."

He wasn't sorry. He was just astonished and slightly appalled at the novelty of a vampire in love with a human. When Carlisle bade him go in peace, he left with some haste. Only I knew that he wasn't heading north, but I didn't care where he went. He was no use to us.

"How close?" Carlisle asked me.

"About three miles out past the river; he's circling around to meet up with the female."

"What's the plan?"

"We'll lead him off, and then Jasper and Alice will run her south."

"And then?"

"As soon as Bella is clear, we'll hunt him." Hunting the hunter. It was right somehow.

"I guess there's no other choice," Carlisle acquiesced. He hated killing.

"Get her upstairs and trade clothes," I said to Rosalie.

Rose didn't think much of that idea. She had always made it clear that she had issues with Bella. I knew that they were mostly jealousy, but I was embarrassed for Bella's sake when Rosalie hissed, "Why should I? What's she to me? Except a menace—a danger you've chosen to inflict on all of us."

You knew she'd refuse, Esme chided me. *I'll swap clothes with Bella. No need to cause a scene.*

I acquiesced aloud, and Esme took Bella upstairs to change.

"You're a piece of work, Rosalie, you know?"

She threw some mental obscenities at me to avoid angering Carlisle, but there was no hiding what really upset her about Bella. If I'd been less anxious about the danger we faced I might have pitied my self-obsessed sister.

We thrashed out the details of our plan. We were going to provide the tracker with two decoys—Esme and Rosalie in Bella's truck, since the tracker already had the plate memorized, and Emmett, Carlisle and I in the Jeep. We all had cellphones, fully charged, and Emmett had packed a backpack with potential weapons and plenty of gasoline and matches. It paid to be prepared—and optimistic.

I had some very specific instructions for Alice. I had relinquished my sworn duty to protect Bella only very reluctantly, and I was going to make absolutely sure that Alice and Jasper stepped up. "Don't take your eyes off her, even for a moment. Watch every minute for decisions and outcomes which change. And remember that she needs to somewhere comfortable to sleep, access to a bathroom at intervals, and regular meals. Jasper, keep her calm and optimistic."

"Yes, Captain," Jasper saluted.

"Alice," Carlisle asked as Bella and Esme rejoined us, "will they take the bait?"

Alice closed her eyes to focus better on what she sensed inwardly. "He'll track you. The woman will follow the truck." She'd seen them both, it was a certainty.

We were good to go.

First, however, I somehow had to say goodbye to Bella, knowing the very real danger she faced, and uncertain of when—even *whether*—I'd see her again. I pulled her to me, drinking in every cell, every molecule, of that enthralling face, drinking deep that enchanting scent, trying harder than ever to read the mesmerising mind that lay behind her beautiful eyes. And then I crushed my lips to hers, and summoned every ounce of my superhuman strength to leave her there.

Our plan was to meander north. Laurent had given Denali as his supposed destination for the same reason we wanted to plant that idea in the tracker's mind: there was safety in numbers. It was logical for the tracker to assume that we would seek the help and support of Tanya, Kate and Irina.

In fact, our primary reason for heading north was that Bella was going south.

Once James had taken the bait and started to close in we would turn and ambush him. But the further north we were at that point, the better. It was a long and complex cat and mouse game.

I worked hard to hear the thoughts of our enemies from the very edge of my range, and phoned Alice when first the woman, Victoria, and then James, took the bait as she had predicted. When Alice called to let me know that they were safely on their way I felt better. So far James only connected Bella with our home and Charlie's place in Forks. Once she was safely away from them, she could be anywhere.

Chapter Twenty

Victoria gave up the chase first. We were running through Snoqualmie National Forest when Esme called me to tell me that Victoria had stopped following the truck and headed instead to Charlie's place. They were staying close to her, protecting Charlie as Bella had wanted.

Then, as we were skirting round Abbotsford heading towards Vancouver after two days of leading the tracker on this long distance meandering wild goose chase, he too lost patience with the pursuit. Or maybe he figured out that Bella wasn't with us.

I had struggled to hear his thoughts and we'd had to stop often to let him catch up and come back into my range. Yet somehow every time we did he seemed to slow down too. It was as though he somehow knew that getting too close to me wasn't a good idea. I caught snatches of his determination, the buzz he felt in the pursuit, but little else.

I drew back one last time and sensed futility. James had realised that chasing me wasn't going to get him anywhere. He had come up with an alternative tactic to bring Bella out. I heard him decide to head for the airport, but nothing else. He was running in the opposite direction too fast. I could no longer hear him.

"Carlisle," I called, and Carlisle and Emmett stopped running and sprang to my side. "We've lost him. He's given up following us." I hoped desperately that we'd bought Bella enough time.

Carlisle nodded, his face grave.

"We have to go back to the house," Emmett said. "We have to put together a new strategy to get him." He still wanted to catch and kill the hunter, but the better part of his declaration was driven by his need to see Rosalie.

"If you know then Alice will," Carlisle said. "She may have more information. We should call her. Edward, what sort of signal do you have?" He knew I needed to speak to Bella. He had no idea how much I needed to hear her voice.

"Not good. Yours is on a different network, it might be better."

Carlisle checked the display, and then dialled Alice's number. "Alice, is Bella there with you? Is she okay?"

I heard Alice's voice, made tinny by the technology. "Yes."

"Edward said James just made a decision and he's no longer following us. We've led him as far north as we can. We'll come straight to you if it would help. If you have any information which could help us, we need to hear it."

"I just saw him," Alice said. "There's a room full of mirrors with a wooden floor. There's a stripe, or maybe a rail, along the mirror walls. He's waiting in the room. And I see him on an airplane, and in a dark room playing a VCR. But I don't know *where* any of these rooms are, or where the plane is headed."

"Alice, you must not let Bella out of your sight. This tracker is smart, and he's determined. You or Jasper—or better still, you *and* Jasper—must not take your eyes off her. Do you understand?"

"Yes," Alice said solemnly.

"Now, Edward needs to speak to Bella." He passed the phone to me.

"Hello?"

224

The relief and joy at hearing her voice again was indescribable. "Bella."

"Oh, Edward, I was so worried."

She was worried about *me*. The delicate girl, fleeing for her life from an unstoppable hunter, was more worried about her indestructible boyfriend. "Bella, I told you not to worry about anything but yourself."

"Where are you?"

"We're outside of Vancouver. Bella, I'm sorry—we lost him. He seems suspicious of us—he's careful to stay just far enough away that I can't hear what he's thinking. But he's gone now—it looks like he got on a plane. We think he's heading back to Forks to start over."

"I know. Alice saw that he got away."

"You don't have to worry, though. He won't find anything to lead him to you. You just have to stay there and wait till we find him again." Easier said than done. He was the tracker, not me, and he could be anywhere.

"I'll be fine. Is Esme with Charlie?"

"Yes—the female has been in town. She went to the house, but while Charlie was at work. She hasn't gone near him, so don't be afraid. He's safe with Esme and Rosalie watching."

"What is she doing?"

"Probably trying to pick up the trail. She's been all through the town during the night. Rosalie traced her through the airport, all the roads around town, the school…she's digging, Bella, but there's nothing to find."

"And you're sure Charlie's safe?"

"Yes, Esme won't let him out of her sight. And we'll be there soon. If the tracker gets anywhere near Forks, we'll have him."

"I miss you," she whispered.

225

I ached for her too. "I know, Bella. Believe me, I know. It's like you've taken half my self away with you." I hoped she didn't vomit again at such a saccharine sentiment.

"Come and get it then," she teased.

"Soon as I possibly can. I *will* make you safe first."

"I love you," she said, her voice gentle.

"Can you believe that, despite everything I've put you through, I love you, too?"

"Yes, I can, actually."

She must have missed the part where I had thirsted for her blood, put her in danger every day, and introduced her to the unstoppable predator who was hunting her even now.

"I'll come for you soon."

"I'll be waiting."

Our goodbyes said with those promises, I ended the call with a heavy heart, but more determined than ever to find and destroy James.

Chapter Twenty-One

We ran back to Forks by the most direct route, not the meandering path we had taken when James was following us. Esme and Rosalie were waiting outside the house to report that the woman, Victoria, had left the area. She was headed east. They'd followed her for as long as they needed to establish that she had moved on and wasn't meeting up with James.

"So now we just find James," Emmett said, banging his fist into his palm. The sound reverberated around the forest.

"How?" Rosalie said. "He got on a plane, but we don't know where it was headed." We were all thinking it, but it took Rosalie to say it. We were at an impasse.

"Can we go to the airport and find out the destinations of the most recent flights? Maybe see if we can get access to the passenger manifests?" Esme suggested, knowing, even as she did so, that it was a long shot at best.

"They won't give us access to the passenger manifests," Carlisle said, "But I think the airport is the right place to be. We need to follow him, and Alice might be able to give us some more information soon. We need to be ready. Esme, Rose, you stay here and watch Charlie."

Esme and Rose nodded solemnly. Rosalie seemed to have forgotten her objections to being part of Bella's protection squad. Maybe it was because she liked Chief Swan and didn't mind putting herself out to keep *him* safe.

Emmett and Carlisle embraced their wives and whispered loving reassurances to them as I waited, my arms painfully empty, at Carlisle's car.

We were just a mile from Seattle-Tacoma airport when Carlisle's cellphone rang. He answered it immediately, switching it to speakerphone. "Alice."

"He's coming *here,*" Alice said quickly, her voice filled with anxiety. "I've seen him in a dance studio. Bella recognises it as one near her home—Fifty-eighth Street and Cactus. And I've seen him at Bella's home. He's on his way *here.*"

"He doesn't know she's there," Carlisle insisted, trying to reassure Alice. But underneath, he wasn't certain.

"You have to move her!" I yelled. "Alice, get her out of Phoenix!"

"We can't," Alice sobbed. "Bella thinks he's come looking for her mother. She won't leave."

"But her mother is in Florida with Phil for Spring Training."

"She's due back. Soon. It could be any day now. Bella doesn't know exactly."

Those words hung in the air between us, sucking away all the hope I had felt that Bella might be persuaded to go somewhere else, somewhere far away where she could be anonymous and untraceable.

"Have you seen Bella or her mother in either of those places with James?" I asked Alice.

"Not yet," she replied cautiously, "But he's planning something, making decisions all the time. Things keep changing."

"Where's Bella now?"

"Asleep. Jasper is watching her. I called you as soon as I could."

"We'll come to you on the next flight," Carlisle said. "We're on our way to the airport now."

"Don't take your eyes off her," I reminded Alice.

"I *know*," she responded, irritably. "Believe me, Edward, we know what's at stake. Jasper has been working really hard to keep her calm."

"We'll call again when we're booked onto a flight."

"We'll meet you at the airport," she suggested tersely. "Then you can take Bella somewhere—anywhere—right away. Jasper and I will stay here to throw the tracker off the scent, make him think she's still with us. Just…don't tell us where you're going. It's safer that way."

"I wish I could take her overseas," I said grimly. "Alice, could you find out whether Bella has a passport? Maybe at her home in Phoenix?"

"She doesn't," Alice said. "She's never left the country."

I was disappointed to hear that. Kolyma might have been a good place to hide. It was remote, obscure, and dark, noteworthy only for its old slave labour camps where gold had once been mined.

I was cheered at least to know that I would see Bella again very soon. Being apart from her had hurt more than I had thought possible. While I could focus on what I was doing, where I was going, I could cope, but once I stopped I felt her absence like a wound. If there was anything left of my soul, it was crying out for hers.

Carlisle secured us three first class tickets on the 4.30 a.m. flight, and we settled down to wait. I liked airports because they, like us, remained alert, active and busy at all hours. Some of the concession stands were closed, but people walked briskly, chatted and shopped just as they would if it weren't the early hours of the morning. It made me feel more normal, somehow. Emmett bought a newspaper and pretended to read it. Carlisle stationed himself at a computer terminal where he could look at some of the latest medical research. I just counted down the minutes until I could be with Bella again.

We phoned Alice again as we were waiting to board the plane. Bella was awake, so we spoke quickly and simply confirmed our arrival time at Terminal 4. They would be waiting for us, Alice promised solemnly.

They were. But Bella wasn't with them.

Chapter Twenty-Two

Anguish ripped through me as horror after horror spilled from
Alice's lips. She had seen Bella in the mirror room with James. They had
brought her to the airport knowing that James was going to find her. And
she had deliberately evaded them somehow, and was now alone and
unprotected somewhere in the city. The anger I felt at Alice and Jasper for
having allowed this to happen and the question of *why* Bella had
deliberately fled the friends who were protecting her were smothered by my
torment at knowing that she was vulnerable and headed straight for her
killer.

"Any clues as to where she might have gone?" Carlisle asked, his
tone dark and solemn.

Alice shook her head. My own despair was only slightly greater than
the desolation and remorse she felt. If vampires could cry, she would have
been in floods of desperate agonized tears.

"We know where she'll end up," Emmett said. "The mirror room.
The dance studio at Fifty-eighth and cactus. We have to go there."

"If at all possible, I'd like to get to her *before* she ends up alone in
that room with the hunter," Carlisle said, but there was no hiding from me
that fact that he had little hope. The tracker had all the special abilities and
skills needed to find one girl in this sprawling city of over a million people.

We didn't. Carlisle's wary glance at me was angst-ridden and almost apologetic.

"The letter," Jasper said, and four heads whipped round to look at him.

"What letter?"

"Bella wrote a letter to her mom. She asked Alice to leave it at the house. It might give us a clue about what she was thinking."

In an instant Alice had produced an unmarked sealed envelope from under the flap on her bag. I didn't have a second thought about the impropriety of reading someone else's mail as I snatched it from her and tore it open.

It wasn't to Bella's mother anyway. It was to me.

Edward,

I love you. I am so sorry. He has my mom, and I have to try. I know it may not work. I am so very, very sorry.

Don't be angry with Alice and Jasper. If I get away from them it will be a miracle. Tell them thank you for me. Alice especially.

And please, please don't come after him. That's what he wants, I think. I can't bear it if anyone has to be hurt because of me, especially you. Please, this is the only thing I can ask you now. For me.

I love you. Forgive me.

Bella

"Emmett's right," I said dully. "We have to go to the mirror room *now*. She's got a few minutes' head start on us."

Carlisle took charge. "Alice, Jasper, go to Bella's home and check that she's not there, then meet us at the dance studio." Alice nodded solemnly, and she and Jasper headed back to the parking garage.

I was already running, at painfully slow human speed, to the exit. "We need a car," I yelled to Carlisle.

"It would be quicker to run there," Emmett growled.

"The sun will be up soon, and we can't be seen running through a city," Carlisle responded impatiently. "But that'll do nicely."

Illegally parked in the shuttle pick-up area was a white Lamborghini Gallardo, its owner, in linen suit and sunglasses, standing casually beside it as he awaited his passenger. It had tinted windows and the keys were in the ignition.

Emmett, in the passenger seat, programmed fifty-eighth and cactus into the built-in GPS. I sat in the back, staring in dismay as the machine calculated our arrival time. It might as well have said, "Too Late" across the little screen. But Carlisle gunned the car, churning up the desert dust on the corners and cutting across the lanes of sparse traffic, and the minutes on the display ticked down quickly.

I'm on my way, Bella! Hold on, Bella! I'll be there very soon. Just be strong for a few minutes more!

We arrived in the dance studio parking lot in a squealing of tires. Without caring who was around at this early hour to see me, I leapt out of the car and ran to the door at inhuman speed, wrenching it open so hard that the hinges pulled out of the wooden frame. As I sprinted into the studio lobby, I was assailed by a scent, which was at the same time enticing, reassuring, and terrifying.

Bella's blood.

She was here, but we were too late.

Emmett saw the tracker through the open door to the mirrored studio, and he and Jasper flew past me, seized an arm each of the hunter, and dragged him away from the broken, cowering figure of Bella below him. An instant later I was at her side.

"Oh no, Bella, no!"

She lay in a pool of her own blood, her head and face lacerated by the shards of broken mirror around her, her leg sticking out at an unnatural angle, looking like a broken china doll. Worst of all she was paler than ever, and perfectly still.

"Bella, please! Bella, listen to me, please, please, Bella, please!" As I heard the death throes of James behind me, I pleaded again and again with Bella to move, to acknowledge me, to give me just something to pin a shred of hope on.

There was nothing.

I called to Carlisle, then broke down in hollow despairing sobs across the body of this perfect, beloved woman.

She moved slightly. Gasped for breath. "Bella!"

Carlisle was at my side in an instant, and in full doctor mode. "She's lost some blood, but the head wound isn't deep. Watch out for her leg, it's broken."

I howled in rage. Breaking her leg was vindictive, pointless torture. I almost wished James wasn't already been dead, lying in pieces just a few feet away as my brothers started the fire which would seal his fate, I wanted to kill him myself right then.

"Some ribs too, I think," Carlisle added, still gently examining his patient. I had never been more grateful for his medical training. If it was just broken bones and a few cuts, she would make a full recovery. And the danger was gone. We could be together again, in Forks.

Bella's lips moved. They were thick and dry, and she had so little breath in her lungs that I could barely make out my name as she spoke it.

"Bella, you're going to be fine. Can you hear me, Bella? I love you."

"Edward," she murmured again.

"Yes, I'm here."

"It hurts."

Not surprising. "I know, Bella, I know." I turned to Carlisle. "Can't you do anything?" Morphine maybe, or a splint for her leg. I hated to see her suffer.

"My bag, please," Carlisle said to Alice. She ran to the car and was back in an instant with Carlisle's black medical bag. I saw her approach with it, then saw her gasp and her eyes widen in alarm. Bella's blood was everywhere, and Alice was struggling. Odd that I, who had been most susceptible to it all this time, barely noticed that I was kneeling in a pool of the blood which had been so impossibly irresistible to me only a few days ago.

"Hold your breath, Alice," Carlisle directed. "It will help."

"Alice?" Bella said, her voice trembling.

"She's here, she knew where to find you."

"My hand hurts," she said suddenly.

She must have cut herself on the broken glass. "I know, Bella. Carlisle will give you something. It will stop."

I was trying to reassure myself as much as Bella, but when her eyes fluttered open and she screamed "My hand is burning!" the hope I'd had began to evaporate. Something was much more wrong than I had imagined.

"Bella?"

"The fire! Someone stop the fire!" she screamed, writhing in anguish. In confusion I looked at the fire Jasper and Emmett had just started at the far end of the studio. Then I looked down at her right wrist, and saw the crescent-shaped wound.

James had bitten her.

"Carlisle! Her hand!"

"He bit her!" Carlisle said in horror. He put down the syringe of morphine he'd be preparing. I tried not to hear the hopelessness of his thoughts, but Alice's were hardly better.

You have to let this happen. You have to let her become one of us, here, now, like this.

I caught my breath in horror at what she was suggesting. She knew my feelings about that. Hadn't Bella suffered enough? She was perfect and precious, and I needed to keep her that way, not destroy her soul.

"Edward, you have to do it," Alice said out loud, brushing the wetness from Bella's lashes with gentle fingers.

"No!"

"There may be a chance," Carlisle said.

"What?" I begged.

"See if you can suck the venom back out. The wound is fairly clean." He carefully pulled some of the shards of glass from her scalp as he spoke.

"Will that work?" Alice said doubtfully.

"I don't know," Carlisle said, "But we have to hurry."

James had bitten her only moments before we burst into the room. The venom hadn't had time to spread far. Maybe it could be extracted. Carlisle made it sound like a medical procedure, but it was far from that simple.

I couldn't do it. I couldn't feed from Bella. Not because I didn't want to—I had wanted to since the day she had first arrived at Forks High School—but because I knew that if I gave in to the terrible temptation I had been fighting for so long the monster in me would surface. If I abandoned myself to my animal urges I wouldn't be able to stop feasting. Bella would die. I would have killed her.

"Carlisle, I… I don't know if I can do that." *Couldn't I just pee on it, like they do with jellyfish stings?*

"It's your decision, Edward, either way. I can't help you. I have to get this bleeding stopped here if you're going to be taking blood from her hand."

Bella screamed my name and her misted eyes searched for me.

"Alice, get something to brace her leg!" Carlisle shouted. "Edward, you must do it now or it will be too late."

I could either kill her myself, or I could let James's poison sentence her to days of indescribable agony as it ate away at her humanity, her soul. But there was a chance, just a very small chance, that I could save her. That neither outcome was set in stone.

Not a small chance, I corrected myself. *As much of a chance as I have resolve.*

If I could be the master of myself, of my instincts, then I *could* save her.

I grasped her wrist, my hands either side of the wound, holding it steady and firm. She would struggle at the intense pain. And then I pressed my lips to her warm skin and drank deep.

The sensation was like being drawn into a warm and comfortable eiderdown, enveloped in contented bliss, which swept away every other sensation. Even with the acrid tang of James's venom tainting it, Bella's sweet, warm blood was the finest nectar, the most exquisite draught, everything I had ever imagined it would be, and so much more. For the first time in nearly a century, the burning craving in my throat was slaked, and replaced by a serene sense of completeness, of wellness. Nothing else in the world could ever be as perfect at the rich syrup forged in Bella's bones and coursing through Bella's veins.

I had been foolish to think that my resolve to save Bella was enough. I hadn't reckoned with the reality of her exquisite blood. Nothing else could ever fill my mind as completely or so perfectly as that rich, thick liquid. I wanted only to drink deep and long and hard, forever.

I was going to kill her. The part of me that wasn't revelling in the high of the drug screamed in horror, grieved, despaired. But I had to kill her, because there was no way I could stop drinking this blood until it was gone, every last drop. Because nothing it the universe could ever be as perfect or as necessary to me.

But I was wrong. Something could be as perfect and as necessary. Bella herself.

"Edward," she moaned, and her voice brought me to my senses.

Carlisle answered for me. "He's right here, Bella."

"Stay, Edward, stay with me…"

Her blood was intoxicating and pure, but for the dull cloying taste of the morphine. With the most supreme effort of will I had ever made, I released her arm.

"I will."

"Is it all out?" Carlisle asked me. He was working on her broken leg, strapping it to the makeshift splint.

"Her blood tastes clean," I told him. "I can taste the morphine."

"Bella, is the fire gone?"

"Yes," she sighed, sleepy from the blood loss. "Thank you Edward."

"I love you," I told her.

"I know," she whispered.

I laughed, because I knew more than ever that it was true. I had proved it. I loved Bella more than I thirsted for her incredible blood. My love for her was the strongest force within me.

As ever, Carlisle was the rational, practical one. "Bella, where is your mother?"

"In Florida," she sighed, and Carlisle shot me a glance of confusion. Her letter had, after all, said that James had her mother. Evidently he had been bluffing. "He tricked me, Edward. He watched our videos."

I didn't understand how Bella's home movies might have led her to believe that James had her mother, but that didn't matter. Bella was safe, and her mom was safe.

Bella opened her eyes again and looked for Alice. "Alice, the video—he knew you, Alice, he knew where you came from."

Alice looked startled, and intrigued, and Carlisle shook his head. Bella shouldn't be encouraged to speak yet. Alice would have to wait for her answers.

"I smell gasoline," Bella said weakly. Our fire was blazing, consuming James, as it would the studio before long.

"Time to move her," Carlisle said.

"No, I want to sleep," Bella protested.

I shot a questioning look at Carlisle. *It's safe for her to sleep now. She's lost a lot of blood and she'll be very tired and weak, but she's no longer in any danger, and there's no need to keep her alert.*

"You can sleep, sweetheart," I told her. "I'll carry you." I scooped her broken body into my arms and held her close to my chest. "Sleep now, Bella."

Emmett and Jasper were waiting for us in the parking lot, savouring the smell of the flames that were just starting to be visible through the blinds in the windows. Before long the fire would consume the entire building. We needed to leave *now*.

"No CCTV in the area," Emmett confirmed as I laid Bella gently across the back seat of the car, her head cradled in my lap.

"Where are we going?" I asked.

"She needs to go to a hospital," Carlisle said solemnly. "But we need to be able to provide an explanation for her injuries."

"I'm on that," Alice declared, climbing into the driver's seat and tossing a small handheld video camera onto the dash shelf. "There's a hotel not far from here which will be perfect. Edward, I need you to phone ahead and check in for immediate arrival. We're going to make a little detour." She handed me her cellphone, the number selected for me to dial.

My sister never failed to amaze me. "How...?"

"I've had longer to think about all the possible outcomes than you have," she said simply. I wondered which other outcomes she had prepared for. "Make the call, Edward. Bella can't get medical help until her cover story is in place."

Chapter Twenty-Three

She looked so fragile, so delicate, lying in the high bed in the white room with bright fluorescent lights highlighting every bruise and scratch, and casting shadows of the many tubes and monitor wires across her precious face.

My ebullience at having defeated James and saved Bella in the nick of time had worn off. Whichever way I tried to frame it, she was lying there, damaged and all but destroyed, because of me. Her broken body perfectly matched my broken spirit.

I wasn't naïve enough to think she would never have come to any harm if she hadn't met me—I had seen her stumble over her own feet often enough—but she would certainly not have almost died in her childhood ballet studio at the hands of a cold predator who thirsted for her blood. Someone not unlike me. I shuddered, remembering the sweet, luscious taste of her blood. Even laced with James's foul poison it had been more delectable than I had imagined anything ever could be.

I shook my head to try to force the memory away, remembering instead that I loved Bella even more than I loved her blood. At first I had wondered whether I was drawn to her because of that alluring and mesmerizing scent. Or maybe it was because she was the one person whose thoughts were closed to me, a mystery I longed to solve. Or it might have been all the good qualities I had seen in her as I grew to know her: her self-sacrificing generosity, her unaffected humility, her artistic intelligence, her natural beauty, or even her endearing clumsiness or unexpected and unpredictable reactions.

It was all of those things. I loved the whole package. She was the focal point, the very purpose, of this endless half-life of mine. But now, because of me, she lay in a hospital bed.

I had tried to stop my mind thinking about the taste of her blood, but now it continued, unbidden, along a path that was even worse. It provided for me the obvious remedy to the danger I had exposed the innocent and perfect Isabella Swan to.

I had long ago discounted the selfish answer to my dilemma; the one where I almost killed her, put her through tortuous pain for three days and stole her soul. But the other answer caused my stomach to twist in pain and the overriding horror to flare. I didn't frame the words. I couldn't bear to acknowledge even to myself that it would take little more to tip the balance, to bring me to a point where I *did* have to think about leaving, to face that impossible pain, for her sake.

To my relief the dark turn of my mind was interrupted by a whirling maelstrom of intersecting thoughts, the most strident of which was the repeated shriek, "Bella, Bella, Bella!" The door to the room burst open and a blonde woman in a fringed hippy skirt and lemon yellow t-shirt flew to Bella's bedside and exclaimed over her as she stroked her hair and kissed her head. "Bella, my baby! My poor Bella!"

Renée's mind was as unique, in its way, as Charlie's slightly obscured and muted one, or Bella's mysterious silence. It might have been just her fear for Bella, but her mind rushed over a thousand things at once, taking in and analysing every little detail. I was glad I didn't spend a lot of time in her company; it would probably be exhausting.

"She's going to be fine," I said, standing up, stretching a little, just as a human would do after sitting at a hospital bedside for five hours.

She whirled round, noticing me for the first time. I saw that she already knew that Bella was going to be fine. She had talked to a doctor. But she was still desperately upset to see her little girl (she used the words in her mind, but didn't picture Bella as anything close to a child) in that condition.

As she looked at me I saw myself reflected in Renée's mind, and heard her crazily random analysis. *This must be the boy. I can see why she likes him. He's dishy, but so pale! Is that what living without sun does to you? Will Bella end up looking like that? His sister looked like that too. Sickeningly stunning, admittedly, but so pale.*

"You must be Edward," she said. I kept my hands in my pockets, hoping that she was too busy stroking her daughter's brow to want to shake my hand.

"I'm pleased to meet you Mrs Dwyer." I nodded politely. "I only wish it were in better circumstances."

"Thank you for staying with her," she said, but her thoughts were elsewhere. *There's something funny about his eyes. I bet he's been crying. That's so cute. And he's not really looking at me, he's looking past me to Bella, but he's not just looking at her, he's drinking her with his eyes as though he just can't get enough. He's in love with her. Am I okay with this? Some guy in love with my Bella. Yes. I like him.*

In her mind my face was suddenly smiling and friendly. In reality I wasn't smiling. Not yet.

"Your sister told me what happened, Edward." And yet, whatever Alice had told her, I couldn't pick it out of her mind. She wasn't thinking about it. Her thoughts were still racing, but our fabricated explanation of

243

Bella's injuries wasn't among them. I picked through surreal images of baseball, kittens and organic vegetable boxes, but couldn't find anything relating to Bella falling through a window. Probably a good thing too. As clumsy as Bella was, our cover story was pretty flimsy and unconvincing.

"She did?" I said, prompting.

"I think I'm to blame." She really did. Crushing remorse mixed with thoughts about her shoes being too tight. I saw that she slipped them off and kicked them under Bella's bed. Her toenails were painted different colours. I wondered whether she would kick off the guilt as quickly.

"How so?"

Renée sighed. "I can see how you feel about Bella. And reading between the lines of her emails I think it's clear how she feels about you. But you know, I lectured her so much when she was a child about the horrors of getting stuck in a small godforsaken town—Forks, in fact—by falling for some guy you hardly know when you're just a teenager. I told her again and again not to make the same mistakes I made. And I think on that date you had she must have realised that she was getting too attached to you, and so she ran. Charlie phoned me, he told me how she'd behaved and what she said, and it was so clear that she was terrified that she was just repeating the mistake I'd warned her about."

I nodded slowly. I liked that explanation.

"When she wakes up," Renée said, her mind slowing its whirlwind path for just a moment as she focussed at last, "I'll tell her it wasn't such a mistake."

"Thank you," I said. I really liked Bella's mother, quite apart from the gratitude I owed her for giving birth to and raising the star around which my planet revolved.

"You want something to eat?"

"I don't think I could eat anything," I smiled.

She returned my smile. "Well, I rushed straight here from Sky Harbor and I'm starving. I'm going down to the cafeteria. I don't need to ask you to stay with Bella for me, do I?"

"I'm not going anywhere," I assured her.

"I'll come right back as soon as I've eaten, assuming I don't get lost again. I suppose I could always get Rosalie to help me again. I like her."

I was surprised and it must have shown when I said "Rosalie?"

"Yes. I met your family in the lobby, and Alice was explaining about the hotel and the window, but what I wanted to know is why Bella came to Phoenix in the first place. So Rosalie offered to show me to Bella's room and on the way she told me all about Bella running out on your date and wanting to be in her own home to sort things out in her head."

I heard Rosalie's smug, *"You're welcome"*. She was just outside the door, listening, but doubtless would be back in the waiting room two seconds from now. Renée already had her hand on the door handle.

"Back soon," Renée said as she left, blowing a kiss to her sleeping daughter.

I was pleased she was gone, partly because the surreal whirlwind of her thoughts was most disconcerting, but also because I wanted to be alone with Bella, to touch her and stroke her again, as her mother had done. I wished I could know whether she was in pain, whether she was dreaming, how conscious she was. I leaned my head closer, resting my chin on her pillow, as though proximity to her hidden mind could help.

Moments later her eyelids flickered, then opened. Her beautiful brown eyes looked up in consternation and I saw her hand twitch towards the oxygen tube under her nose. I reached out and took that warm and wonderful hand. "No you don't."

Her head rolled to one side as her eyes sought my face. "Edward?" Her eyes met mine. "Oh Edward, I'm so sorry!"

It was one of those unexpected reactions I loved. What did she have to be sorry for? "Shhhh. Everything's alright now." And it really was. She was alive, and she was awake.

"What happened?"

She had forgotten. Probably for the best. I filled her in on my stupid, unforgivable failure to protect her, her mother's presence at the hospital, Alice's smoothing things over with Charlie and the extent of her injuries. She wanted to know what had happened to James, and whether Alice had seen the tape. If there was one good thing to come from this terrible series of events, it was that Alice now knew something of her origins, as shocking as they were.

"Ugh," she said as she saw the IV in her hand.

"Afraid of a needle," I mused, shaking my head. "Oh, a sadistic vampire, intent on torturing her to death, sure, no problem, she runs off to meet him. An *IV* on the other hand…"

She rolled her eyes. "Why are *you* here?"

I was confused at the question—did she really imagine I could leave her? She clarified, "I meant, why does my mother think you're here? I need to have my story straight before she gets back."

"I came to Phoenix to talk some sense into you, to convince you to come back to Forks. You agreed to see me, and you drove over to the hotel where I was staying with Carlisle and Alice—of course I was here with parental supervision—but you tripped on the stairs on the way to my room and…well, you know the rest. You don't need to remember any details, though; you have a good excuse to be a little muddled about the finer points."

"There are a few flaws with that story," she said. "Like no broken windows."

I smiled to myself, remembering how quickly, thoroughly and efficiently Alice had set the scene. By the time the ambulance arrived, there was nothing to suggest that it hadn't happened exactly as we claimed. Except possibly the fact that it really is quite difficult for a normal human to break through a window, especially accidentally. "Not really, Alice had a little bit too much fun fabricating evidence. It's all been taken care of very convincingly—you could probably sue the hotel if you wanted to. You have nothing to worry about. Your only job is to heal." I stroked her soft cheek gently with the back of one finger, and smiled as I heard her heartbeat speed up, echoed by the gentle beeping of the monitor.

"That's going to be embarrassing," she muttered.

"Hmm… I wonder." I leaned in slowly and the beeps grew closer together again. I kissed her—and they stopped. I pulled back, and with relief heard the rhythmic thumping and beeping again. "It seems I'm going to have to be even more careful with you than usual."

"I was not finished kissing you," she complained. "Don't make me come over there."

I obliged, and this time the monitor reported a flutter of frantic happy heartbeats.

"I think I hear your mother." The maelstrom of thoughts hit me long before her scent or the sound of her footsteps did.

"Don't leave me!" she demanded, looking fearful for a moment, as if she imagined that I *could*.

"I'll take a nap," I suggested, and settled into the recliner at the foot of her bed.

"Don't forget to breathe," she said sarcastically as I closed my eyes.

I heard the door open and Bella exclaim "Mom!" in delight and relief. I heard Renée tiptoe gently to the bed.

"He never leaves, does he?" she whispered.

"Mom, I'm so glad to see you!"

"Bella, I was so upset!"

"I'm sorry, Mom. But I'm fine now, it's okay."

"I'm just glad to finally see your eyes open."

"How long have they been closed?" Bella asked in confusion.

"It's Friday, hon, you've been out for a while."

"Friday?" She sounded shocked.

"They had to keep you sedated for a while, honey—you had a lot of injuries."

"I know."

"You're lucky Dr. Cullen was there. He's such a nice man...very young, though. And he looks more like a model than a doctor..."

"You met Carlisle?"

"And Edward's sister Alice. She's a lovely girl."

"She is," Bella agreed.

"You didn't tell me you had such good friends in Forks."

Bella moaned suddenly, and I opened my eyes in alarm. Renée was gazing intently at her daughter, worried. Apparently any movement was painful for Bella. Renewed guilt washed over me.

"It's fine," she said, "I just have to remember not to move."

I closed my eyes again, reassured.

"Where's Phil?" Bella asked.

"Florida—oh, Bella! You'll never guess! Just when we were about to leave, the best news!"

"Phil got signed?"

I felt Renée's chagrin that Bella had guessed so easily, especially when she knew almost nothing about baseball. "The Suns, can you believe it!"

"That's great, Mom."

"And you'll like Jacksonville so much. I was a little bit worried when Phil started talking about Akron, what with the snow and everything, because you know how I hate the cold, but now Jacksonville! It's always sunny, and the humidity really isn't *that* bad. We found the cutest house, yellow with white trim, and a porch just like in an old movie, and this huge oak tree..."

As Renée raved about the house I fought back my despair. It was right that Bella should move to Jacksonville. It was what had to happen. It was safe, and fitting that she should go somewhere sunny and bright, to live in a yellow house with her bubbly mother. Her new life would be the perfect counterpoint to her time in Forks. No more rain and mist, cloud and gloom. No living in an insular little community in a tiny house with a shared bathroom. No vampires. I wondered how I would live without her, but I had known for some time that, for Bella's sake, I had to.

"Wait, Mom!" Bella interrupted. "What are you talking about? I'm not going to Florida. I live in Forks."

"But you don't have to anymore, silly," Renée responded. Blaming herself for Bella's hatred of small-town life only went so far, then. "Phil will be able to be around so much more now...we've talked about it a lot, and what I'm going to do is trade off on the away games, half the time with you, half the time with him."

"Mom, I *want* to live in Forks. I'm already settled in at school, and I have a couple of girlfriends and Charlie needs me. He's just all alone up there, and he can't cook *at all*."

Renée didn't believe Bella's reasons any more than I did. Apart from anything else, I distinctly remembered Bella telling me that her mother was an 'unpredictable cook'. If Charlie's poor culinary skills were a reason for Bella to live with him, then Renée had at least as much claim on her daughter's cooking prowess.

"Bella, honey, you hate Forks."

"It's not so bad."

"Is it this boy?" Renée whispered.

"He's part of it," Bella admitted. "So, have you had a chance to talk with Edward?"

"Yes, and I want to talk to you about that."

I wanted to hear what she had to say about me as much as Bella did.

"I think that boy is in love with you," Renée whispered.

"I think so, too," Bella agreed, and I heard the laughter behind her voice.

"And how do you feel about him?"

"I'm pretty crazy about him," she admitted. I tried not to smirk.

"Well, he *seems* very nice, and, my goodness, he's incredibly good-looking, but you're so young Bella…"

"I know that, Mom. Don't worry about it. It's just a crush."

I'd tease her about that later.

"That's right," Renée declared, satisfied.

She left soon afterwards, eager to take an expected call from Phil. Once the nurse who came to check Bella's IV had left too, I was at her side.

"How was your nap?" She asked me.

"Interesting…I'm surprised. I thought Florida…well, I thought that's what you would want."

"But you'd be stuck inside all day in Florida. You'd only be able to come out at night, just like a real vampire."

I was so touched by her ingenuousness that I let the *real vampire* thing pass. "I would stay in Forks, Bella. Or somewhere like it. Someplace where I couldn't hurt you anymore." I watched warily to see whether she understood what I was saying, whether she was aware of how guilty I felt over what had happened, and how keenly I was aware that she would not be safe until I was no longer part of her life.

As she stared at me, uncomprehending, another nurse bustled in. Cursing her timing, I sat still and quiet as the nurse tried to persuade Bella to accept more pain meds. Her voice weak and tremulous, Bella refused. She was trying to hide her distress, but I knew her well enough by now to recognise the signs. She was upset by my revelation.

I moved to the bed the moment the nurse left, and took her perfect face in my hands. I needed to reassure her of my love, even if I couldn't do much more.

"Don't leave me," she begged in a broken voice.

"I won't. Now relax before I call the nurse back to sedate you. I'm not going anywhere. I'll be right here as long as you need me."

"Do you swear you won't leave me?"

Against my better judgement, I leaned close to her so that she could look me in the eyes as I declared, "I swear."

Her heartbeat and breathing slowed; her body began to relax. When I enquired whether she was feeling better she confirmed that she was. I muttered to myself, "I can't believe that my words alone could have such a dramatic physical effect. Talk about an overreaction."

"Why did you say that?" she asked quietly. "Are you tired of having to save me all the time? Do you *want* me to go away?"

251

"No, I don't want to be without you, Bella, of course not." That was certainly true. "Be rational. And I have no problem with saving you either—if it weren't for the fact that I was the one putting you in danger...that I'm the reason you're here."

"Yes, you're the reason," she said. "The reason I'm here—*alive.*"

"Barely. Covered in gauze and plaster and hardly able to move."

"I wasn't referring to my most recent near death experience," she said. "I was thinking of the others—you can take your pick. If it weren't for you, I would be rotting away in the Forks cemetery."

Tyler Crowley's car, I remembered. I shouldn't have saved her, but I did.

I chose to ignore that. "That's not the worst part, though. Not seeing you there on the floor...crumpled and broken. Not thinking I was too late. Not even hearing you scream in pain—all those unbearable memories that I'll carry with me for the rest of eternity. No, the very worst was feeling...knowing that I couldn't stop. Believing that I was going to kill you myself."

"But you didn't."

"I could have. So easily." Regret and shame filled me. I still knew that she would never be safe while I was in her life.

"Promise me."

"What?"

"You know what."

I had made that promise already, and should not have done. But I did so again. "I don't seem to be strong enough to stay away from you, so I suppose that you'll get your way...whether it kills you or not."

"Good. You told me how you stopped. Now I want to know why."

I was taken aback by this change of direction. "Why?"

"*Why* you did it. Why didn't you just let the venom spread? By now I would be just like you."

Alice or Jasper? Whichever one had told her, I was furious. I didn't want her to know that she had that option, because as far as I was concerned, she didn't. I said nothing.

"I'll be the first to admit that I have no experience with relationships, but it just seemed logical…a man and a woman have to be somewhat equal…as in, one of them can't always be swooping in and saving the other one. They have to save each other *equally.*"

"You *have* saved me," I told her. If she only knew what my life had been before she came into it.

"I can't always be Lois Lane, I want to be Superman, too."

"You don't know what you're asking."

"I think I do."

How much had Alice told her? Our world was alien and terrifying enough without destroying her innocence still more with these unpalatable truths. I had always tried to protect Bella from the worst side of our nature. "Bella, you *don't* know. I've had almost ninety years to think about this, and I'm still not sure."

"Do you wish Carlisle hadn't saved you?"

"No, I don't wish that, but my life was over. I wasn't giving anything up."

"You *are* my life. You're the only thing it would hurt me to lose."

I was determined "I can't do it, Bella. I won't do that to you."

"Why not? Don't tell me it's too hard! After today, or I guess it was a few days ago…anyway, after *that*, it should be nothing."

"And the pain?" I asked. I remembered it all too clearly. There was no way I could put Bella through that torture.

"That's my problem. I can handle it."

"It's possible to take bravery to the point where it becomes insanity." Bella, who had walked calmly into a vampire's lair, should know that.

"It's not an issue. Three days. Big deal."

I was going to have to have serious words with Alice. Three days in intense, deathly agony *was* a big deal, and Alice had evidently underplayed that truth. But there were other issues at stake too.

"Charlie? Renée?"

That silenced her. She watched me thoughtfully for a while. Finally, she said, "Renée has always made the choices that work for her—she'd want me to do the same. And Charlie's resilient, he's used to being on his own. I can't take care of them forever. I have my own life to live."

"Exactly," I said, seizing on her words. "And I won't end it for you."

"If you're waiting for me to be on my deathbed, I've got news for you! I was just there!"

"You're going to recover," I pointed out. Neither Esme, Rosalie, Emmett or I had had any hope of life.

"No," she said calmly. "I'm not."

I struggled to understand. I had been with her almost constantly since she had arrived at the hospital, and never far away even when the nurses had demanded privacy. When had they been able to tell her something which I wasn't privy to? Or did she have pain somewhere which she hadn't confessed to the medical professionals around her? "Of course you are. You may have a scar or two…"

"You're wrong," she insisted. "I'm going to die."

Again I protested, because I couldn't allow it to be true. "Really, Bella, you'll be out of here in a few days. Two weeks at most."

She glared at me, and made her point. "I may not die now…but I'm going to die sometime. Every minute of the day, I get closer. And I'm going to get old."

I considered that as I had considered it before. I felt no differently. "That's how it's supposed to happen. How it should happen. How it would have happened if I didn't exist—and I *shouldn't exist.*" I should have died decades ago. Bella should never have met me. Even now she should be making prom plans with Mike Newton. The thought was abhorrent.

She snorted. "That's stupid. That's like going to someone who's just won the lottery, taking their money, and saying, 'Look, let's just go back to how things should be. It's better that way.' And I'm not buying it."

"I'm hardly a lottery prize."

"That's right. You're much better."

"Bella, we're not having this discussion anymore. I refuse to damn you to an eternity of night and that's the end of it."

"If you think that's the end, then you don't know me very well. You're not the only vampire I know."

I was going to have to have a serious talk with Alice. "Alice wouldn't dare." I remembered, however, that Alice *might* dare. Because Alice, more than anyone, thought it was inevitable.

"Alice already saw it, didn't she?" Bella exclaimed, reading my expression. "That's why the things she says upset you. She knows I'm going to be like you…someday."

"She's wrong. She also saw you dead, but that didn't happen either."

"You'll never catch *me* betting against Alice."

We fell silent. It was strange, arguing so passionately, yet so quietly. Bella because she couldn't speak easily, and me because I didn't know whether Rosalie was nearby, listening. I reminded myself that our fight—if

255

it could be called that—was because there was so much love between us. Bella wanted to be with me forever. I wanted that too, but not at any cost. First and foremost I wanted her to have a good, happy, fulfilling life, and I knew that I couldn't provide that for her.

"So where does that leave us?" she asked.

"I believe it's called an *impasse*," I concluded. "How are you feeling?"

"I'm fine," but she looked uncomfortable.

"I don't believe you."

"I'm not going back to sleep."

"You need rest. All this arguing isn't good for you."

"So give in."

"Nice try." I pressed the call button and suggested to the bored voice which answered it that it might be time for more pain medication for Bella. She continued to protest.

"I'm not afraid of the needles," she admitted at last. "I'm afraid to close my eyes."

I smiled, and gently cupped her face in my hands. "I told you I'm not going anywhere. Don't be afraid. As long as it makes you happy, I'll be here."

She smiled back, calmer now. "You're talking about forever, you know."

"Oh, you'll get over it," I teased. "It's just a crush."

Bella shook her head. "I was shocked when Renée swallowed that one. I know *you* know better."

"That's the beautiful thing about being human. Things change."

"Don't hold your breath."

I was still laughing at the irony of that when the nurse entered with the syringe and injected the medicine into one of the tubes which fed into Bella's veins. I saw almost immediately her eyelids become heavy, and her breathing slow.

"Stay," she slurred to me as the nurse left the room.

"I will. Like I said, as long as it makes you happy…as long as it's best for you." That was quite a codicil. I hoped she was too sleepy to notice.

"'S not the same thing," she mumbled. Even in her drugged state, nothing escaped her notice.

"Don't worry about that now, Bella. You can argue with me when you wake up."

"'Kay."

"I love you," I whispered into her ear.

"Me, too."

I laughed at that. "I know." And I kissed her gently.

"Thanks."

"Anytime."

Her eyes were closed now, and she struggled to speak. I had to listen very closely to make out what she was saying. "Edward?"

"Yes?"

"I'm betting on Alice."

She drifted off to sleep, and as I had so often, I watched her, taking in every perfect angle of her face, drinking in her delicious scent, revelling in her existence and her nearness and her love for me, unworthy as I was.

I didn't know whether Alice was right or not. Unlike her I had no idea what the future might hold. But I knew that however long I had with Bella, whether it was a mere seventy years, or eternity, it wasn't long enough.

Epilogue

I took her to prom. It wasn't easy—I had to trick her into it—but it was a dream of mine to walk into the dance with a beautiful and beloved girl on my arm. Maybe every seventeen-year-old boy has that dream, but not every seventeen-year-old boy has attended innumerable proms before, aloof and alone despite the vapid girls who fawn at his feet.

As though trying to make up for my past indifference I let my teenage ebullience have free reign. Maybe I was a little crass in my reaction to the jilted Tyler Crowley, but I was still giddy at my success at tricking her into going to prom. I had had to battle Bella's intense dislike of high school dances—even ones which were a rite of passage rooted in years of tradition—and I hadn't thought Charlie would ever let me take Bella anywhere again.

Bella even seemed to relax a little when we arrived, maybe even start enjoying herself.

Until Jacob Black arrived.

Gangly, awkward and uncertain, he cut in despite my better judgement. I hoped he'd deliver his message and then leave. I watched from a safe distance, listening carefully to everything Black said and thought.

Billy Black had paid his son to attend the prom, and bribed him with car parts, of all things, to deliver a message to Bella. That might have been faintly amusing, especially since the lad didn't understand the message, except that his mind was barely on the words he had been told to deliver anyway. He was here, primarily, because he wanted to see Bella.

I wasn't unused to that, of course. When she first arrived at school, almost every boy on campus had indulged in lustful flights of fancy in which Bella took centre stage. What troubled me more, with Black, was that his mind was without the usual lasciviousness and coarse images. He truly admired Bella. He had fond memories of her, and he respected her and felt happy her company. He was, I concluded, on the cusp of falling in love with her.

I would have to nip that in the bud.

His warning message had been delivered; I took my rightful place again, startling Black somewhat as I claimed Bella between songs.

"Don't be mad at Billy," Bella said. "He just worries about me for Charlie's sake. It's nothing personal."

Actually it *was,* but she wasn't to know that. "I'm not mad at Billy, but his son is irritating me."

"Why?"

I couldn't tell her that the lad wanted to steal her from me. It wasn't a big deal anyway, and I didn't want to sound petty. "First of all, he made me break my promise. I promised I wouldn't let go of you tonight."

"Oh. Well, I forgive you."

I chuckled at that. "Thanks, but there's something else. He called you *pretty.* That's practically an insult, the way you look right now. You're much more than beautiful."

She laughed. "You might be a little biased."

"I don't think that's it. Besides, I have excellent eyesight." In my ninety years I had seen many attractive women, and even with her leg in a heavy cast, Bella outshone them all.

"So are you going to explain the meaning of all this?" she asked as we danced. In reply we headed for the back door of the gym, and once outside in the fading sunlight I scooped her into my arms and took her to a peaceful part of the school grounds—a pine bench beneath the fragrant madrone trees.

"Twilight again," I observed. "Another ending. No matter how perfect the day is, it always has to end."

"Some things don't have to end," she said pointedly.

I sighed. "I brought you to the prom because I don't want you miss anything. I don't want my presence to take anything away from you, if I can help it. I want you to be *human*. I want your life to continue as it would have if I'd died in nineteen-eighteen like I should have.

"In what parallel dimension would I *ever* have gone to prom of my own free will? If you weren't a thousand times stronger than me, I would never have let you get away with this."

She made a valid point. "It wasn't so bad, you said so yourself."

She said nothing, and I took that as capitulation. She was inwardly, secretly, glad that I had tricked her into coming to prom. She might have been hiding that thought from herself, as well as from me, of course, but it was there nevertheless.

"Will you tell me something?" I asked.

"Don't I always?"

"Just promise you'll tell me."

"Fine."

"You seemed honestly surprised when you figured out that I was taking you here. I'm curious—what did you *think* I was dressing you up for?"

She didn't want to tell me. She blushed deep red, and tried to get out of answering. She didn't want me to be mad, she said. Still I demanded to know.

"Well...I assumed it was some kind of...occasion. But I didn't think it would be some trite human...prom!"

"Human?" I was confused. What other sort of occasion could there be?

"Okay, so I was hoping that you might have changed your mind...that you were going to change *me,* after all."

I recoiled in horror at what she had expected, and at the very idea that she could imagine that I would casually pick her up and take her away to destroy her. But the humour of it won through the anger and shock.

"You thought that would be a black tie occasion, did you?"

She scowled. "I don't know how these things work. To me, at least, that seems more rational than prom does."

The idea that it was fitting to dress in finery to be condemned to excruciating and soul condemning pain was not only macabre and twisted, but demonstrated—as though I needed further demonstration—how unusual and unique Bella's mind was. She had expected some other *rite of passage,* something horrific and obscene.

I decided to treat the whole thing as a joke.

"I am serious," she told me.

"I know. And you're really that willing? So ready for this to be the end, for this to be the twilight of your life, though your life has barely started? You're ready to give up everything?"

"It's not the end, it's the beginning," she said, under her breath but of course I heard her.

"I'm not worth it," I told her.

"Do you remember when you told me that I didn't see myself very clearly? You obviously have the same blindness."

Hardly. "I know what I am." I didn't grow, breathe, reproduce or excrete—by every technical definition Mr Banner had given in our shared biology classes I wasn't alive. That meant that if Bella was asking to become like me, she was asking to be dead. She was asking me to kill her.

Another impasse. She was evidently blinded by the image of perfection I presented, and failed completely to see the monster within. Maybe I needed to show her.

"You're ready now, then?"

She was startled, I saw, but she answered without hesitation. "Yes."

"Right now?" I inclined my head, brushing my lips gently against her neck. She was tense, her heartbeat and breathing were quick and erratic, but she was determined.

"Yes." She closed her eyes against the expected pain.

I chuckled and moved away. Did she really think I would give in here, at school, during the prom? "You can't really believe that I would give in so easily."

"A girl can dream."

"Is that what you dream about? Being a monster?"

"Not exactly," she replied. "Mostly I dream about being with you forever."

I melted at those words. She didn't *want* the pain, the power, the thirst, or the isolation. She didn't *want* to be a vampire. She just wanted to be with me.

I wanted to be with her too. For the whole of her life.

"Bella, I *will* stay with you—isn't that enough?"

She smiled as my fingers touched her lips gently. "Enough for now. Look, I love you more than everything else in the world combined. Is that enough?"

"Yes, it is enough," I agreed. "Enough for forever."

And I leaned down to kiss her beautiful throat.

Made in United States
Orlando, FL
06 December 2025

73960618R00148